Sydney stumbled into a p around, she tried to turn b midst of the noise of fighting the brush, a new sound came to An animal sound. Something snuffling, then dry leaves and brush crackling under heavy feet.

The noise came from behind and slightly to her right. Pinpoints of sunlight came through the branches overhead, and as she watched, a form shook itself. More snuffling as it moved toward her at an angle. Did it sense her?

It snorted as if in answer and stood still. Should she run? Try to move away quietly – impossible under the circumstances. Or stand very still and hope it went away.

Whatever it was, it was wild or feral and probably dangerous. Maybe a bear or a wild hog, which she understood lived in the state. Maybe even a feral dog, but its dark form seemed too bulky for that.

It turned away from her at a sound in the brush farther to the right.

Go. Get whatever it is, she urged silently.

It raised its head and tested the air, snuffling loudly.

With its attention diverted, Sydney took a careful step forward. There was no longer time to try to get around the dense thicket ahead of her. She was determined to plow through it at a rush, hoping not to fall. She pushed off her back foot and began running . . . branches stung as they slapped her cheek, her forehead . . . .

In spite of the noise she was making, she could hear the animal behind, crashing through the brush, pushing her to desperate speed. She decided that the thing was a wild boar. She'd read stories of what one could do to a person if roused, but never heard of any in Oklahoma. This one must have been wakened by her progress through the underbrush, and he sounded in a foul mood.

Gordian Knot Books is an imprint of Crossroad Press Publishing

Copyright © 2017 by Cary G. Osborne
Cover by David Dodd
Design by Aaron Rosenberg
ISBN 978-1-946025-17-3

All rights reserved. No part of this book may be used or reproduced in any manner whatsoever without written permission except in the case of brief quotations embodied in critical articles and reviews.
For information address Crossroad Press at 141 Brayden Dr., Hertford, NC 27944
www.crossroadpress.com

First edition

OKLAHOMA WINDS: BLACK ICE

A SYDNEY ST. JOHN MYSTERY

*Best wishes
Cary Osborne*

CARY G. OSBORNE

CHAPTER 1

The nose of the car pointed directly at the red disk of the setting sun, squeezed between a layer of dark clouds and the darker curve of the earth. Late twilight with visibility at its worst.

Professor Tallidge drove carefully under the speed limit as she headed home from her office on the Oklahoma State University campus. The temperatures were low, near or below freezing, with patches of black ice scattered along the road. They were impossible to see unless the headlights reflected from them. A bit of sleet fell during the day, without warning, and she only knew about the ice because it was mentioned on the radio. Oklahoma weather, unpredictable as always.

She tried concentrating on the road, but her mind kept returning to what she'd found earlier in the day in her research. She was working on a book about Indian cowboys in Oklahoma, a state with more diversity in the Native American tribes than any other. She taught Oklahoma and western history, among other subjects, at OSU. She hoped this book, her latest project, would be published at the end of the spring semester.

A couple of days earlier, she had her first look at papers in the Filmore County Historical Archives. Several collections originated with the early settlers, Boomers and Sooners, and had accounts of individual ranch hands or lists of their names as hired hands. The last collection she started looking through was that of the Blair Bar Ranch owned by the Blair family, who settled in the northern part of the state during the last land run in 1893.

When she made plans to look through those papers, she was told that another patron, Professor Berger, was also interested. She called him to discuss the differences or similarities in their projects, but there was no problem. He was working on the one ranch, while she was looking only at the Indian cowboys.

Several names were found in the records, but the collection was not well organized, and it would take time to sort out the information she needed. It took a couple of days of thought and a conversation with the archivist to figure how best to tackle the search.

The second day, she came across a folder with several pages cut from a bound journal. The story those pages told concerned her. She discussed them with Dr. Berger, hoping he might have insight as to whether she could use the information and if she should report the events to someone, like the police. He'd promised to contact her after consideration on his part. She'd also tried to contact Senator Blair, the grandson of Carl Blair, whose papers she was searching. In the meantime, she planned to continue searching the documents.

Her attention was jerked back to the road by very bright headlights ahead. There was so little traffic that she'd let her mind drift from the task at hand, and the brightness of the lights startled her.

Blinded by the light, she slowed. When the light blinked off, she guessed that the vehicle had turned. Suddenly the lights were right in front of her. She jerked the wheel to the right, heading for the shoulder. The light followed her. She shut her eyes against it. The car tilted as the shoulder dropped lower. She fought the wheel and slammed on the brakes. The car rolled over. Once. Twice.

The seat belt and shoulder harness dug into her body. The air bag deployed. The violence of the roll, however, snapped her neck. Professor Tallidge died almost instantly.

CHAPTER 2

The gun fired and they were off. Hundreds of settlers, on horseback, in wagons, some on foot, heading into the promised land. At first they drove straight ahead, then individuals broke away, taking different directions. Every way, except back. No one wanted to go back to where they came from. Within hours, flags would be planted, claims would be made, townships would be staked out.

Sydney St. John was reading about the last Oklahoma land run in 1893 when she was jerked back into the present by Doctor Berger rapping on the door frame. The old school clock in the hall struck three. It was his research of the Blair Bar Ranch that had her studying the land run.

"Yes, sir. Another box?" Sydney asked.

"No," he said. "I'm finished for the day. But I'd like to show you something. Or, rather, I'd like for you to read something from one of the folders."

"What is it?"

He pulled a standard acid-free folder from behind his back and placed it on her desk. "Just read the journal pages, please. You'll find it interesting."

Leaving a folder out of a box was against the archives' rules, as he well knew, so what he'd found must be very unsettling. A few minutes later she unlocked the front door for him. As he started through, he told her he wouldn't be back for at least another week. He was their most regular researcher, and as she closed and re-locked the door, she wondered when he would run out of subjects to write about. Numerous articles were published under his name, and currently he was working on a history of the Blair Bar Ranch and the Blair family, first established in that last Oklahoma land rush. It was a mostly neglected subject as the more popular 101 Ranch was better known, with a flashy history similar to Buffalo Bill's traveling extravaganza.

The Blair Bar Ranch once ran to thousands of acres and was a popular dude ranch in the 1930s and 40s that offered popular entertainment for the time with its rodeo-style performances, trick riding, and roping. The descendants still owned the property, but it was now a much smaller working cattle ranch with some oil wells. The children and grandchildren of the first father and son went on to other professions, but the ranch represented their roots in the state.

The collection was one of the older ones in the archives, and its organization left a lot to be desired. For a short while, there were two researchers, and she'd tried hard to help both Dr. Berger and Dr. Tallidge find the information they needed. Dr. Tallidge's death, when her car slid on ice last week, had shocked both her and Dr. Berger. She'd just started her research and neither of them knew her well, but the sudden death of someone you know was always disturbing.

Life always went on, though, and Route 66 was Doctor Berger's next subject, although so much published material already existed about the iconic highway that Sydney wondered how he would be able to find more to say. Several of the collections contained a lot of information, though, and the professor was very good at ferreting out details that were never covered in other works. She had already started a list of boxes, photos, and other material that he might find useful for the new project. It would be several weeks, however, before he completed the Blair project.

She sat back in her chair and looked out at the street running in front of the building. Gansel was such a small town, with all of the advantages and disadvantages that means. Businesses closed at five, except for the five restaurants. One of those closed at eight, three at seven, and the bar, which also served food, at nine. Grocery items were available at the three convenience stores, which meant mostly junk food and milk and bread.

There was one insurance office, the sheriff's office, a small public library, a florist shop, a funeral home, and Eastland's, still called a variety store. Several buildings and store fronts were empty, the former businesses victims of recessions and movement to the larger towns. Four churches served the religious needs of the community. The courthouse on Main Street saw plenty of use, since all of the county offices were located there. Except for the sheriff's office, that is.

The county kept threatening to close the one elementary school and send local children to the school in Guthrie. Older children were already bussed down to Guthrie and Edmond for middle school and high school. However, a branch of the county library had recently opened. She hoped it was a sign that Gansel wasn't dead yet.

Most of the people were long-time residents, descendants of the original settlers. Three main residential areas surrounded the downtown area. Around the town center, older houses, some dating back to the late 1890s. To the north were houses built in the 1950s and later. The newest, to the west, made up a bedroom community for the larger towns to the north and south. She rented a 1950s house, thinking when she first moved to Gansel that she might not stay long. Her newer house in Norman was currently rented out to a professor at OU, which paid the mortgage and her own rental.

Shopping was nonexistent. Usually, when she needed something she drove down to Edmond or even to Norman, where she lived for several years, the last two when attending OU's library school. She still felt very comfortable there, even though Stillwater was a bit closer. Visiting with friends in Norman was an added benefit, and she would sometimes spend the night at someone's house, especially if she and a bunch of her friends attended a play or concert.

Her only friend in Gansel was Julia Vincent, who owned the florist shop. As small as the town was, she managed to keep the shop going, not getting rich, but making money. Weddings and funerals were her big stock in trade, events that kept the four churches and the flower business busy.

Sydney knew a lot of people in the town. She occasionally met with city and county officials, at times representing Doctor Arnold when he and his wife were off on one of their mysterious trips. Over the past year, she'd seen them less and less.

In spite of Arnold and some of the headaches the job presented, she loved living in Gansel and working in the archives. She also found that the usual depiction of life in small towns didn't fit, as she found the people here friendly, helpful, and they didn't try to interfere in her life in any way, other than repeated invitations to attend one church or another, which still happened after five years of politely saying "no, thank you."

Light pollution was low, so she could see thousands of stars at night. The nights were so quiet that the roar of big trucks on Interstate 35 could be heard if the wind was out of the east, which it rarely was. Wildlife sometimes came in and out of town. She'd seen a few deer and even a pair of coyotes in the field behind her house on occasion, and lots of birds, when the field was planted with barley and when it lay bare in the winter.

Although she treasured her friends, she didn't go out of her way to make new ones. That wasn't her style. She accepted friendship when offered. Given her current circumstances, it was fortunate that she enjoyed her own company and that of books and her research. Still, she enjoyed human companionship, and that thought made her think of Ben.

She re-focused on the scene outside the window, where a couple of people walked past, heading east. They were bundled up against the Oklahoma wind and she couldn't tell who they were. February was often the coldest month of the winter, storms covering the roads with black ice, treacherous conditions, especially on the Interstate. After the storm moved through the night before, the light rain froze on bushes and trees, but the roads remained mostly clear since the ground wasn't frozen yet. Up until a week earlier, the winter was mild, and everyone enjoyed that. However, February might prove to be a bitch.

As for herself, she had a love-hate relationship with winter in Oklahoma. She hated the ice storms and refused to leave the house until she knew the roads were totally clear. The wind could cut through anything, including the seals around the windows in her small house. She kept warm by turning the thermostat up on the natural gas heat, and burning wood in the fireplace in the living room. She'd always preferred a cooler house, and this one did not disappoint.

Among all the things to worry about, she'd recently begun thinking of buying a house in Gansel instead of continuing to rent.

It looked like she would be working in the archives for years to come, something she wasn't sure of when she first moved north. Four years had passed, and the work was as fascinating as ever. Her one hesitation was due to her relationship with Ben and not knowing what the future held for the two of them. Working for Doctor Arnold was also a problem. She learned over time that he was a bully who thought he knew everything and who listened to his red-headed wife's opinions on the archives rather than Sydney's. For four years, she'd managed to fend off his uninformed interference, and there was no reason she couldn't keep handling it, except being worn down by it. But if she stayed, she would have to find a better living situation. And she and Ben would settle for a long distance relationship.

The old school clock chimed in the hall and she looked up to see that it was four o'clock. An hour left to clear everything up and lock up and go home. As she started cleaning off her desk, she spotted the folder Doctor Berger asked her to read. His concern was obvious and she was very curious about what was so interesting.

CHAPTER 3

Sydney could see her own reflection in the dark window as she finished reading and sat back in her chair. She took a deep breath and let it out slowly. Out of curiosity, she'd opened the folder before leaving the office, just for a quick look, and in the following hour, she read the three pages of small, close-spaced writing twice, leaving her wondering what she should do.

Doctor Berger was right. This was interesting stuff. Too interesting.

It wasn't unusual to find incidents from the past that still had meaning in the papers of an individual or a business. They were real people with everyday problems and issues, many of them or their descendants living full lives with the usual frailties of the human race.

But this. It was the second time she had come across evidence of a serious crime.

What should she do? What would Doctor Arnold tell her to do? She hesitated to tell him, to ask for his advice, because she knew him to be a dishonest man. His wife would have something to say about it too, which always made matters worse.

She gathered up the pages and went into the hall to the copy machine. She ran copies of the four-by-seven-inch sheets, cut from a bound journal of some sort, with their neat handwriting in brown ink. She wondered if whoever cut them out meant to destroy them. And was the rest of the journal somewhere in the boxes of the collection?

She slipped the copies and her notes into her portfolio, put it in her book bag and put on her coat. Gathering up her purse and book bag, she made her way to the side door, which opened out to the parking lot on the east side of the building. It was once paved, but the surface now consisted of patches of asphalt with ragged stones jutting out. The years erased the lines for parking slots, although there was a sign for her designated space. The lot occupied the northeast corner of the block. The only light came from a street light on the opposite corner, so her car—an older, green Honda CR-V—sat mostly in darkness.

The air was calm and had grown even colder. Not yet freezing, she thought, but the temperature would probably drop overnight. There wasn't much moisture on the street or the parking lot, so there might not be ice in the morning.

She pressed the button on the remote key to unlock the doors and put her burden on the floor behind the driver's seat. Opening the driver's door, she stood for a moment, breathing in the cold air and listening to the quiet. A thousand stars shone in the sky, and there were thousands more if only there were less ground fog and the one street light weren't so bright. Actually, Gansel had so little light pollution compared to the larger cities and towns to the south and north, the night sky revealed more of its beauty.

She blew out, hoping her breath would exhale in a cloud, but it wasn't cold enough or humid enough. As a kid, it was how she pretended to be smoking, a real habit she picked up for a number of years. She'd been smoke-free now for twelve years. Smiling with self-satisfaction and happy in her life, she got in behind the wheel, and headed home. Her rental house sat on the northwest edge of town on a small rise in an older residential area. The field behind, to the north behind her, lay fallow. The farmland was flat, and from her back porch, she could see for miles. Nearly identical houses sat on either side of hers.

Most nights, weather permitting, she went out on the back porch and sat with a cuppa—hot chocolate or coffee in winter, iced tea in summer—and listened to the silence or the wind, whichever occurred that night. Tonight, she was home later than usual, and the temperature had dropped, so instead, she heated up a bowl of Hungarian mushroom soup left over from the weekend. There was one bowl left that she might save for tomorrow night or finish off tonight, depending on how hungry she was when she finished the first one.

As the soup heated in the microwave, she set her bound notes and the copies from the older journal on the kitchen table with a highlighter, pencil, and eraser. Before the microwave dinged, she sliced a piece off the Tuscan loaf of bread. She'd eaten half of the loaf and the remainder was beginning to get hard. She decided to slice the rest so she could either toast it or soften it in the microwave over the next few days.

The meal was warming and satisfying. The reading material, however, left her curious and unsatisfied. More than that, she wasn't sure what she should do about it. Was the guilty person still alive? Had the statute of limitations run out? Was it her responsibility to report what she'd found? Or, rather, what Doctor Berger found. There were all sorts of ethical considerations. Was there anything in the "best practices" for archives to cover this situation?

Curiosity came from not knowing the whole story. It was the driving force behind her career and her life. It drove her to look for more information, find the intricate details of the lives of those people whose legacies were in her hands. One day, someone else would be responsible for the documents and the stories of people, the history of their days. But now, she was the one who preserved the papers and memorabilia, the words of people, many long dead. It was a big responsibility in many ways, but it was never daunting. It was a true labor of love.

She rinsed the dishes and put them into the ancient dishwasher. The rest of the soup and the bread she put away for tomorrow.

She sat back down, munching on a homemade chocolate chip cookie, and looked over the pages again, studying the highlights and notes she made. Her questions were noted in the composition book she used for such tasks. All she knew for certain was that, if she did report what she'd found, it wouldn't be to Doctor Arnold first. She didn't want to be responsible for any decision he might make.

Of course, nothing had to be decided tonight, nor for a whole week, since Doctor Berger would be gone that long. The one person she should ask was Alexander Otis, the county sheriff, but once she did that . . . well, he would be obligated to investigate. How far should she go with this? For tonight, though, she wasn't going anywhere.

She went into the bedroom to get ready for her shower, pulling the sweater over her head, just as the phone rang. In her haste to answer the call, she got all tangled up in the sweater. She threw it on the bed, only to hear the answering machine in the kitchen pick up the call. The voice leaving a message was Ben's. She picked up the extension in the bedroom.

"I'm here," she said. "Give me a moment."

Hurrying into the kitchen, she hit the stop button on the machine.

"Okay?" Ben asked from the other end.

"Yes. Someday I'll tell you about the struggle I had."

"Tell me now."

"No. You don't need to know everything yet. Maybe I'll keep some secrets forever."

"I'll bet not."

Sydney laughed. "We'll see." She went into the living room and dropped into the overstuffed chair. "What's up?" She jumped back up to close the blinds on one of the windows, not wanting neighbors to see her shirtless.

"Not much. It's been another cool day here, surprisingly. The weather has been awfully mild."

"Enjoy it while you can."

"You bet."

They compared winter weather for a bit and then he asked her about the archives. He had done a bit of research when he returned to Oklahoma the year before to check on his grandfather's collection. His stepmother donated Josiah Bartlett's papers, telling everyone she was the only living heir. It turned out there were two grandsons, Ben and his brother, Arthur. When he first showed up, Sydney feared that he might make a fuss about not being consulted regarding the gift, but "the trouble" wasn't directly due to him.

"I was wondering," he began during a lull in the conversation, "if you would like some company beginning next week."

"Is everything all right?"

"Oh, sure. It's just that most of the work I'm doing right now I can do anywhere. Truth is, I miss you. If anything comes up, I can handle it from there."

She took a deep breath. For a moment, she told herself not to appear too eager. Next moment, she berated herself for thinking and acting like a teenaged girl.

"I'd love to have your company. How long do you think you'll stay?"

"A few days at least. Maybe a week."

"That would be great. But you know," she added, "I'll be working."

"I know. But we'll have nights and a weekend. What shall we do?"

"Depends on the weather," she said and laughed.

February being such a treacherous month, she knew they would have to play it by ear until very close to the day he arrived. So far, winter was cold, sometimes windy, but no snow and only a bit of freezing rain. The possibility of being confined in the house with Ben for a few days was not a bad prospect.

He planned on leaving California the next Wednesday. He'd checked fares, and leaving on that day gave him a cheaper fare.

"I might look through more of my grandfather's papers if that's convenient."

Having completed sorting and processing the collection she was eager for him to see the difference since his last foray into the boxes. All metal, such as staples and paperclips, was removed. Copies made of vulnerable papers. Everything neatly placed in acid-free folders and boxes, and a comprehensive finding aid in the binder.

She told Ben she'd be delighted for him to look it over. As they talked about his visit, she glanced at the material from the Blair collection still lying on the kitchen table.

"I have an interesting problem in another of the collections. I'd like to get your input on what to do."

"You're not going looking for murderers again, are you?" he asked.

He referred to events of the last spring. Days before he appeared at the archives, Sydney's intern, Irene, was killed in the processing room of the building. That was the beginning of a dangerous adventure for both of them. Also known as "the trouble."

"No," she said with a laugh. "No murderer. If you're interested, I'll discuss it when I know more."

"I'm at your disposal."

They chatted more about what was going on, then reluctantly

said good night. Sydney sat thinking about the revelation in the few sheets she'd read. She'd told Ben there was no murder, but she couldn't be certain of that. If she were the only one who knew what it held, she could ignore it. But someone else, a researcher, found it first. That meant consideration must be given to the impact of the revelation on the reputation of the archives and her own reputation, as well as on any descendants, several of whom were still alive. The archives were always at the forefront of her concern, of course.

It came back to her that she was sitting in her living room in her bra and that the shower awaited. In a few minutes, standing under the hot water, she let herself relax, thinking nothing but good thoughts. The last thing she needed to do was make trouble for herself.

She slept well that night, and didn't remember the problem until she gathered up everything to take to work the next morning. Once in her office, she called her fellow archivist at the Carl Albert Center at the University of Oklahoma. Louise Zimmer was the one who had trained Sydney in archival work when she was attending library school, working on her master's degree.

"I have a hypothetical question for you," Sydney said, after the usual catching up. She described what she'd found in general terms. When she finished, she asked, "What are our responsibilities as archivists when we discover something like that? I mean, if we find evidence of a crime that happened decades ago, are we required by the ethical standards of archives, to report it?"

"Are you still involved in that murder back in the 40s?"

"No, it's . . ." She started to say "something new." Instead, she said, "It's only hypothetical. But having gotten involved in that earlier business, I want to have a better idea of what my responsibilities are."

The newspapers spread the story of her encounter with Violet Parsons and her grandson, which made her and the archives well-known for a short while. Thankfully the furor died down in good time.

"Understood," Louise said. "I think that, regardless of how long it's been, if it's a serious crime, especially if where the statute of limitations is a factor, then we need to at least consult with legal authority. If someone else finds it, a researcher or someone, and we haven't . . . well, we could be liable in some way. It could also be that the whole situation was solved at the time and you may need do nothing."

"Okay."

"You can't tell me what it is?"

"No, I want to keep it hypothetical. I don't want you to be involved in some way that might not be to your benefit."

"Thanks," Louise said. Sydney knew by her tone that she was smiling. They had gotten to know each other pretty well during her year at Carl Albert as a graduate assistant, and the memory of those months was sweet.

"You're welcome," Louise said. "Give me a call next time you're down here and we'll catch lunch."

"I will. Promise."

They said goodbye and hung up. Sydney sat thinking for some time. She gave Louise only a bit of the information from the file, not wanting to pinpoint the incident, nor wanting to get her erstwhile boss and instructor involved any more than was good for either of them.

She opened the folder on the top of her desk and re-read everything. Although the collection came from the Blair family, the documents in front of her originated with Carl, the patriarch. His father established the family in Oklahoma in the 1893 Cherokee Strip Land Run, the next-to-last land run in the Unassigned Lands of the territory that became Oklahoma. It was Carl who built the business and ranch to its heights.

Whether they were Sooners—those who entered the territory prior to the start of the land run—she did not know. She wasn't in Oklahoma when the collection first came into the archives, nor had she ever done any extensive research in it. The papers sat on the shelves for years before she took on the position. However, she gathered a good bit of background information from public records, newspapers, and other sources, setting up a three-ring binder for researchers to use. That was her way of not only assisting researchers, but also learning as much as she could about the originator of a collection and the circumstances of their lives in Oklahoma history.

The collection was important because Carl Blair managed to

build a substantially larger ranch than the one hundred sixty acres his father claimed in the land run. He then turned that ranch into a dude ranch with some shows similar to the 101 Ranch, except the Blair West Show was smaller and never traveled. A lot of visitors came from the east and elsewhere, wanting to see real cowboys roping and riding. Some went out on horseback during their stay to play cowboys in a real roundup, roughing it on the prairie for three days and two nights, eating chuck wagon food. The most popular attraction was a staged Indian raid on the camp, which the guests fought off with cap pistols.

Blair's two sons ran the show for a while, but their goals changed. Lawrence, the elder son, became a lawyer, specializing in land disputes, with his offices in Ponca City. Once oil became a big commodity, land claims became ever more important.

Grayson, the younger son, decided to become a wildcatter, drilling for oil and natural gas all over the state. His company, GB Petroleum, failed after a few years and he moved back to the ranch.

The youngest of the three children was Lily, born with many health problems. Her parents worked hard to give her the care she needed; whatever the doctors recommended they tried. Something worked, as she grew up strong in both body and will, although she looked delicate and very pretty in the photographs. She could rope and ride with any man on the ranch and took great pleasure in riding off into the wilderness on her pinto, leading a pack horse, being gone for as long as a week. Although nothing in the journals so far indicated outright that this habit was not approved of by her parents, there were strong hints. It appeared the need to be totally alone for periods of time was overwhelming to her. No one knew exactly what she did on those rides, but one of them may have led her to the events that made her family disown her. She disappeared from the story at the age of twenty-three.

Another reason the collection was important, and perhaps more immediate, was that Carl's grandson, Grayson, Jr., was a member of the state legislature. He was now a state senator, who before being elected to that office, served six terms in the Oklahoma House of Representatives before the law establishing term limits was passed. The current term in the senate was his last. Most of this information came from his official website and a small amount of data Sydney found on the Internet. She assumed there was much more in the papers themselves.

She also read through the "deed of gift." The strange thing about their getting the collection was that another grandson, named Carl after his grandfather, presumably, donated the papers as executor of the estate. Lawrence, the eldest son, objected strenuously, to the point of hiring a lawyer to try and prevent it. However, Carl and his lawyers managed to fight off the efforts of his father.

The events described in the journal pages found by Doctor Berger occurred before Lily's disappearance. She would have thought such violence was relatively normal in those early days before statehood. However, the good doctor knew more about Oklahoma history, and his reaction led her to believe that maybe it was more serious than she knew. Her own knowledge was gleaned from family papers and history of the land runs from books and the Internet.

The phone rang, bringing Sydney back to the present day. When she answered, it was Doctor Arnold's voice on the other end.

"The county supervisors have authorized funds to upgrade the alarm system in the archives," he said, speaking over her "hello." "The installation will begin next Tuesday. A Mister Langford will be calling you to get the details of what we discussed and what should be installed."

Finally, she thought. After someone broke in and murdered the intern last May, she raised the question of security. The upgrade should have been done months ago; in fact, the installation was scheduled, but Arnold dragged his feet in honoring the request of the supervisors. It was Grady Lively, one of the supervisors, who pushed him to arrange for the upgrade.

"Mind, there will be no additions or changes, nothing that will cost more than the amount allotted," Arnold continued.

"How much is that?"

"Enough. Just make sure they have access to the building and whatever else they need."

"How long will the installation take?"

"A day, or so they said. Why?"

"I may need to notify researchers who are scheduled to come in."

"They won't be interfered with. Eleanor is certain there will be little noise or bother."

Ah, yes, Eleanor. His wife. She who knows everything.

There was a click on the line and he was gone. No "goodbye" or "how are you." For an instant, it crossed her mind that this was a good opportunity to tell him about the events uncovered in the Blair papers. His sudden ringing off convinced her that there was no need.

But Sydney decided to talk to Sheriff Otis at the earliest opportunity. Her first loyalty was to the archives, and she had no intention of shirking that duty. Besides, she was curious.

CHAPTER 4

Otis looked uncomfortable, as the chair on the other side of the desk was too small for him. That was probably Sydney's perspective. He seemed not to mind, being accustomed to having to accommodate to a world designed for smaller people.

He stood six foot, four inches, and probably weighed in the neighborhood of two hundred seventy-five pounds. What most often drew people's attention were his very large hands that looked capable of crushing a large melon to mush. The full-sized pencil he currently held appeared half its size. She knew from experience that the man himself was gentle and intelligent, in spite of his size and his good ol' boy Oklahoma personality.

Sydney told him she only wanted his opinion on something. She wasn't issuing a complaint or anything. But he pulled out his ubiquitous little spiral bound notebook with the pencil poised to take notes if necessary.

"Like I told you on the phone, Otis, the questions I have are about something in one of our collections." He hated his first name, which was Alexander. No one ever called him that. Ever.

Otis nodded, watching her face thoughtfully as she went into teacher mode.

"It's sensitive because one of our state senators is the grandson of the man who created the collection." Otis's eyebrows rose and his forehead wrinkled. "The papers belonged to his grandfather, Carl Blair, and his grandson is Senator Grayson Blair, Jr., Carl's father, James, homesteaded in the land run of 1893, and Carl started the Blair Bar Ranch on that land. You know about the Blair Bar Ranch, I'm sure." Otis nodded. He was Oklahoman, born and bred.

Sydney took a deep breath and told the sheriff briefly what

she'd found in the few pages of a journal written by Carl Blair. She handed him a clean copy of the journal pages. On the originals, the handwriting was neat, the ink brown and still dark, the words clear, so the copies were also clear.

He read the words Carl used to describe how he and his two sons flogged a man nearly to death. They believed that he had slept with Lily, Carl's daughter, accusing the half-breed, Johnny Whitefeather, of raping her. Reading between the lines, Sydney suspected that the girl was a willing participant, that she met Johnny on many occasions when she went out on her forays into the prairie. She may have been in love with him.

There were no hints of how they found out, but again her instincts told her that Lily might have been pregnant and eventually couldn't hide it. She could have been followed on one of her treks, of course, but the men certainly waited quite a while to do that. There wasn't a hint that she had accused Johnny of rape. It wouldn't have mattered to the men of her family either way. Johnny was half Indian and half black, and he must be punished for presuming to consort with a white woman, their sister and daughter.

Otis finished reading then looked up. "The statute of limitations has most likely run out," he said. "I'll check on that. If this Johnny Whitefeather died later, however . . . well, that's another story."

"Would you say that finding what happened to him is impossible?"

"Probably. People of mixed blood, especially coloreds, were not documented as well as whites. If he belonged to a tribe, that might make it easier. But I won't know until I do some looking." He glanced back down at the pages in his hands, then handed them back to her. "No one else knows about this?"

"Only Doctor Berger and me. Oh, Doctor Tallidge might have read that part, but she died in a car accident over a week ago. I haven't even told Doctor Arnold."

"For the moment, let's keep it that way." She nodded agreement. They both knew that Arnold couldn't keep things to himself, especially if they were the least bit exciting. He liked to appear to be in the know. "Could you get me a copy of those pages?"

"Take these. I made them for you." She handed them back to Otis.

"Do you have any idea where the rest of the journal is?"

"No. It might be somewhere in the collection, but I haven't done a thorough search for it, yet. This collection was processed before I came here, and I haven't done much with it. I think Doctor Berger and Doctor Tallidge might be the first to look through it."

"You might want to look for it. See if there's anything else, like a list of cowhands. See if this Johnny's name is on it."

She nodded, having planned to do exactly that. After a few more pleasantries, the sheriff left her to her work.

Curiosity was what drove her to spend hours seeking information hiding in original documents. Now, she couldn't help reflecting on the possibility of finding more of interest in the Blair collection. Ben warned her when she told him about the Blairs over the phone. "Remember the last time." She remembered all too well. But this time was different. She had turned it over to Otis and would do the same with anything else she might find. She hoped that a list of workers on the ranch was somewhere in the boxes. Searching for it could be easy if the original inventory contained good detail.

Friday afternoon came with its promise of a work week ended and a weekend free of the archives and responsibilities. Work responsibilities, that is. Since she often left work well past six in the evening, she rarely had time to do any of the errands required for taking care of a house and a life. Living in Gansel made it necessary to drive several miles south to grocery shop, or any other shopping for that matter. Except for insurance, legal help, flowers, gas, funerals, and religion.

She marveled that her friend Julia's flower shop survived, much less did a roaring business. The restaurants also managed to survive, none of them large chain establishments or even a fast food provider, except for the Dairy Queen. Chuck's Bar served food, had a bad reputation, and she never went inside it, although she was curious, which she curbed for safety's sake.

She kept forgetting about the newly opened branch of the library, in one of the store fronts located not far from the florist shop. She had yet to visit it, but had the impression that their collection was small and limited.

She turned her chair from the window with its view out onto the nearly empty street. The three-ring binder with the finding aid for the Blair collection lay open about half way through. She'd looked through it during the week, and several pages of the first half bore sticky tabs, marking where she found journals or possible journals listed. The entire inventory of contents of the boxes was drawn up haphazardly, with less detail than usual. It would have to be re-done one of these days, but not until she could get another unpaid intern. Not one student showed interest when the position was posted at most of the Oklahoma universities for the past two semesters. Who would want to work in a place where the last intern was murdered?

Sydney looked around as if the question was spoken aloud. Being alone most of the time had her talking out loud to herself or to Lewis, her part Maine coon cat, habits she kept trying to break. Most people would consider that very odd, indeed. Most of her life she'd had few friends, never fitting into whatever common mold she found either among schoolmates, co-workers, or social acquaintances. In her generation, most women married young and settled down. She and Leo married relatively young, but chose not to have children, a decision that separated them from everyone they knew. After her husband died, she became restless and moved to three different cities. After a romantic involvement ended, the one that brought her to Oklahoma, she went back to school, earning a master's degree in library studies. It was during those two years that she worked as a graduate assistant in the Congressional Archives at the University. The jobs she took right after were part-time and more for the learning experience than the small salaries they offered.

The sort of gypsy life she had chosen led to short friendships or none at all. She'd made friends in Norman, especially classmates, many of them her own age. After moving north, however, she was lonely sometimes. But she enjoyed her own company and books helped take the edge off. Lewis was a great companion, too, although typically demanding. Her work also filled her days in a way that she enjoyed and found exciting. Most people would think her crazy to think that the archival world was exciting. Then there were occasional trips south to join friends in seeing movies or plays, even live music.

She mentally brushed away these thoughts and brought herself back to the task at hand. Since Sydney brought the flogging incident to his attention earlier in the week, Sheriff Otis called back once to see if she'd made any progress in finding the full journal. It had only been two days, she explained, and there were sixty boxes of papers and ephemera. Carl Blair not only was a rancher and showman, he also represented his district for two terms in the state legislature in Oklahoma City, after the state gained statehood in 1907.

The organization of the papers was haphazard and the box list was of little help. Personal and family records, business records, and political records resided in the same boxes. She began by looking through lists of boxes containing what appeared to be mostly personal records, thinking that would be the most logical part of the collection to search. She did find three journals, but not the right ones. It appeared that Carl was in the habit of writing accounts of life, both personal and business, for his whole life.

If the box list was detailed and complete, it was the best way to find them quickly. The gaps in the dates soon made it clear that not every one was listed. To ensure finding them all, she would have to pull every box instead of those few she was able to identify from the list.

It was just another example of how having little time for going through the older collections that she had inherited limited their usability. They were supposedly organized and in good shape, and there were a few that could be so described. Several newer collections needed preliminary inventories and eventual sorting. But most of the collections needed a great deal of work. She did take time for the usual background research for the Blairs, which helped her to understand some of what was listed in the finding aid, and added background to what researchers found in the collection.

There was plenty of work, not to mention the security people coming to install the upgrade to the alarm system. Checking, she assured herself that appointment was on her calendar for Tuesday. She double checked, too, that Doctor Arnold wasn't on her schedule. He would not appreciate her search for the journal for Sheriff Otis since it took her away from working on the more current projects. Thank goodness the Bartlett collection was mostly finished. Only posting the finding aid online remained.

When five o'clock came, it was difficult to pull herself away from looking for evidence of the journals in the finding aid, which she had gone back to, intending to look for only a few more minutes. It was always like this when she started researching in general or searching for specific information. This was the work that suited her personality and her skills, including her need to organize. Only a few of her friends understood the need and the curiosity satisfied by her work, mostly those she'd met in graduate school.

For her part, she grew weary of hearing many of her friends and co-workers always talking about children and grandchildren. Not that she didn't love children. She did. However, some talked about the kids so much, one would think nothing else mattered in their lives. Some of them pitied her for being childless, to which she would respond, if only to herself, that at least the world's population didn't increase on her account. She did not regret the decision not to have children. Lewis made enough demands on her time and patience.

But life could get lonely without family. She tried not to think about that. Besides, Ben was in her life now. True, it was on a part time basis, which suited her just fine.

These were thoughts that often ran through her mind as she prepared to leave the archives and head out to an empty house on a Friday night. Well, not entirely empty. Lewis would be there demanding his kibble and, even more, her undivided attention.

She turned toward the door, headed for the side exit and parking lot. Turning back suddenly, she grabbed up the binder with the Blair finding aid to look through at home and stuck it in her book bag.

She piled the bag and her purse in the back of the SUV as usual and climbed into the driver's seat. She dialed up Julia on her cell phone at the flower shop to see if she might be having dinner alone. They both liked Molly's Café, which served pretty good home-cooked meals, usually enough for two. And since Julia liked to pick at the food on other people's plates, there was a chance she was just the right dinner companion.

This time, though, there was no answer at the shop. Julia must have gone home early. She debated going to the café by herself, but decided on leftover soup at home.

The most important task for the evening, after feeding the cat, was to make out her shopping list. Saturday she would drive down to Edmond, her retail mecca of choice, have lunch maybe at 501 Café, then come home and put her purchases away. She wrote herself a reminder on a Post-It note to take the cooler along to put the frozen and refrigerated items in and attached it to her purse. She forgot the cooler the last time and, although it made little difference in the condition of the food, she wanted to keep in the habit of taking the cooler.

Saturday night, Sydney looked through more of the finding aid and came upon an item that might just be what she was looking for. Sunday morning, she went into the archives; with the excitement of a treasure hunter, she didn't want to wait until Monday to find out if she was right.

When Ben called Saturday night, she told him about the find. He reminded her again of the dangers of getting involved in looking for clues of a crime, but she shrugged off his warnings.

"There's little chance of anything happening a second time," she'd said. "And I'm just looking for information for Otis. I haven't initiated anything."

"Well, I'm just saying . . ."

She liked that he worried and that he was coming soon to see her, and even more, she liked that they were not in each other's laps all of the time. She could take a visit for a while, even the man she was beginning to adore. But she had lived alone for so long—too long—to be comfortable with constant company. So when he said that he would have to postpone his visit, her disappointment surprised her. A project came up for a long-time client and he couldn't put him off. She understood that perfectly well, but the delay was more disappointing than she wanted to admit.

Work was a good distraction. That and her curiosity took her into the archives early Sunday. The streets were empty. All of the stores and offices were closed. Most of the residents were in one of the churches in town or in one of the surrounding towns. She and the regular patrons at Chuck's Bar and Grill were the few heathens living in Gansel.

She put her bags down on her desk and made her way into the stacks on the first floor. Racks of metal shelving stood nearly as high as the twelve-foot ceiling, leaving just enough room to place a Hollinger archival box on the top shelf with a few inches above for air flow and to satisfy the fire marshal. The boxes were of a size such that either legal size folders or letter size would stand upright.

The shelves were arranged so that the fluorescent lights hung between the racks, to make it possible to read the writing on the ends of the boxes. Each one was labeled in dark pencil with the name of the collection, which was the name of the person who created the documents, the year, series, and sub-series. Only a few required more detailed labeling. Some of the older boxes bore typed labels that were glued on, a practice that was old form, as the glue dried out and the labels were often found on the floor.

The box she was looking for sat in the third row from the back, third shelf from the bottom. She pushed the library book cart close to the shelf and put the box on the top, wheeling it into her office next to her worktable. Lifting the top off, she started searching through the folder titles until she came to a journal slipped between two of them. It was tall and slender and filled with figures relating to business. She wrote a brief description of the item on a "Pulled" card, the size of the folders, and put it in place of the journal.

Continuing from there, she found two more. She pulled both of them, but the third one was the one she was looking for.

She laid all three on the table, marking their places in the box with "pulled" cards, then replaced the box on the shelf. Selecting the journal that she'd been seeking, she opened the cover. Noted on the first page in black ink was the range of dates for the notations in the journal, which included the date of interest. She felt the thrill of discovery that always came after a long search. It wasn't gold or anything else that most people would find of value. But to her, specific information, facts from a person's life, from history, was as exciting.

The leather binding of the journal was tight, the pages clean, the neat writing inside in brown ink covering every page except the last five. The page numbers were pre-printed in red on the upper corner of the outer edge, the lines in blue. Vertical margin lines were also in red, but some notes were written outside the margins, added thoughts, sometimes in pencil or blue ink.

Each section of writing was dated on the top line of the page. She riffled the pages, looking for July 22 or 24, 1941. The pages Doctor Berger found loose were dated the twenty-third.

Seeing Lily's name she stopped. The date was May 19th.

A tornado came through this day around 5 in the pm. Not much damage to the ranch. An outlying building destroyed, but that was it. Worried about Lily. She went out on one of her jaunts morning before and hasn't gotten back. Figured she would come back soonest after the storm. Will go looking tomorrow if shes not back.

The next day's entry began with Carl sending some of his men to the north pastures to check on the cattle. Lily had not reappeared by noon, so he and Grayson, who apparently had returned home after his business failed, went looking for her. They headed west, which was the direction she usually took from the ranch. They suspected where she might have camped, a place she often spoke of as one of her favorites. She was always a bit secretive about exactly where she went, and they took advantage of being able to see long distances from high spots.

Headed for Potter's creek and the pool it forms just below the bluff. Cottonwoods and a willow or two grow there, pretty tall. No trace of the tornado passing through, nor of Lily at first. My horse lifted its head at the scent of water and called out, trying to rush straight for it. Since we'd watered the horses good before leaving, it seemed odd he was that excited. Then heard an answering call from the trees.

The father and son rode down side by side toward the trees. As they got closer, they saw three horses, one unsaddled and tied to one of the smaller cottonwoods beside the pack horse with its burden spread about the campsite. The third horse was being saddled in a hurry, but the man stood stock still on seeing them so near. Carl spotted Lily standing a short ways apart, hands on hips, watching them ride up. So, they found out about her liaisons this way.

I saw that it was Johnny Whitefeather saddling the horse. I asked what was going on. Lily said she had been camping in the grove when the storm started up. A while later, Johnny had come up looking for shelter. Grayson challenged the bastard, accusing him of molesting his sister, which he denied. Lily denied it too. She swore she told the truth. We warned the half-breed off, telling him if we ever found him near Lily again, we would kill him. He left in a hurry.

Rode home with Lily and Grayson. Told her she would not be going out alone again. She argued and I told her I'd horsewhip her if she did. She said no more and neither did I, seein as how she knew I meant what I said.

No more was written in the journal about Lily until a month later. Sydney had found the rest of the story. Lily was pregnant and admitted that the child was Johnny's. They were in love and she continued seeing him, sneaking out when she could, mostly when her father and brothers were out tending to the cattle. Carl's words pressed into the paper, the sentences short and terse. Sydney felt surprised that he'd written about it at all. True, his journals showed that he wrote down nearly everything important in his life—ranch happenings in the official journals, personal events in the smaller journals. The three pages with the description of Johnny's flogging came from the personal journal.

Sydney checked the time. It was after two and she still had laundry to do at home, plus some cleaning around the house. She was a creature of habit and often bristled at having to change her routine. But this . . . this story was too compelling to just leave. For one of the few times in her career, she put the journals in her book bag and carried them home to finish reading. First, however, she wanted to find the next journal in sequence.

Whoever organized the collection didn't work very hard at getting things together. The next journal turned up an hour later in another box far removed from the one in which she found the first part. It was later than she liked when she left the archives and headed home.

First thing was to feed Lewis, who was unhappy with her for being so late. He fussed and rubbed against her legs, nearly tripping her in her rush to get his food down for him. She then hurried through the chores, leaving laundry for the next day, and fixed a quick dinner of stir-fried kielbasa and vegetables. Afterwards, with a last cup of coffee, she sat at the kitchen table to read the journals and make notes. The table top gave her more room than the top of her desk in the separate office. She made certain that the table top was free of any food residue and set her coffee cup on the nearest counter. A spill would be so damaging if it got on the journal when she spread out materials, thus the extra caution.

She placed the loose pages back in place in the earlier journal, then picked up the later one. She started reading at the very beginning, not wanting to miss any possible mention of events relating to Lily and Johnny and what her family might have done. Sydney was certain that the outcome could not have been good.

CHAPTER 5

The front bell rang and Sydney jumped. For the past hour she sat in her office waiting for that very sound, and when it came it was too loud and jarring. She'd called Sheriff Otis only minutes after getting into the office. He was out at the time, but the deputy promised to give him the message. While she waited, Sydney tried to concentrate on the documents currently in process, but it was hard going. Every noise outside and inside the old bank building sent her gaze through the window onto the street.

Relieved that he was finally here, she went to the door to let the sheriff in, only to find that it was a stranger wanting to know if this was where she could find county birth records. Sydney directed her to the county court house on Main Street. The name of the Filmore County Historical Archives fooled more than one person looking for official records. The woman thanked her and walked away just as the sheriff's huge black SUV pulled up to the curb. Otis climbed out on the driver's side and walked around toward the door.

"Mornin' Sydney."

"Mornin', Otis."

She pushed the door further open and stepped aside to allow for the sheriff's bulk to get through the door and followed him into the office.

"You found something else?" he asked as they sat down.

"Yes. I don't know if it will help, but I found a later journal. It turns out that Lily was pregnant and Johnny Whitefeather was the father."

"She admitted it?"

"Yes. I haven't found any more about Lily for at least two years. I haven't gotten any beyond that yet. And nothing more on Johnny, except a short sentence saying that Carl and Grayson went looking for him."

Otis nodded and thought for a moment. Sydney tapped the eraser of her pencil on the desktop while she waited.

"They probably sent her off to have the baby somewhere. They used to have homes for unwed mothers where such babies were born then adopted out." She nodded and waited again.

"Do you know if there were any relatives back east?" he asked after some thought.

"Probably were, but I haven't come across any mention of them. I know young women might also be sent to live with other relatives when they got into trouble. Or Lily could have just run away. She was very independent."

They talked over other possibilities, listing them more than discussing which was most probable.

"I've got requests out for information on Johnny Whitefeather," Otis said. "But if I start an inquiry about Lily Blair, it'll be official, at least too official. The papers could get hold of it, and I wouldn't want to stir up anything at the moment. Senator Blair is retiring this year."

And in another year, maybe he would run for governor, at least according to rumors, although his age might make that unlikely. She certainly did not want to be the source for a scandal or even a speculative story that could ruin his reputation. That would not reflect well on her or the archives. But her curiosity was up and running.

"You can probably be more discreet, inquiring about the whereabouts of Lily and any child she had," he continued. "My inclination is to just let the whole thing drop, but if there was a crime involved . . ."

"Wouldn't Johnny's death because of the flogging count as a crime?"

"Probably not in the day because of who they all were. But I know about it and it's my job to follow up. I also know you. Your curiosity is buzzing and you want to know what happened, no matter what I decide to do. But move carefully. I'm sure you can come up with some sort of background for asking questions, seeing as you're an archivist and all."

"Yes."

"But it won't be official. Be casual about it. And keep me apprised about anything you find."

"Yes."

"I'm not fooling, Sydney. You nearly got yourself killed once."

"Twice," she corrected, referring to the efforts of Violet Parsons last spring. Otis frowned. "I know. I'll be careful. And I'll keep you apprised."

Otis stood and looked down at her. "Promise," he said.

"I promise."

He got up and went to the main door. She had left it unlocked when he came in and he opened it, stepped outside, then turned toward her.

"How did you know?" he asked. She arched an eyebrow in question. "That Lily was pregnant?"

"I've been doing this for a long time. You get to where you read between the lines."

He nodded and strode to his car.

The rest of the day she continued studying the inventory of boxes in the Blair collection, making a list of those that might contain information pertaining to Lily and the time period in which she seemed to have disappeared. With that finished, she turned to her computer to see what she could find on Senator Grayson Blair, Jr. The current organizing project was forgotten.

According to the biographies, he was born in 1941, the year after his Aunt Lily disappeared. He was the grandson of Carl Blair, founder of the Blair Bar Ranch, and two-term state representative. Carl died in 1975. His father, Grayson, Sr., was born in 1909, died in 1983. His Uncle Lawrence was only mentioned by name, and nothing about Lily. Grayson, Sr., married a woman named Gladys Smith, Grayson, Jr.'s mother, who died in childbirth in 1941. There was nothing else on her, not even her birthplace or parents' names.

Sydney made a note to check on official records for birth, death, and marriages. The state's vital records online weren't accessible by the public except with permission of the subject or family. The exceptions were in death records occurring seventy-five years ago or births occurring 125 years ago. Her name was listed with the site as an archivist, but they still required her to jump through some hoops to do many searches. It helped to have memberships in several genealogical search sites and several other websites where she could search vital statistics. She spent much of the rest of the week intermittently searching through the records she could access.

By the end of the day Tuesday, the alarm installer came and went, taking less than a full day to accomplish the task. All of the journals noted in the inventory were pulled from various boxes; however, she suspected there might be more not on the list, given the gaps in dates. Reading through three of them, she discovered two amazing facts about Carl Blair. One, he was a hard man, even cruel at times, both with his family and with those who worked for him. There were a few favorites among the ranch workers, those who curried his favor, but even they didn't seem to stay around very long. As for his family, in the late 1800s and early 1900s, all rights belonged to the husband and father.

The second discovery was even more bizarre: He wrote it all down in his journals. Disciplining of the hands he wrote down in the ranch journals along with details on the stock, water, weather. The incidents were described in cold detail, as if everything within his sphere possessed no feelings, could feel no pain or humiliation. Corporal punishment was ordered for many infractions of his rigid rules, carried out by himself or his foremen, of which there were several.

He didn't spare his family, either. The two boys were given whippings for talking back and a good number of other infractions. Once, he ordered fourteen-year-old Lawrence to stand out in the rain for an hour, holding a dead calf in his arms. Earlier, the boy accidentally let the calf get out of the pen. There was no reason given for why the calf was dead. The last line read, *He won't be that careless again.*

Sydney felt cold herself when she read that account late Wednesday afternoon. What sort of men did those boys grow up to be? What they each did for a living was no indication of whether their ethics or sense of compassion were warped. Nor, she realized, was there much mention of Lily or Carl's wife, Alice. As females, were they unimportant? Or did they manage to deflect his anger somehow? Did they have any place on the ranch other than cooking and cleaning and perhaps hosting parties?

The fact that Carl was angry enough to flog Johnny Whitefeather for his liaison with Lily indicated that he thought of his daughter as a possession. A loving father might be tempted to do the same thing, but not write about it so boldly, almost proudly, in his journal. But then, Sydney, reading the words from a safe distance in time, never experienced much violence, nor had she ever known a man like Carl.

Once she read through the few journals she found, they were placed in boxes and a new inventory begun. When the inventory was finished, it would replace the original on the website and be labeled "finding aid." For now, she simply made an adjustment in the posted inventory so that any potential researchers would see that they existed and that they were accessible. After she hit the "save" button for the last time, she did wonder if someone was checking the archive's website and if the finding aid might provoke someone to action. It was still difficult to believe that her Internet traffic, over and above the website, was monitored. She also didn't believe that there was any danger. Sure, danger existed last year, but that was because of a deranged person.

After the events of the past year, "Remember Violet Parsons" became her mantra. However, she had a job to do, and the online finding aid was a big part of that.

Doctor Arnold made no further appearance for the rest of the week, for which she was grateful. His occasional interference, based on his lack of knowledge of archival practices, and the opinions of his wife, could make her job more difficult. Happily, she was learning to work around his demands, proposals, and suggestions in ways that satisfied him and, in the end, gave her free rein. One of her tactics was to do certain tasks when he was absent from the archives. Of course, she told herself, the current lessening of interference was due in part to his wife's being in southern Europe for a month. How that woman hated cold weather.

The one making the most demands on her time these days was Lewis, her cat. His behavior was becoming so worrisome that she made an appointment with the vet first thing Saturday morning. Friday night he seemed more active and she toyed with the idea of putting off the appointment. Checking his records, she found that his regular checkup was due next month, so she decided to just get it over with.

She also decided to take the journals home to work on over the weekend, much against her better judgment, but her curiosity needed satisfaction. Ben called as she started to leave the office to postpone his trip again. He wanted to let her know as soon as possible. The disappointment she felt lessened her interest in the information still unread in the journals. Closing up shop, she decided to run over to Molly's for supper. Friday night was chili night in the winter, and she loved Molly's chili. Not too hot, not too mild. Just right.

She was sounding like Goldilocks, which made her smile in spite of herself. Should someone laugh at her own jokes? Especially if they were silly?

Molly's was crowded as usual on a Friday evening. Several people greeted her as she made her way to her favorite booth. The end of the work week for most in Gansel meant a night out. Maybe even a movie in Edmond or Stillwater.

She ordered her chili and water, then opened her computer to check her personal email. Coffee came later at home while she did some more research online. Saturday nights Ben and she spoke for an hour or more on the phone. They were both old enough to prefer the telephone to any of the other methods of communication. She'd never learned how to Skype, although it was on her computer. And live chat was so distorted to her eye that she felt very uncomfortable watching it. After they hung up, which was around ten p.m. her time, she often stayed up researching, reading, or watching a little TV if she could find something on.

Researching was often her downfall. It was just too easy to follow the leads found in one source, to others, to others. Just like reading the dictionary, which she did when she was young. Now, she found herself looking up words—most everything, really—on the Internet. She hated that, yet found it so easy and quick that she couldn't help using that resource. For facts and general information, over and above spelling and synonyms, she started with the Internet, then followed up with books, libraries, and official records. However, even the latter were often available online these days.

She closed her computer and was about to get up out of the booth when the café door opened and Julia Vincent walked in. She stopped just inside the door and shouted to all and sundry, "It's cold out there!" Some people nodded agreement, others agreed out loud, as Julia grinned. She spotted Sydney and wound her way between tables.

"Oh, you're finished," she said.

Julia often did not order her own meal, just picking at other people's food. She always claimed that she "wasn't really hungry," and that she "never gained weight." In reality she was slightly overweight, but not enough to be a problem. Her still-blond hair was cut short and tonight she wore a stocking cap to keep her head warm.

She sat down, rubbing her hands together, and shrugged out of her fake fur coat. She reached for the menu standing against the wall behind the napkin holder, and actually ordered chili-cheese french fries. Sydney ordered coffee, figuring she would be another half hour or so, now that there was someone to talk with.

"What's up these days?" Julia asked as Patty, the new waitress, walked away.

"Just the usual." Sydney resisted the temptation to tell her friend about the Blair secrets. There might be little to it, and it would do no one any good to spread suspicions around. Julia was a good and honest friend, but she loved a good story, both in the telling and in the hearing. Instead, she talked about the alarm installation and the collections currently being organized.

"How's Paul doing?"

Julia's husband, Paul, had driven north, last she'd heard. He made very good money, and between that and the flower shop, they made a good living.

"He's stuck in Nebraska. I guess you heard about the snowstorm up there a couple of days ago." Sydney nodded. "They couldn't even get the warehouse doors open so he could unload. Frozen shut under a huge snow drift. The roads are still too bad for him to risk driving home."

"He'll be up there over the weekend?"

Julia nodded. She hated spending the weekend by herself. She was one of the friendliest people Sydney ever knew. Everyone who met her loved her. Yet, she seemed to have few close friends. Sydney and she often met for dinner and a few times saw a movie together. There were thirteen years between them—Sydney being younger—but they interacted as equals.

"So, how are things for the weekend?" Sydney asked.

"Oh, I've started a project in the house. Painting the spare bedroom. Paul was supposed to help when he got home, but . . ." She shrugged.

They discussed paint colors and what to use in various rooms and the best techniques. Under all the small talk, Sydney thought of her own weekend, wondering if she might go down to Norman and visit with some of her friends there. Sometimes it felt as if those friendships were fading away, partly because most of her friends thought Gansel was too far to drive.

She stayed with Julia as she finished the french fries, taking a couple for herself. She refused a refill on the coffee.

"When will you see Ben again?" Julia asked.

"He was supposed to come this week, but he got tied up with a client. We changed it to next week then postponed again."

"Again?"

"Yes." She shrugged. "It's hard to tell when he'll be able to make it."

"I thought tax season was slowing down for him."

"There was a problem for one of his clients and he has to be there to meet with the IRS. Then another client found out he was still in town."

She must have sounded really bummed about the postponement because Julia reached over and squeezed her hand.

"It's okay. He'll get here." She moved her hand back and ate another french fry. "Wanta come over and help me paint this weekend?"

Sydney started to say no, but there was no real reason not to. It would keep her busy and her mind occupied on something mundane for a while.

"I'll let you know. The weather might get bad."

Julia finished her fries and they both paid their bills. Outside, they hugged and climbed into their cars. It was so cold that Sydney was afraid the moisture from her breath might ice up on the inside of the windshield. She sat with the motor running for a short time, letting it warm up. The drive to her house was too short to generate much warmth.

It wasn't surprising that this winter turned so cold. Last spring started very warm, with thunder storms and tornadoes followed by the summer warming very quickly. The summer heated up, staying in the nineties through August, even hitting the hundreds several days in a row. A cold dreary winter often followed that sort of summer and fall. One morning black ice covered the roads as the ground stayed cold, but so far this year, no damaging ice storm.

She pulled into the driveway of her rented house and turned out the headlights. Climbing out, she looked up. Here, on the edge of Gansel, there was even less light pollution than there was downtown, and the sky was black. Stars sparkled against the soft velvety background in the heat of summer. In winter, it more closely resembled black ice, making the stars brighter and sharper.

She shivered in the slight breeze but continued to look up as she leaned back against the side of her old CR-V. Directly above, she identified Orion with Betelgeuse at the left shoulder. In a few minutes she was too cold to stay out. She opened the back door behind the driver's seat and retrieved her purse and book bag.

The house was warm, and Lewis was insistent that she was letting him starve to death. The Maine coon part of him meant he was quite large, and his appetite matched. It was not easy feeding him sensibly so he didn't get too fat. Tonight, she was feeding him much later than usual, and she would pay with his persistent yowling.

Within fifteen minutes, she put her purse and book bag down, shrugged out of the leather jacket, and put Lewis's food down on the floor. She undressed in the bedroom, putting on her long flannel gown, and in minutes, sat at the computer in the small bedroom she used as an office. First, she checked her email, reading one from Ben first. He was so sorry about having to postpone again, but when he called later in the evening, they could plan on his coming east in two weeks. He went on to say how much he missed her and couldn't wait to see her. Jokingly, he said something vague about the possibility of his moving to Oklahoma and flying to Los Angeles to conduct his business, which was usually seasonal.

She answered just as vaguely about his moving, tentative as usual about getting so involved with someone. She was still leery of that, even though she wanted to see Ben as often as possible.

The phone rang at nine o'clock, an hour earlier for Ben on the west coast. Wind rattled the windows and the bare branches of the tree in the backyard in bursts, reminding her of the sound of Pick-Up Sticks that she played with as a child. Hot coals glowed in the fireplace, a glass of Moscato sat on the table beside her, the afghan lay over her legs, and Lewis had tucked himself in against her. This was what made winter tolerable, even enjoyable if she was honest with herself.

She liked to use the speaker phone, and Ben used his landline connection through his computer, leaving his hands free to look things up on the computer, or thumb through magazines or books. He loved to read articles to her or bits from books he was reading, one of the things they enjoyed sharing. For her part, she liked not having to hold a phone handset up to her ear while her hand went numb, just one of the signs that she was older. As a teenager, she talked on the phone with friends for hours, accepting the discomfort as part of the experience.

They told each other the week's events. Long conversations on Friday or Saturday nights became their ritual, without planning it. Ben went first, describing the wonderful weather and that he met one of his clients near the beach in San Diego. She scolded him for boasting about the wonderful warm weather, while she suffered in the Oklahoma wind and freezing temperatures. Still, he worked eight to ten hours each day with a few extra hours in the evenings, so she forgave him. It was a busy week, and he'd enjoyed it. Even so, he regretted not being in Gansel with her. His plans were still not set, but he was working on it.

Sydney described the cold and windy weather and that the weatherman said there might be ice early the next week. She briefly repeated the conversation with Doctor Berger, how he'd been worried about what he'd read, and that she contacted Sheriff Otis to see if the archives had any responsibilities regarding the knowledge of the commission of a crime over seventy years before.

The next week was going to be even more hectic for Ben as a couple of his other clients found out he was still in town. When she said how much she looked forward to working on the Blair collection, he expressed concern. She promised to only discuss information she found on Johnny and Lily with Sheriff Otis and to leave the rest to him. Any further research was for the sheriff's benefit, after all.

They talked for a while about the things they wanted to do when he was finally able to come to Gansel. He promised that this time he would do some cooking for her. His repertoire contained only a few dishes at which he was very competent. They laughed, planned what wines she should get, and he wished her good luck with Lewis the next day at the vet's. When they finally hung up at eleven her time, an hour later than usual, the wind had died down, leaving her wrapped in silence, except for the crackle from the glowing coals and the circle of light of the single lamp standing beside the sofa. Gradually, the sound of a train whistle came to her out of the darkness to the west, bringing to mind the old Hank Williams song about the lonely whippoorwill.

She stretched out on the sofa, lying back against the pillows, and stroked Lewis. He was asleep and didn't move, letting her adjust his position, but his purring could be heard from the other side of the room.

Her thoughts went to the Blair family. Pictures of Grayson, Jr., were online, of course, but she didn't know what his brother Lawrence looked like. Grayson was tall and thin, stern-looking and wearing what appeared to be a designer suit. Pictures of Carl were in the collection, although she needed to locate them. She had one picture of Lily as a teenager, she thought. Finding a picture of Lawrence would be her next task. There were no photos listed of his two children, which meant little as she'd found that the original inventory was incomplete and in some ways inaccurate.

She threw off the afghan and slid from under Lewis, letting his large self rest on the sofa. His head came up for only a moment, then he lowered his chin to his paw and went back to sleep.

In the office, Sydney turned on the computer and went into the kitchen to pour a glass of orange juice. Settling into the desk chair, she clicked on her Internet icon and began searching. Two hours later, she sorted through the few pages she printed out and began studying them.

There were several photographs of Lawrence from newspapers in Ponca City and Oklahoma City. Most of them dealt with his legal work. He'd even argued one case before the state Supreme Court, which occasioned a story in *The Oklahoman*, Oklahoma City's newspaper. The oldest one was of him and his new bride, blurred with age. They both looked rather ordinary and self-conscious as they posed for the camera.

The more interesting photos, however, were even older. They were of the Blair Bar Ranch and some of the entertainment the family arranged for tourists. People frowned, laughed, looked awestruck at the skills of marksmen and riders. What she hoped to find was one that might name Lily in the picture.

Glancing at the clock on the computer screen, she realized that it was after two o'clock. Her eyes were burning from not taking a break away. She couldn't really make much sense of the pictures any more. Time to go to bed and work on this tomorrow. Before turning off the computer, she checked her email one last time.

Looking through the list of messages, she found one of interest in the spam folder. The name "Blair" was included in the subject line, reading in full, "No more looking at blair family."

She placed the curser on the message, hesitating to open it. How would anyone know that she looked at Blair family history? Why would anyone think it was a bad idea? She was the archivist in charge of Carl Blair's papers, after all. Of course, not everyone would know that. Still, it seemed impossible that anyone knew she'd been searching for information, much less the reason for it.

She pressed the button and the message opened. It contained a link, but no explanation. Opening a link in an email from someone she didn't know was the height of folly. And yet, she did just that.

CHAPTER 6

"Might anyone in your office know about our interest in the Blairs?"

Sheriff Otis frowned at the suggestion in a way that made Sydney think he already considered that possibility. It was Monday morning, and she called him about the strange email. He came right over.

"Yeah. I had my best Internet person looking for information. But would she tell anyone? I don't think so. She's been with me for fifteen years and most of my deputies have been with me for a decade or more."

"Are any of them connected to the Blairs in any way?"

He shook his head. "Two of them aren't even native Oklahomans."

She sat thinking a moment. The only inquiries she made were through ordinary data bases on the Internet, and the likelihood that someone might have intercepted those queries was very small. First, no one would have any reason to be checking her online work on a regular basis, yet they knew about her searches. Second, the county paid for high security on their Internet service. Yet, she couldn't help remembering something similar happening when she was involved in the Bartlett collection. At that time, the IT people went over their systems and found nothing out of the ordinary.

"Let me see the email again."

She gave him back the copy. The tone wasn't exactly threatening, just mildly warning:

There ain't no one wanting you to be messing around with the Blairs. So, just stop.

There was a link to an article from *The Oklahoman* newspaper about Senator Blair and his plans to retire and how popular he was. His last act, a very popular one, was to get a project authorized to create a monument to his father.

"It sounds as if someone was trying to make it look like they were uneducated, don't you think?"

He nodded agreement. "Almost as bad as one of those grammar nazis on Facebook who misuse "its" and "it's" to make a point."

"You're on Facebook?" She couldn't keep the note of surprise out of her voice.

"Yeah, for some time now. Lots of law enforcement offices are on there. We chat about problems, changes in technology, things like that. We even caught a thief by monitoring the chats."

"Really? Did you by chance mention the Blairs on there?"

He shook his head. "Don't think so. Maybe I should check with everyone in the office."

"Maybe. I've been careful myself, but my involvement in Oklahoma family histories isn't a big secret. Anyway, you can have that copy of the email. You understand why I'm a bit nervous about it, I'm sure."

"After what happened last year, it's no wonder. I'll bet no one ever thought of archival work as being dangerous."

"I sure didn't."

He grinned and got up. "I'll check with my deputies and get our IT people to see if they can track down the source. Let's hope that there's nothing to that note."

"Yeah, let's."

She let him out the door facing the street where his marked SUV sat at the curb. He was one of the few people Sydney felt should have one of the big vehicles, given his size. He wasn't fat, just big. In his uniform and with the shiny badge pinned to his shirt, he was extremely imposing.

Back in her office, she went back to the finding aid for the Bartlett collection that she'd been neglecting. There was little left to do, and she needed to be able to give Dr. Arnold a positive report, should he ask.

Then there were the newer collections. She would have to review the work done thus far, but she remembered that one of them consisted mostly of business records, which raised the question in her own mind as to whether the archives might become the repository of a lot of such records. They could be of great historical interest, of course, but being a dumping ground for business records was not what she saw as her mission. On the other hand, Doctor Arnold had no such mission or vision in mind, and he agreed to take the collection when the business closed its doors for the last time, without asking for any input from her.

She would have at least liked to do an appraisal before they accepted everything they had. Plus there was no evidence of the deed of gift yet, and she couldn't help wondering if one existed. Until it turned up, she would not spend one minute on organizing it.

She'd found only some of the journals that were scattered throughout the boxes of Blair documents; she intended to search for others. Having looked through those few boxes, though, she now had an idea of how haphazard the organization was.

She sighed. Of late, there was so much to do, and without help of some kind, a lot of the collections would have to wait. She smiled as she picked up the original Blair inventory. It was created by a previous archivist when the boxes were received. There was no box list created by the Blairs to compare it with.

These days, in particular, she was what was called in the profession a lone arranger, a description that suited her to a tee. Over the past year, at least since Irene's death, she lost the part-time student and no one was found to come in as an intern. Charlene Hooks, retired librarian and part-time processor, came in when needed. Dr. Arnold insisted on approving any hours she worked, and requesting that approval was getting high on her list of options.

The original Blair inventory consisted of box numbers, folder numbers, dates, and a few vague words describing the content of each box, such as "Ranch, letters." No mention of subject, names, or any of the usual descriptions. Lack of organization in the boxes of the collection proved the biggest frustration, especially the mixture of dates in multiple boxes, too many of which didn't correspond to the inventory. There was little hope of finding specific information quickly.

Before starting, Sydney took a moment to call Julia. She had not called her over the weekend to say that she wouldn't be helping with painting and now felt guilty. They chatted for a few minutes, Julia forgiving her as usual. Her husband didn't unload his truck until Sunday, and then picked up another load that morning heading west. He wouldn't be back until Friday.

Then Julia asked, "Did that researcher find you this morning?"

"What researcher?"

"This man came into the store asking where the archives were located. I'm guessing that he didn't make it there."

"No, I've not seen anyone today."

"Odd. He seemed very keen on knowing where you were."

Sydney glanced at the clock on her computer screen. It was past one o'clock.

"What did he look like?" There was a pause. "Was he nicely dressed? Young or old? Tall or short?" Julia interrupted before she could add any other comparison.

"Pretty nondescript. Wearing jeans and t-shirt, I think, but his jacket was zipped up. Nothing really notable."

"When did you see him?"

"A little past nine. Just after I opened. Maybe he stopped to get breakfast at Molly's or something. Or maybe he got a call or . . ."

"It doesn't matter," Sydney said, filling the following silence. "He'll probably be here sooner or later."

"Probably."

After agreeing to meet for lunch or dinner soon, they hung up. Sydney sat looking out the window in deep thought. The wind picked up as predicted on the radio earlier in the morning, making the world feel much colder than the actual temperature, even inside her office. A few papers skittered down the street, mesmerizing when she was deep in thought. As she was now. She couldn't help wondering about someone asking for directions to the archives, but not arriving. Admittedly, the conflict with Violet Parsons and her grandson made her gun shy, but that sort of thing almost never happened in real life.

Ever since Violet came near to killing her, Sydney wondered what she should have done—or not done—to prevent it all. She could have left the whole thing to the police, but her expertise came into play in finding details in the case. Most of all, though, she was spurred to action by the lack of interest displayed by the police.

They believed it a simple break-in gone wrong, but Sydney never believed that. Following her instincts and her curiosity led down the path to murder and attempted murder.

Irene's murder resulted simply from the Bartlett collection being given to the archives, not from initial curiosity on her part. The intern was dead because the collection arrived and she was in the wrong place at the wrong time. Happenstance. Yet, Sydney still felt guilt, as if she could have prevented her death somehow.

No, she reasoned, turning her chair back around to the desk. Irene's death was a mistake all around. No matter how much she tried to own it, the guilt was not hers. It was her persistence which led the police in the right direction.

This time, however, if anything happened she could not escape blame. But then the danger would be all hers, too.

That night, after she told Ben about her workday, she mentioned the mysterious email and Otis's reaction.

"Sydney, I'm worried," he said when she finished.

"I don't think there's any need."

"That email wasn't sent as a joke."

"Carl Blair is dead and what happened was a very long time ago. His sons . . ."

"Are politicians. At least one of them is. The other is a lawyer. Reputation is everything to both of them."

She sat silently, miffed that he was talking to her as if she didn't have enough sense but pleased that he cared.

"Most politicians will do almost anything to protect themselves. They might see any questions about that incident as an attack against them. Especially Grayson. He's leaving office and wants to leave behind a pristine record."

"I know but . . ."

"And putting that information about the journals online. If someone is keeping an eye on you or the archives, that's the first place they'll look."

"But they'd have to know what was in the journals to be concerned."

"Not necessarily. It's knowing what *might* be in the journals that will worry them. Just like Violet Parsons."

He apologized for sounding like he was giving orders, saying he was concerned for her safety. The memory of the earlier threats and the danger to them both was clearly on his mind. He could have died, too, and that made his concern for her even more intense.

"I'll be careful," she said, not wanting to argue about it and feeling as if she was giving in, both to his fears and hers. Her own teased her, now that he had expressed his so strongly. Was she being foolish or unrealistic?

Before hanging up later, he asked her to be careful and to think about what he'd said. They'd forgotten to discuss plans for his visit and exactly when it would happen.

Sydney fixed herself another cup of tea, knowing full well that two cups before going to bed would have her up to pee once or twice during the night. She liked something to drink while she worked on the computer, which would be only for a few minutes. Tonight, she was tired and distracted and found concentrating difficult.

A sharp bang startled her. It came from the front porch. She remembered how sounds in the house seemed threatening right after it was broken into. She told herself it was only the house itself, creaking and groaning in the wind, but this sound was too loud. She got the .32 caliber semi-automatic out of the bottom drawer of her desk and went to the front door. She stood in the semi-darkness, listening.

The wind shook the storm door. The roof rattled overhead. Maybe something was blown over by a strong gust. Not wanting to take any chances, she turned on the porch light. By itself, that would probably make any prowler take off. She pulled the venetian blinds away from the window and looked out, but her view was limited to a small section of the front porch.

Taking a deep breath, she unlocked the deadbolt on the door and opened it slowly. A gust of wind nearly tore the storm door handle out of her grasp, but she held on. In one corner, a potted plant lay on its side on the wooden floor of the porch.

Putting the pistol in the pocket of her robe, she stepped out and pushed the storm door closed. Another gust of wind caught the hem of her robe and raised the whole skirt around her. Her hair whipped to one side. Quickly, she pushed the robe down. Then, she set the plant upright and moved it against the house wall, where it would be more protected. Putting her hand in her pocket and feeling the coldness of the gun, she looked around the yard and down the neighborhood.

It was the last street on this side of Gansel, with only one street light at the corner to the west. Hers was the only house with lights on at that time of night. A car sat along the curb to the east and she thought she saw movement inside, but couldn't be certain. She opened the storm door and went back inside the house.

In spite of the tension—or perhaps because of it—she started yawning. She accepted that it was well past time to go to bed. Being so tired, she was probably imagining things. She looked outside, unwilling to go to bed if the car was still parked in the street. It was gone.

That's okay, then, she thought, without totally believing it. She climbed into bed and, to her surprise, dropped off immediately.

The expensive chocolates moved back onto the shelf as if of their own volition. Sydney sighed, but silently congratulated herself for her willpower. The vet bill was enormous. In light of that, spending that much extra money on candy was too frivolous.

Doctor Fremont had examined Lewis carefully, taken blood, x-rayed him, and prescribed supplements, which he provided there in the office in Gansel. Lewis, the good doctor said, was getting older and wasn't digesting his food as well as he should. The supplements, in the form of tasty treats, would help with that. Most of the tests showed the cat to be in good health otherwise, but results from a couple of the tests wouldn't be back until next week. She'd paid with her debit card, and all the way home, wondered how she was going to make up the extra expense.

She got Lewis into the house, gave him a treat, then headed south on I-35. In Edmond, traffic was horrible as usual on Saturdays, and the stores were crowded. Her first stop was at a store selling household items. She needed a new timer for the kitchen. There was one on the cook stove, but she sometimes used two at the same time for different dishes. There wasn't one on the old microwave oven, and the ancient wind-up one finally stopped working.

Her second visit was to the Post Office where she mailed a couple of sets of copies to researchers and bought stamps for her personal use. Not that she used them much anymore, except to send checks to pay bills. As with most people, communicating was done on Facebook or by email these days. She missed getting real mail, but didn't miss hand writing letters. She limited that mostly to cards for birthdays and Christmas and the checks. Like most of her friends and relatives, communication was through the Internet, one way or another.

After the Post Office, she stopped into her favorite local restaurant and ordered half of an order of lasagna. She pulled out her current novel and began reading, at the same time enjoying a good cup of coffee. Suddenly, a lot of hollering and rushing in and out of the kitchen caught everyone's attention. A moment later, she smelled smoke, but no one shouted for people to get out, although the smoke alarm went off just then. It all lasted only a couple of minutes and someone came from the kitchen to announce that there'd been a small fire. Everyone settled down to their meals amid occasional nervous laughter and shaking of heads.

She ate only half of her meal and left with the other half resting safely in styrofoam. Next, she made her way to the market for her last stop. In spite of the current financial situation, she bought a few extra cans and frozen items, just in case the new cold front actually moved into the area in two days' time as predicted. The experts were calling for freezing rain, as temperatures were supposed to plummet. It appeared that a lot of other people were doing exactly the same thing, as every cart was at least half full and items on some of the shelves were thinning out.

Her preferred store, a locally-owned chain that specialized in organic vegetables and meats and health foods, was crowded. The outrageously expensive candy she congratulated herself for putting back on the shelf was special dark chocolate, a treat that she enjoyed immensely. Besides, she rationalized, she should be trying to lose a few pounds. The drive home from Edmond always seemed longer than the drive down, this time worsened by a light rain. When she pulled into the driveway at her house, she felt tired. It took all of her energy to get the bags inside as she dodged raindrops, and then got everything put away.

Lewis, forgetting that he was mad at her after the vet visit, jumped up beside her on the sofa, purring before she even reached over to pet him. He was a very forgiving cat. Sydney stretched out on the sofa and he moved to accommodate her. He lay half on her right leg and half on the sofa, his purring vibrating against her thigh.

She woke abruptly with that confusion of not knowing where she was. Napping was not a normal thing for her, and she wondered if she was coming down with something. There was supposed to be some flu going around, and there were always colds this time of year. Getting up and walking to get rid of the stiffness, she felt a bit groggy, but that wore off as she got the blood circulating better.

Lewis followed her into the kitchen, expecting his dinner at any time. She pulled down a can of cat food and emptied it into his dish. He liked it spread around so that he didn't have to take bites out of the whole thing.

When she set the dish on the floor and straightened up, she swayed as dizziness swept over her. She closed her eyes, holding onto the counter's edge until it passed. Yep, she might be coming down with something.

Even so, she felt hungry. Pulling the styrofoam takeout box from the fridge, she emptied the contents into a dish, then set it into the microwave to warm the lasagna.

The rest of the evening she rested. Not exactly sick, she just didn't feel well enough to do much. She'd eaten only half of the leftovers. Lewis begged for a share, so she wrapped the remains in a plastic bag and tied it up so he couldn't smell it anymore.

She changed into her long flannel gown right after she ate and then stretched out on the sofa again. Propped up on several pillows and with the afghan spread over her, she watched television for a while. A sudden spasm in her abdomen, and she belched.

Oh, no. Not an intestinal virus.

She sat up straighter, and in a moment, another spasm doubled her over. It was followed quickly by another. She shoved Lewis off of the sofa and raced for the bathroom. She vomited, but only a little. Spasms brought more pain and she collapsed onto the sofa again.

Nothing more happened for a few minutes and she went into the kitchen and got out an old dishpan. Setting it on the floor beside the sofa, she leaned back and pulled the afghan over her. She was cold and sweating. Lewis sat on the arm of the chair across from her, watching with his eyes half closed. She closed her own.

A spasm woke her, the pain too sharp to ignore. She wanted to stand up. Maybe that would ease the pressure. Her legs didn't want to cooperate. Her arms trembled and wouldn't push her upright. A deep belch made her bend over and reach for the dishpan. Although she gagged, nothing came up.

A series of spasms hit her, and she thought she might pass out. There was a bitter taste in her mouth, and she wanted more than anything to rinse her mouth out. Try as she might, she couldn't push herself up from the sofa.

She awakened again with pain in her abdomen. When it passed, she wondered if she fell asleep or passed out. Did it matter? Probably. She tried to focus on that question, but pain in her stomach was nearly constant now. She wrapped her arms around her lower abdomen and groaned.

Lewis jumped down from the chair and came over to her. Did he sit there all this time? A wave of pain and nausea washed over her and she bent over, nearly putting her chin on her knees. Lewis jumped up beside her and put his own chin on her thigh, concern reflected in his eyes. She imagined it, of course, but he did seem distressed.

She reached over and stroked his head. He pressed upward against her hand. The next wave of pain and nausea made her cry out and he looked startled, but didn't leave her side.

This might be a virus, but she needed help. This was not something she could just go to bed and sleep through.

She reached for the cordless phone and dialed 911. She pressed the speaker button. Nothing happened. She hit "stop." And started to dial again. There was no dial tone.

CHAPTER 7

The phone slid to the floor as Sydney doubled over with another spasm. Her mind couldn't grasp the reality. The phone was dead.

Where was her cell phone? It took a moment to remember. It was in the office on the charger. She couldn't even stand. How was she going to get to the office?

Gritting her teeth, she forced herself to her feet, pushing up on the arm of the sofa. Lewis backed away as she swayed. Shuffling her feet across the wood floor, she started toward the hall. She was damned if she was going to crawl.

Dizziness swept over her. Her knees buckled, but she managed to stay on her feet. She kept moving forward. Her world, all of her attention, focused on moving her feet. Wave after wave of cramps drained her strength and concentration. Even the reason for moving forward no longer mattered.

When she finally dropped into the chair at her desk, she was soaked with sweat. She squinted, trying to see through the haze of pain. Nausea burned her throat. She reached for the trash can as she gagged. This time, she vomited for more than a minute, although it seemed like five.

Reaching for a tissue from the box on her desk, she wiped her mouth. The sour taste was stronger, enough to make her gag again, but nothing came up.

Picking up the cell phone, she pulled it loose from the cord. Blinking several times she got her vision cleared enough to see the buttons and screen. Slowly, she pulled up the keypad and dialed 911.

"What is your emergency?"

"Ambulance, please. Hurry."

"Yes, ma'am. May I have your name?"

"Yes, it's Sydney . . ."

Another wave of cramps and nausea cut off the words. Sydney leaned over the trash can again.

"Sydney? Is that a last name or first name?"

She retched once and remembered nothing else.

Voices spoke her name from far away, but answering was too difficult. There was bright light, and she tried to cover her eyes so she could sleep.

When voices spoke again, the words were for someone else. The light was still too bright, and she moaned as she lifted her arm to shield her eyes. Someone grabbed her arm.

"Not yet," a voice, nearer than the others, said.

"When?"

"Soon." A hand was placed on her forehead. "She's coming out of it."

It was now recognizable as a woman's voice, soft and soothing. The last words were sharper, addressed to someone else.

A man's voice asked, "How are you feeling?"

She hadn't thought about it. There was an overall discomfort, hurting even, that seemed all-consuming. It was everywhere, impossible to define.

"Does your throat hurt?"

She swallowed and groaned. "Yes."

"How about your stomach?"

She tried to reach a hand down to her belly, but again another hand stopped her.

"Hurts," she managed to get out.

"I'd imagine it does. Did you take any pills?"

She meant to shake her head, but didn't know if she'd managed it. "No," she said weakly, just in case.

"When will you know what she took?" another man's voice asked.

"I don't think she took anything. It doesn't appear to have been a medication of any sort."

"What then?"

"We won't know until the toxicology report comes back. What

we got from her stomach doesn't show any pills. Have your officers found anything at her house?"

"No, nothing."

She hadn't taken anything. The last thing she ingested was the lasagna. Was it food poisoning then?

"Food . . ." she managed to say, but they continued talking to each other.

She tried to open her eyes. The eyelids kept sticking together and felt a bit grainy. The light was still too bright, and she shut her eyes immediately. She opened them a sliver, peeking out from beneath her eyelashes.

Within her line of sight were a man and a woman, one a doctor in a white smock, the other a policewoman in uniform. She thought the latter was with the Edmond Police Department, but that was not entirely clear from the insignia on her uniform. What she did know was that she wasn't from the Filmore County Sheriff's Department. Wrong uniform.

She blinked, opening her eyes a little further.

"Food poisoning."

The voice was husky and each word hurt her throat as if it had been rubbed raw.

The doctor looked down. "Food poisoning? Could be." He nodded. "You rest now. We'll check in on you a little later."

Sydney closed her eyes. Just those few seconds made them burn and feel as if there was sand in them. She drifted off to sleep, her body relaxing in spite of the tubes and wires attached to her. She was aware of them, and at the moment, unconcerned.

"Are you doing all right now?"

Julia guided the SUV through traffic getting out of Edmond. She volunteered to come down, bringing some clothes, and pick Sydney up the moment she heard what happened. She asked few questions, except how did she feel and what did she need. With all the medication she was given, Sydney slept most of the trip.

She was tired and her body ached. As she learned that morning, the emergency room staff had pumped her stomach. That was the cause, in part, of her sore throat. That and the violent vomiting, which got rid of much of the poison still in her stomach. They still weren't certain what she had ingested, but they seemed to accept that she hadn't taken something knowingly.

Turning off the interstate onto the ramp leading into Gansel woke her up. Again, she felt surprise at where she found herself, uncertain where it was for several minutes. She pulled her coat closer around her, wishing the car's heater would warm up. Putting her hand in front of the vent, she was surprised at how warm the air was.

She sat back with a sigh.

"Okay?" Julia asked.

"Fine. Just can't seem to get warm."

"We'll fix that once we get to your house. I got some soup at the store before I left for Edmond. There's chicken broth for today. You'll have a hard time keeping anything down I would guess."

Sydney nodded. The only thing the hospital gave her to eat that morning was Jell-O and some lukewarm tea. What passed for broth and more Jell-O arrived for lunch just before she left. Neither was satisfying, but she felt hesitant about eating anything at all.

"Did you call Ben?"

Downtown Gansel looked deserted. It was Sunday morning and most of the cars were parked at the churches.

"No. I decided to call him after I get home."

"You should've called him. He'll wish you had."

"Probably. But I didn't want him thinking he needed to fly back or anything. I'm fine and, frankly, I'd rather be alone." Not to mention that her voice was so husky it would probably be difficult for him to hear her over the phone.

"Well, you won't be alone for a while, Missy. I'll get you home and heat up the broth. And . . ." she went on, keeping Sydney from commenting, ". . . I will stay the rest of today. Maybe overnight if I decide you need someone with you. The doctors said . . ."

"Hang what the doctors said," Sydney said, more vehemently than she'd meant to. "Sorry, Julia. I do appreciate your help. And if I need you there tonight, you may stay."

Julia turned to look at her, about to retort, then laughed at the expression on her friend's face. "I'm staying," she said. "No use taking any chances."

Sydney nodded. She really did appreciate Julia's willingness to help her. It was only that she did so much on her own, taking care of herself and everything she needed, that it was difficult to accept help. From anyone. That was what worried her about her relationship with Ben.

He always wanted to help with something when he was in town. And Julia was right. He would be upset with her for not calling sooner and letting him know what was happening. He would probably understand once he knew that she'd been unconscious or asleep most of the evening and night. She could also use the excuse of not having her cell phone with her. That probably wouldn't be acceptable since a call was made to Julia. It was just such expectations that made her so hesitant. When you were in a relationship, the other person expected certain courtesies. She wasn't sure she could do that, sharing her life with anyone. And now she had to accept Julia's help. She was grateful, but . . .

They'd reached the small house, stopping that stream of introspection. Julia parked in the driveway behind the CR-V.

"You just wait," Julia said as she climbed out and came around to the passenger's side. Sydney slid to the ground on her own, pausing to make sure her legs would hold her. To her dismay, she needed to lean on her friend to get into the house.

Lewis was standing on the chair next to the door, waiting to see who would appear once it was opened. He meowed when he caught sight of Sydney and jumped down to rub against her legs. She talked to him as people who live with cats will do and Julia helped her out of the coat and then to the sofa.

Julia very sensibly chose a long cover-up for Sydney to wear home. That way she could just take off the coat and be ready to lie down immediately. Which was exactly what Sydney did. The ride home tired her more than she expected, even though she'd slept for hours at the hospital and most of the drive. In spite of her efforts to stay awake, sleep came quickly.

When she woke, the smell of chicken soup filled the house, and she felt truly hungry. Before she could eat, though, Julia insisted that she call Ben. First, she checked voicemail. He had called Saturday night, said that he figured she was out with friends, and asked that she call when she could. She dialed the number, and at first he was relieved to hear her voice. Then she told him what happened.

"Why didn't you call me?"

She gave him the reasons and excuses and he reluctantly accepted them. He asked how she was feeling, was someone with her, and the worst question of all, "Do you want me to fly back?"

She assured him that Julia was there and would take care of everything. His concern came over the line and she found it heartening that he really did care. In spite of her desire to always remain independent, his willingness, desire even, to jump on a plane and be at her side, was warming.

As for the poisoning, she gave him what details she knew, which was essentially very little. He asked if it was food poisoning for certain.

"It must have been. I think it must have been in the lasagna. That seems to be pretty certain."

He was silent for several seconds and she guessed he was thinking about the last time her life was in danger and her current research project. He asked again for her promise to be careful, and after some more chatting, she grew tired and they said goodbye. Before he hung up, however, he got a promise that she would call the next day.

She managed to drink some of the chicken broth before the phone rang. Thinking it was Ben calling back, she asked Julia to answer it and tell him she was asleep. It was not quite a lie as she was having great difficulty keeping her eyes open.

"It's Sheriff Otis," Julia said, handing her the phone.

"Oh." Sydney put down the cup and rubbed her eyes, hoping to get rid of the sandy feeling. "Hi, Otis."

"Heard you had some trouble yesterday."

"Yeah, a bit. Who told you?"

"The state police called. They're investigating."

"State police? I thought the Edmond police were handling it."

"Since no one knows where the actual deed was done, Edmond handed it over to state. They in turn called me for some background and to make me aware of what happened."

"Do they even know what happened?"

"They told me it might be intentional poisoning."

"What? How?"

"The poison might have been pokeweed. It grows wild and with the leaves chopped up, it might look like parsley or something. It's fairly fast-acting, causes stomach cramps and vomiting. They're still waiting for the tox results, but the doctors took a poll as to what might cause the symptoms that was also readily available."

"Could it have been a mistake? Pokeweed isn't green this time of year, is it?"

"Not likely. But who knows. Do you still have any of the lasagna?"

"Yes. The styrofoam box is in the trash."

"I'll be by later to pick it up to have it analyzed."

It was too much to take in. Someone may have tried to kill her. Or at the very least, tried to make her very ill.

"Is there anything you are doing other than researching the Blairs? Anything that someone wouldn't want you doing?"

"No. It's been very quiet. We've gotten a couple of new collections that I'm working on, but I haven't seen anything that might provoke someone this much."

"Well, someone's not happy with you."

"Yeah."

He asked more questions, most about to whom the other collections belonged, which she described in as much detail as she could. He didn't recognize the names, so it seemed like a dead end. In spite of the evidence and what Otis said, she didn't want to believe that the poisoning was done deliberately. For one thing, that might mean Ben was right.

"If you think of anything, gimme a call," he said.

She promised and hung up.

"Sounds like you're in trouble again," Julia said.

"Yes, it does. But I just can't imagine how or why. They think it might have been pokeweed."

"It's winter," Julia said. "Where would anyone find pokeweed this time of year?"

"That's what I asked him. I'll look it up on Wikipedia later."

They discussed several possibilities, such as someone drying some of the weed or having an indoor plant, but none of it made any real sense. Sydney found out later that the roots were the most toxic part of the plant and that it has berries that are also poisonous.

"What's this research project you mentioned?" Julia asked, turning their attention away from the source of the poison.

Sydney hesitated to tell her about the Blair family papers and what she'd found. Informing Sheriff Otis was her duty. With Doctor Berger being the one who found the entries in the journal, there was little choice. If she didn't follow up, he probably would. But Julia had no stake in the issue and knowing details might put her in danger if the Blairs found out their history was under scrutiny. If they or some of their supporters wanted to keep the story from getting out.

"The Blairs are one of the older Oklahoma families," Julia said when she'd finished. "They pretty much do whatever they want to."

"But how would they have found out I was checking on them? The collection's been in the archives for years. It was processed long before I ever got the job."

"Well, someone knows, and it looks like it's one of the Blairs or someone who supports them. Even a state senator wields some power, especially in Oklahoma."

Sydney dozed off as the debate continued on what they knew and what could be guessed. Julia got her up and to bed, followed by Lewis who hardly left her side. His added warmth, tucked against her stomach, was comforting.

Julia woke her early enough Monday morning for her to call Doctor Arnold to let him know she would not be in the archives that day or the next. She got his voice mail as usual and he never called back. Arnold would be unhappy, but he should know.

Late morning, Otis came by and picked up the styrofoam box, still tied up in the plastic bag. He didn't stay long. Bad weather was moving in again and he and his deputies had to get things ready for problems over the next few days.

Off and on during the day, Sydney worked online, trying to find more information on Lily Blair and Johnny Whitefeather. Many official records of that period were available on the Internet, but huge gaps appeared everywhere. Her memberships in several databases gave her access to a lot of records, but it sometimes took three or four websites to answer one question.

Julia cooked their meals and every so often Sydney lay down for a nap. Her strength sagged until she could not hold her head up. She figured it was due in part to the trauma and physical shock of what happened. Some of it was due to the medications they gave her in the hospital and for her to take at home. Julia proved to be both an excellent nurse and a good cook. By Monday night, Sydney was eating solid food, not too rich or heavy, but very tasty.

That night bad dreams woke her about two a.m. The details were gone next morning, except that she was trying to do something or get somewhere and didn't know how. Pretty much the same as her efforts during the day.

As she searched through website after website, the one thing that stumped her most was the inability to find out anything about Grayson's wife, Gladys Smith.

The best source was probably Grayson, Jr.'s birth certificate, but finding it proved difficult, too. She started making plans to head to Newkirk to check out the records in the county clerk's office and Ponca City's historical museum. She also wondered if Alice Blair kept births recorded in a family Bible somewhere. Families were prone to do that back in the day. If one existed, it was not listed in the inventory. It was probable that one of Carl's children had it at one time.

She made notes, searched the Internet, and slept on Tuesday, in about equal amounts. She wanted to be back at the archives on Wednesday morning, but weakness and dire warnings from Julia convinced her that one more day of rest would be better for her.

Julia decided that her friend was well enough by Wednesday morning for her to return to her own home. It was decided somewhere in their conversations that Sydney would stay home for the rest of the week. Bad weather was threatening and she was still weak. Julia had stocked the fridge with plenty of food the day before, and there was always plenty of coffee and tea. The stack of wood for the fireplace was high. With many hugs, "thank yous," and "take cares," she climbed into her SUV, leaving Sydney alone for the first time in several days.

The house was too quiet for the first hour. She was restless, wandering from room to room, unable to focus. It was a feeling she hated and which only occurred after she'd spent a considerable amount of time with someone. By one p.m. she decided to call Ben, something she rarely did in the middle of the day. He would at least be interested in the fact that Julia had gone and things were returning to normal.

To her disappointment, the call went to his voice mail. She left a message with all the information about how things were going, in spite of her first inclination to just hang up. It was hard not to take personally the fact that the one time she called him during the day, he wasn't there. Totally irrational. After all, she talked with him the night before. *He's working*, she told herself. That was why he was still there and not in Oklahoma. Plus the fact that she had not asked him to come.

She went to the computer and tried to concentrate, but it was no good. Slumping in the chair at her desk, she pouted. She hated it when she pouted; it was so unattractive in a woman of her years, but she couldn't help it. It was ridiculous to feel so put out by his not being there when she called today. For goodness' sake, where was her independence now?

Gradually, she realized that something was hitting the roof of the house. Peeking out of the front door, she found that it was raining and sleeting. Looked as if the bad weather arrived a bit early. Back inside she turned on the TV, finding a local channel with a weather map. She also consulted the weather app on her cell phone showing a different perspective. Both described exactly what was happening now and at least until noon on Thursday. Road conditions would be bad with a chance of icy surfaces. If there was ice in the morning, she wasn't going out of the house for any reason.

Then her eye caught the mailbox at the street. The mailman had probably gone by now—he usually showed up about eleven-thirty—and she was a sucker for getting mail. If only mailboxes were still mounted on the wall beside the front door, she wouldn't have to go out in the weather. If only Julia had checked before she left. If only.

She could just ignore it and find something else to do, but knowing there might be mail was a lure she always found hard to resist. There was nothing for it but to put on her coat, grab her umbrella and get out there. She would never be able to concentrate on anything otherwise.

The front porch was still relatively clear when she stepped out in her colorful rubber galoshes. Very carefully, she stepped down to the first step then to the sidewalk. They were both wet, but not yet icy. The sleet pattered noisily against the umbrella. Taking short steps, she made her way to the mailbox attached to the top of a post.

Sleet hitting the metal box tapped out a song. When she tried to pull down the door facing the street, it was frozen shut and refused to budge.

She took a firm hold on the tab and wiggled and pulled it. It resisted. Just as she was about to slip the umbrella handle under her arm and use both hands, it jerked open. She nearly fell backward into the street. The door swung all the way down to reveal no mail at all.

All that trouble and nothing to show for it.

She looked up and down the street as she closed the box. To the east, three doors down, the white postal delivery vehicle was just pushing mail into their box. Two more houses and he'd be at her house. She turned her back to the falling rain and sleet and waited.

"Hey, George," she said as he pulled up even with her. There was so little light and his skin was so dark, she couldn't see his face.

"Hi, Miz St. John. Kinda cold to be standing out here."

"Tell me about it. Any mail for me?"

"Yes, ma'am." He pulled a bundle of envelopes and a magazine out of the bin on the seat beside him and handed it over to her.

"Thanks," she said.

He saluted with two fingers and drove east to her next door neighbor.

The wind caught the umbrella as she turned and nearly pulled it out of her hand. She shivered, taking small steps again to regain the porch. *Stupid. Was a bit of mail worth getting this cold? Especially as ill as I've been.*

She berated herself all the way to the door while clutching the mail to her breast. She collapsed the umbrella, pulled the storm door open, and turned the doorknob. It wouldn't turn. When she'd moved in, she installed all new locks on the front and back doors. The knobs locked automatically when she closed the doors and there was a dead bolt on each. She was sure, though, that she left the door wide open.

She looked down the street to see if the mailman was still in sight, but he was gone. She tried the knob again, but it wouldn't turn at all. The back door was locked, too. It hadn't been opened for several days, at least since Saturday.

A shiver ran through her, not entirely due to the cold. Staying out in this weather for any length of time was at least uncomfortable, at worst, dangerous. Most of her neighbors worked and were not at home. Balancing the mail and the umbrella, she checked all of her pockets to see if she just might have her cell phone with her. No luck.

Nothing to do but break one of the windows, a prospect that did not appeal to her, but neither did freezing to death.

She set the mail on the metal chair that always sat to the left of the door and propped the umbrella against it. One of the flower pots might be good for breaking a window. Just then a car horn sounded behind her. Looking toward the road, she saw George sitting at the end of the sidewalk in his Postal vehicle.

"Something wrong, Miz St. John?" he called out the window.

"Oh, George. Thank goodness you've come back. I've locked myself out."

"I forgot a package for you," he said, holding up a box wrapped in brown paper as he ran up the sidewalk. "It's too cold for you to be standing out here."

"Tell me about it. Can you get a locksmith for me?"

"I'll do better than that," he said with a grin. "If you'll hold the storm door open for me."

He put the package down with the rest of her mail and pulled out a credit card and began maneuvering it between the door and the frame. He left it wedged there and pulled a very small screwdriver and another tool from his breast pocket.

"Never know when I might need these," he said as he worked. "Looks like it ain't just the doorknob. Dead bolt's locked, too."

"Really?"

There was no way that could have been thrown. She was still certain that she'd left the door open and closed only the storm door.

With a click, the door opened. George stooped down to pick up the credit card from the floor.

"I'd appreciate it if you didn't tell anyone 'bout this," he said. "I worked as a locksmith a few years back and practice it ever' so often. You never know when it might come in handy."

"Very true, George. And I promise I won't tell a soul."

He picked up the mail from the chair and handed it to her. "Be more careful, now, ya hear?"

"Thanks, George, I will. I owe you big time."
"Nah. Glad to help. Get yourself inside now and get warm."
"Thanks, again, George."

George sat in his vehicle, pulling away from the curb only when she closed the door from the inside. She opened the umbrella and set it on the door mat for it to dry, then took off her boots, coat, and hat, dropping all on the same rug. Stepping in front of the fireplace, first she faced it, letting the heat warm the front of her body, then she turned and warmed her back. The moment she turned away from the fire, that side got cold again. Shivers ran up and down her body, leaving a feeling of permanent chill. All of the heat was outside, yet her skin was cold to the touch, even her hands that were like ice. She was certain she had never been colder in her life.

Someone once told her that when you're deeply chilled, you shouldn't take a hot shower or bath. She didn't remember why that was not a good idea, and she wanted to feel hot water running down her body in the worst way. But she refrained, not daring to try it, not knowing what else to do. After a few more minutes of toasting in front of the fireplace, she went into the kitchen, filled the kettle with water, and put it on the stove to heat. She got down the Brown Bess teapot on the top shelf of one of the cabinets and a tin of breakfast tea.

As the water heated, it occurred to her to check the back door to see if it was actually locked. It not only wasn't, it was not closed tight. She started to push it to and lock it, then thought better of it. Turning on the porch light, she looked out. Rain drops and sleet bounced off the front third of the wood floor. Wet footprints, coming and going, stood out on the few feet of dry surface, disappearing on the wet surface on both the porch and the step.

The kettle began whistling and she pushed the door to and locked it. She poured the boiling liquid over the tea bags in the pot, not bothering to pre-warm it. The pot was too hot when she tried to wrap her hands around it. In the meantime, she checked the tile floor of the kitchen and the wood floor of the living room for wet footprints. There were several not her own.

Her hands shook slightly, and she was very careful as she poured herself a large mug of the tea a few minutes later. She added honey and cut and squeezed a lemon. Tea with honey and lemon were supposed to be good for what ailed you, and hopefully it might keep away any drastic illness.

It was hard, but she managed to wait until the tea was moderately cooler. Blowing on the surface, she then took a sip. It was strong and with just the right amount of sweet and sour. She went into the living room, sat on the end of the sofa nearest the fireplace, and pulled the afghan over and around her. The fire crackled and popped cheerily, not caring that cold occupied every fiber of her proverbial—and physical—being.

Gradually, though, between sipping the hot tea and the heat from the fireplace, she began to feel warmer. Warmth brought sleepiness. She shook her head, thinking that there was something she needed to do. It took a moment to remember, then she forced herself to get up and check the front door. It was locked, both the doorknob and the dead bolt. Finding the back door unlocked earlier and the wet footprints, both inside and outside, scared the bejesus out of her. There were no recognizable signs that the lock was picked; it certainly wasn't forced open since the frame was without a scratch.

Taking small steps, she made her way back to the sofa. She stretched out, pulling the afghan over her. Lewis jumped up, purring as if everything was right with the world. He wedged himself between the back of the sofa and the backs of her legs.

Sydney continued to worry about who unlocked the back door. Neither she nor Julia went out to the back the whole time Julia was there. The door wasn't forced, no splintering of wood, no broken glass. Then she remembered George's unlocking the front door. Probably anyone could learn to be a locksmith.

The last thing that came to mind as she fell asleep was wondering where she left her tea mug.

CHAPTER 8

The sun came out Thursday morning for a while, then clouds moved back in during the night. The temperature hovered around twenty degrees, making the heat and glow from the fireplace especially welcome.

Having decided that another day's rest would be good for her, especially in view of the bad weather, she tried to call Doctor Arnold. Again, it went directly to voicemail. And he hadn't once tried to get in touch with her. She knew for a fact that he'd not left any messages since she could access the voicemail in the office from home.

The mug of hot chocolate warmed her inside and out as she wrapped her hands around it. Sheriff Otis, sitting across from her, took a swallow of his, too. She'd given him the largest mug in her cupboard and still his hands dwarfed it. The overstuffed chair, however, looked as if it was made for someone of his size, unlike the office chair in the archives.

He set his mug on the small table beside the chair, using the coaster she kept there. He looked from the front door to the fireplace, then at her.

"Why didn't you call me yesterday afternoon?"

"All I could think of was getting warm. I still feel chilled deep down inside."

"You haven't told me how you got back inside."

"Otis, I promised I wouldn't tell anyone."

"So, someone else got you inside?"

"I can't say."

"Musta been George, the mailman."

"You know about him?"

"Of course. He's helped us several times. Everyone in town knows he was once a locksmith."

"Then why..."

"I guess he thinks it lends him an air of mystery. There isn't an ounce of larceny in him, though."

"Well, he certainly saved my life."

"Probably. You couldn't have survived staying out in that weather very long."

"It turned out the back door was unlocked. I could have gotten in there, but I thought it was locked. You did see the footprints in back, though," she said, bringing the conversation back to the purpose of his visit. In daylight, they were plain to see in the earth made soft and mushy by the rain.

"Yeah. They led to the back fence. Kent is following them from the fence to see where they lead. I suspect they curve around and come out down the street somewhere. Did you see any strange cars on the street?"

"Not last night. There was a car I didn't recognize one night last week. Very late. The night it got really windy. One of my plants out on the porch was turned over."

"Anything you would recognize again?"

"No. It was very late and very dark. The car was dark, too. I thought I saw someone inside of it, but..." she shrugged.

He emptied his cup and looked over at her. "Thanks for the hot chocolate."

"You're welcome."

"I've been thinking that maybe you should quit looking into the Blair business. I didn't want to make it an official inquiry yet, but it looks like that was a mistake. You may have alerted them to the fact that someone's looking into things. And they think it's you. You didn't do anything wrong," he added quickly as she started to protest. "Still, someone somewhere found out enough to make them nervous and come after you."

"Then you do believe that the two incidents are related and deliberate?"

"One accident I can believe. Two in just a few days—too much coincidence."

His cell phone rang, and while he talked to whomever was

calling, Sydney took the mugs into the kitchen and rinsed them. She caught enough of Otis's side of the conversation to believe he was talking to one of his deputies. She went back into the living room when she was sure that the call was done.

"Looks like I was right," he said as she sat down. "The tracks went to the west a ways, then doubled back to the next street. Whoever it was walked between two houses down there and probably to a waiting car. No way to tell on the pavement where he might have parked."

She nodded. This was apparently an attempt on her life, along with the poisoning, or at least a warning. It didn't really make much sense. She knew so little about any Blair secrets, so far, mostly because there was little to be found. The Internet produced little information. Most of what she knew was from the collection. The collection!

"Otis, can you have one of your deputies check the archives? If someone is so desperate they'll come after me, why wouldn't they also try to get the papers?"

He made the call on his cell phone, telling Kent to drive over to the archives and see how things looked. The call came back in less than fifteen minutes. The doors were locked and the blinds all down. No sign of illegal entry or damage.

"All of the blinds?" she said. Otis asked, then nodded. "The blinds in the break room shouldn't be down. Can you take me?" It was Friday afternoon and snow was predicted later in the evening. The roads were already bad, icy in places, especially in her neighborhood.

"Sure. Probably a good idea."

"Give me a moment."

She went into the bedroom, closing the door, and changed into warmer clothes. She dug out her fluffy boots, got her coat and scarf out of the coat closet in the living room. Grabbing up her purse and making sure the keys were in there, she was ready. The blinds in the break room were never lowered. There had never seemed any need, and the sunlight coming through the window—when there was sunlight—made the small room cheery.

In good weather, you could get anywhere in Gansel in fifteen minutes. With bad road conditions, it took twenty-five. How deputy

Kent had made it so quickly was anyone's guess. Although Otis's four-wheel drive vehicle had good traction, the going was slow. The roads were even worse than the official reports on the radio, and as they traversed the nearly empty streets, snow flurries powdered the windshield.

Otis parked the SUV on the wrong side of the street in front of the archives as the sidewalk was partially cleared. It had been salted, but it was too cold for that to work yet. The deputy stood at the door, his vehicle parked across the street. She inserted the key into the dead bolt first. It wasn't locked, but the lock on the doorknob was. She turned the key in the doorknob and opened the door. Otis pushed past her and she followed to enter the code on the alarm control pad on the wall just inside.

The entrance was just as she'd left it a week ago. When they turned the corner to the left, looking into the stacks, all was a blur of papers and boxes.

Some boxes lay upside down with papers spread on the floor. Some rested on the edges of the shelves, papers hanging out and scattered across the floor. Several box lids lay about.

"I thought the alarm system was updated," Otis said.

"I thought so, too."

She turned from the mess and selected another key on the ring to unlock the door to her office. Nothing was amiss there. Putting her bag down, she shed the coat, gloves and hat, and made her way toward the stairs. She turned into the utility room to check the alarm panel and pressed the button for the readout on the screen. It showed that the electricity went out last night, and the backup power was activated. Any other information would have to come from the security company's computers.

She went back to the stairs and climbed to the second floor. She flipped up the light switch at the top of the stairs. The main lights were rather dim, giving just enough illumination for a person to move from the stairwell into the hall without bumping into anything, although there was nothing in the way to bump into. Otis followed at a respectful distance as she went into the stacks to the left then to the right, flipping on more lights as she went. All was well, and she breathed a sigh of relief. The burglars somehow knew or figured out that all of the boxes of the Blair collection were together on the first floor. That could mean they knew how archives were organized, or at least knew how this one was.

"Did that alarm control tell you if the intruders tried any other door or window?"

She nodded. "No, only that the front door was opened."

"We need to get Kent back in here to check for fingerprints."

They went back downstairs, and he stepped outside for the one other person who was qualified with the fingerprint kit. The deputy grabbed the kit from the back of his SUV and started at the front door. Sydney felt sure that there would be few prints to eliminate. Her prints were in the database, as were those of everyone who worked in the archives, either part time, or, like the alarm installer, through their employer. While they waited she considered calling Doctor Arnold to let him know what was going on.

Suddenly, she wanted to call Ben. He would understand her frustration and would be upset about the break-in at her house. Part of her didn't want to upset him, so far from the scene, as it were. Another part of her didn't want to listen to him telling her how to solve the various issues all of this raised: she needed a safer house; she should move out to California; he should move back to Oklahoma.

Kent quickly finished the task at hand. Fingerprints of all kinds would be on so many things within the archives that he only took those on the doorknob, the edge of the door, and the shelving where the boxes were stored. He finished, and the lights were turned out and the doors were locked. They all stepped out onto the sidewalk. Sydney didn't argue when he said he would take her home. The archives were, once more, a crime scene and the police would be checking everything.

They climbed into Otis's SUV. It took longer to get back to her house, as the snow was accumulating on top of the ice that had melted very little. They didn't talk much as he drove, each trying to make sense of what was happening.

Her thoughts were confused. She almost never acknowledged the need for help or comfort from others. Not since Leo died. Her husband was a caring man with whom she'd had a very close relationship. They knew each other's thoughts and feelings. They had anticipated what was needed in moments of crisis or stress.

When he died, she had no one to help or even to listen. She had believed their friends would be there for her, but she ended up alone with no one to lean on. Eventually, she stopped relying on anyone but herself. Not wanting to bother others with her problems, was how she thought of it. Yet now, faced with one of the greatest crises of her life, she did not want to be alone to handle it by herself. She'd already considered calling Julia instead. But it was Ben she needed. She blamed this weakness on having been so ill with the poisoning, and being trapped out in the weather weakened her further.

Reaching her house, Otis walked her to the door, made sure she got inside safely, then left. She'd wanted to shout, "Don't leave!" Instead, she closed and locked the door. She resisted the urge to close all of the shades and blinds. She liked the house bright and airy; even though it was still snowing outside and the sky was grey, the house was brighter with everything open. Yet, it no longer felt as if it was the sanctuary it once was, as if whoever was after her could and would stand outside and watch her through the windows and get in any time they wanted.

She shivered as she took off her coat and boots, leaving them on the rug inside the door to dry. Her life wasn't going to change to accommodate the fear they were trying to instill in her. So, the shades and blinds stayed up, snowflakes drifting to the ground in slow motion on the other side of the glass.

The coffee maker was still on and she poured a cup with lots of honey and cream. Then she sat at the kitchen table, trying to puzzle out what was happening and her feelings. Nothing made any sense at all at that moment, and she gave up and picked up the phone.

Before she dialed the number, she realized that the message light was blinking. Ben had called while she was out with Otis. His voice was bright and cheerful.

"Hey, Beautiful. Sorry I missed your call. I forgot my phone at home when I went to meet a client. I guess you're at work, but I won't try to call you there. Plus, I'm fixin' to go to another meeting in just a few minutes. Give me a holler tonight after you get home."

She slammed down the handset. Why couldn't he be there when she needed him? It was hard enough to admit that need, that she couldn't, or didn't want to handle the situation all by herself.

Her hand shook as she punched in his phone number. A deep breath brought the beginnings of calm. Realization was beginning to seep in that she was frightened, not only by the attacks, but by the break-in at the archives, and by this sudden need for comfort from someone. She started to hang up, then heard the first ring of the phone.

Maybe he wouldn't be able to answer.

"Hello."

"Ben. Hi."

"Good afternoon. What's up?"

"Do you have time to talk? Things are happening here."

"What kind of things?" His voice lowered a bit, as if he had sat up abruptly and was now fully focused on her.

She told him about being locked out of the house and calling Otis. He made only short comments as she continued telling him about Otis coming when she called him and their rush to the archives. In spite of herself, she got choked up when she described what they found there.

When she stopped, there was a moment of silence. "Damn!" he said. "I had no idea being an archivist was so dangerous. I'll bet you never did either."

His words brought a slight smile and lifted the tension from around her heart. She'd heard that before

"That's true."

"I think I should come back there. My being with you might discourage some of these . . . what? Attacks? Are they trying to hurt you? Or are they just trying to discourage you? To frighten you?" She noticed he didn't say "murder," or "kill."

"I don't know. But they are frightening me. Even if they didn't mean to kill me, there was a chance I could be dead."

They discussed the situation, first emotionally, then settling into a more reasoned consideration of what they knew. They deduced from the facts, guessed at motives, for more than half an hour. The most puzzling thing of all was how someone put pokeweed in the lasagna. That might be explained by the fire in the kitchen as a distraction, but there was no way to know. However it was arranged, it was premeditated. In the end, she felt exhausted and knew they were no nearer to solving the mystery than when they started. A calmness settled over her, though.

"I know what you should do," he said finally.

"What's that?" She wasn't at all sure what he was going to say.

"Well, two choices. First, you move out here with me and find a safer archive in which to work. Or two, you at least move into a more solid house that would be more secure."

"You're joking."

"No, I am not joking. At least think about it." When she didn't say anything, he went on. "Look, this is the second time you've been in danger because of something in that archive. It's not normal."

"I've been working here for four years, and nothing happened until last year."

"Yeah, but now things *are* happening. And you're probably getting some sort of reputation that makes people think you're a risk to them and their secrets. Your boss probably isn't too happy about all this either."

Doctor Arnold wouldn't be happy once he knew the whole story up to this point. She still needed to talk to him, but she'd wait until he finally called her back. If he ever did.

She told him she hadn't been able to get in touch with Arnold. As they went on discussing events, she and Ben didn't exactly argue, but they certainly disagreed. All of her life she'd moved from one place to another. The conversation made her realize that in Oklahoma, she had finally put down roots. In spite of everything, she not only didn't want to move again, she didn't want to leave Oklahoma, even with all its problems. The state's history was fascinating, including the lives of those whose papers were under her stewardship.

They hung up with her agreeing to think about what he'd suggested. Buying a safer house wasn't a bad idea and she was going to give that some serious thought. Trouble was, Gansel didn't have much in the way of newer homes and few new homes were being built. She'd always felt it was a bit far from the main urban centers to be a bedroom community, especially with other towns between it and Tulsa, Oklahoma City, even Stillwater. Yet, there were two newer communities in the county. One was even gated.

The thought of Tulsa reminded her that she still wanted to get to the birth records in Ponca City and in Newkirk to see if she could find anything on either the elder Grayson's wedding, or birth records for Grayson, Jr.

The one thought Ben brought to her mind was how people who donated collections to the archives might view all of this. Would they see her as a threat, or worse still, would they be worried about what those papers might reveal?

CHAPTER 9

Friday and the weekend, she stayed home, wrapped in her afghan and sitting in front of the fire. Even when using her laptop, she stayed in the living room, warm and cozy. She did spread fertilizer on the front sidewalk so she could get out to the mail box. On Monday, Sydney planned to check out the mess in the stacks.

Doctor Arnold finally returned her calls. Mostly the message was, "We'll talk about this when I get back." Getting started on the cleanup was more important. The mess was not quite as bad as she remembered from the quick inspection on Thursday. She suspected that the intruder pulled the top off a box, looked at the folder titles, then dropped it. Some fell to the floor, often upside down, but some became wedged between the shelf it sat on and the one above, leaving the box dangling over the edge. Hopefully, that would make it easier to match box and contents, since things weren't shuffled around.

Otis had asked that she give him an accounting of what might be missing or damaged. The work would be done with that in mind. However, the work could be difficult, given the inaccuracies in the finding aid and her lack of familiarity with much of the material. She knew generally what was in the boxes from her earlier search; however, the details proved to be more of a mystery.

She'd used the weekend at home, while the forensics people did their work, to draw up a plan for the task. It wouldn't be foolproof since she didn't have an exact idea of how much disorder was created. Now that she knew the pattern, and using the original inventory, the task didn't seem quite so daunting. Obviously, there were a few items that would have to be guessed at, but it would be relatively easy to find a logical placement.

Before she touched anything, she called Charlene Hooks, her part-time assistant, to see if she could come in and help. Charlene never turned down the opportunity before, and she didn't on this occasion, either, in spite of the road conditions. All Sydney told her was that vandals got into the archives and left a mess.

"Don't even try if your roads are dangerous," Sydney said.

Doctor Arnold would probably be furious since she didn't check with him first, but she could always remind him that he didn't return any of her earlier phone calls until days later. Not to mention that the new alarm system failed. She would have to call the security company and see why. Just one more thing for Doctor Arnold to fuss about.

She shrugged off that issue for now, planning to make time to address it later. Sydney studied the inventory again. Not much more than a box and folder list, it gave a lot of room for rapid re-sorting of most of the papers. She ran two copies of the box list after making notes, keeping the original intact.

The final task would be to examine each box not emptied to make certain that nothing was obviously amiss inside. The bulk of the work would be pulling the papers back together into the boxes they came out of.

It was frustrating having to bring the collection back together without actually re-organizing it. Still, it would take quite a bit of time. Yet, she'd been given a perfect opportunity to become even more familiar with the contents and look for anything pertaining to the search for information on Lily and Johnny. She grabbed a couple of boxes, pushing some folders back in and picking up others from the floor, and took them to her office. As always, she found herself getting lost in reading documents, knowing full well that she couldn't afford the time. It took an effort to concentrate on working as quickly as possible. Still, the people became even more real, living and breathing. This was a big reason she was an archivist in the first place.

One box was completed and the second begun when Charlene arrived, her usual quiet efficiency lending further calm to the task. Sydney gave her the second copy of the inventory, marks indicating the boxes Sydney wanted her to work on, none of them including the dates of most interest in her search, then set her up in the reading room instead of the processing room downstairs. No researchers were expected and it would be easier for the two of them to compare notes. Plus, it was warmer on the first floor than it was in the basement. Charlene began with boxes numbered five and seven. Box six had not been touched by the intruders.

The random nature of the damage seemed to indicate they had no idea what boxes to look in. The incomplete finding aid posted on the website would have helped, if they knew it existed. The fact that they did select only certain boxes had at first made her think they had consulted the finding aid. The website was one of the first things she marked for improvement when she took the job. It was well organized and fully searchable, which, to her mind, made it one of the best she had seen. However, it was the details that were lacking.

She checked the list again and confirmed that all of the boxes in which she found journals were among those dropped onto the floor. The rest were probably pulled because none of the journals were in boxes where they were expected. Instead, they were lying on her desk in the office here or in her book bag at home when the intruders broke in.

That thought made her stop. Had the intruder at home looked for the journals? Was his sole purpose to harm or scare her? Did he not know about the journals and how important they were? From the actual details of recent events, it was impossible to tell what these people knew and didn't know.

Sydney double-checked the journals still sitting on the desk. All of the information she gleaned on the Johnny Whitefeather and Lily Blair events came from them. They were all there and seemingly untouched, which was not terribly strange since the door to her office was locked and they didn't bother with it. Or, so it appeared, since it was still locked when the damage was discovered, and the key to the front door didn't work on her office door. Of course, whoever got in knew how to pick a lock and may have been looking for something other than the journals. If they found what they wanted, there would have been no need to search further. Or the intruder was in the archives when Deputy Kent checked the building and sneaked out the back, leaving the search incomplete.

From now on, the journals would be stored in the vault, at least until everything was resolved. She took a moment and did just that, taking those in her book bag first, then gathering the ones on her desk, she found a box the right size to put them in and placed the box on one of the shelves of the vault.

Before settling back into the work, Sydney picked up the phone and called Desideria Diego. Desi, as everyone in town called her, was the only realtor with an office in Gansel. Just a few years earlier, she and her domestic partner Linda Zabat built a brand new house just outside Gansel for themselves and their two children. It was time to test the waters for herself, not only as a security measure, but also as a financially sound move. If she stayed in Gansel, as she was planning to do, owning a home instead of renting should be her next move. And after four years, it looked like she would be staying put. Her home in Norman would have to go up for sale, and with the proceeds as a down payment, she could afford it. Ben's other choice for her she shoved into the back of her mind for the time being.

Desi was delighted with Sydney's interest in a new home, and they discussed the options. At that moment, there were only five homes up for sale in town and two beyond the city limits, most of which needed a good deal of updating. They made plans to visit them the next day. In the meantime, Desi said, a few builders were becoming interested in possibly starting up building projects. With greater interest in oil and natural gas in the northern part of the state, people were moving into the area, and Gansel was in their sights. She'd heard that a new housing addition was being planned, but it was only speculation at the moment.

The phone rang just as Sydney let Charlene out the door to go to lunch. She was going to follow immediately and almost left the call to voicemail.

Caller ID showed it was Doctor Arnold calling. He asked what the hell was going on. She started to explain, but he cut her off.

"You do seem to have difficulties keeping out of trouble," he said, his tone reasonable, but icy. "Too bad the alarm system installation wasn't completed."

"It wasn't?"

"No. That Mr. Langston needed other materials since some of the wiring in the building is so old. He'll finish the installation today."

She nearly laughed out loud. She'd been so worried. Of course, no one had told her about the delay.

"Anyway, if he'd kept to his schedule things might not have happened the way they did."

"Of course." She certainly wasn't going to comment further.

It was usual for her boss not to inform her of scheduling changes and time was wasted worrying about the system. That didn't change what happened, but not being kept informed certainly rankled. She planned to give Mr. Langston a piece of her mind.

"How many days were you out last week?" he went on.

"All week."

"Surely food poisoning isn't that bad."

"It wasn't exactly food poisoning."

"No? That's what you said in your message."

"Yes, that's what everyone . . ."

"Anyway, not too many people were out and about with the way the weather's been, so hopefully, no harm done."

"Right."

"I'll let you know when Langston calls to finish the installation."

That would be nice, she thought, then remembered he'd said it would be today.

"Anything else?"

"I called Charlene in to help with straightening up the mess with the papers."

"Oh, good. Keep me posted."

He said goodbye this time and hung up. Sydney sat looking at the telephone in her hand for a long moment in amazement. He didn't once ask how she was. But he also didn't complain about the length of time she was out of the archives. Nor about why she was calling Charlene in. Well, if he said nothing today, he probably would when it came time for her annual review.

She gathered up her things and, locking all of the doors behind her, stepped through the front door onto the sidewalk on Logan Avenue. The wind coming out of the south penetrated her coat, and she wondered if walking to Molly's Restaurant was a good idea. She gritted her teeth and walked anyway. After all of the days of inaction, she could use the exercise. At least the sidewalks were cleared; otherwise, she wouldn't consider it.

Her teeth were chattering by the time she got inside, where it was warm and cheerful. Fewer diners than usual sat in booths and at tables. The cold was either keeping people home from work, or they ate earlier. Looking at her watch, she realized it was later than she thought.

Molly's beef stew with corn bread was especially good and she lingered over it, until she remembered that Charlene would be returning to the archives any time. She had her own key to the front door and could let herself in, but the idea of her being in the building alone for any length of time was unsettling.

She got back to find Charlene already back at work, totally unconcerned. She'd been there only a few minutes, she said, so no harm done. The rest of the day passed quickly, and the work of straightening up the mess went smoothly. Most of the upended boxes held material from the late 1920s to 1940, lending more credence to Lily and Johnny Whitefeather being at the center of the search.

An hour before closing time, Sydney found a folder of special interest. It contained letters and other papers erasing Lily's name from any inheritance of the Blair Bar Ranch and all businesses pertaining to it. Lily was dead to them, apparently. But did she actually die? Or did she get away? If she were dead, was there any need to expunge her claim to an inheritance? Then there was her baby. Did it survive? If so, what happened to it?

None of the papers said anything about where she was, or whether she gave birth. Nor did they specify the reason for her disinheritance, although that was clear, given what Sydney already knew. The details were probably in the personal journals.

Sydney continued working, deeply engrossed in what she was finding, even though there was nothing more on Lily or Johnny. Five o'clock came and Charlene said goodbye. Sydney let her out the main door, locking it securely behind her.

The sun was down with just a glow on the western horizon, and the archives were dark inside. Most of the lights were turned out in the stacks; only the night lights glowed, making more shadow than light. She checked the building, making sure again that everything was locked up tight.

She also tested all of the windows on the first floor. None of them were easily raised; some on the second floor were still painted shut.

When she first took over as archivist, she insisted on being able to raise the first floor windows as a safety measure; however, two of them had not yielded to their attempts. The papers, journals, boxes, and most other material were highly flammable. If people were inside when a fire broke out, they might escape through one of the windows on the first floor. No one except staff should ever be in the stacks on the second floor, and escape from there required getting to the west side of the building where there was a fire escape. That door was steel and double-bolted. If anyone was trapped on the east side of the second floor, they would have to break a window and jump.

She pushed on the lower sashes and twisted the locks. Finished, she looked down the nearest aisle between shelves. Someone could be hiding in the shadows in most of the aisles. Should she call Otis and ask if one of his deputies could come check out the stacks upstairs? Since she'd been in the stacks downstairs all day, she doubted anyone could be in there. The floors creaked after all, in spite of the reinforcement that was done when the building was renovated. Boxes of papers were very heavy, especially when there were hundreds of them.

The cell phone in her pocket chimed and she jumped. She dug it out of the pocket of her wool slacks and leaned against the window sill.

"Where are you?" Ben's voice asked when she answered.

"In the archives. Where are you?"

"I'm actually home early for a change. I was thinking about you and tried the house phone first."

She smiled and said it was good to hear his voice, and meant it. As they talked, she began walking back toward her office. He was chagrined when she told him about the phone conversation with Doctor Arnold. She relaxed in her chair as they continued to talk about their days. The front bell rang, startling her again. Someone was at the door.

"Just a minute," she said. "Someone wants in."

"Don't answer it!"

"I'll take you with me, and I'll check before I open it."

Standing on the sidewalk out front was Kent, Otis's deputy. She opened the door and greeted him.

"I saw the lights still on and thought I'd better check."

She was holding the cell phone so that Ben could hear the deputy.

"Everything's fine," she said. "But I wonder if you could check around, especially upstairs. Since you're here"

"Sure, I can do that."

She stepped back to let him in.

"I'll call you back," she said into the phone.

"Okay. Be sure you do."

She disconnected, turning on the lights so Kent could see his way up the stairs. The light came on in the hallway and she stayed at the foot of the stairs and listened. The floor creaked with his every footstep. The light in the aisles between the shelves was dim even during the day with the blinds all down. Light was the enemy of paper preservation. The former bank building was a good choice in some ways for an archive. There were few lights in some parts. The building was well constructed, but there were windows in all of the walls except the west wall on the second floor. When the walls between the former offices were taken down, light through the windows became more of a problem.

He came back downstairs, announcing that nothing was out of order.

"I'll be off then. 'Night, Miz St. John."

"'Night, Deputy."

He went out the front door and she picked up her bags, ready to follow. The journals were safely locked up in the vault, the stacks on the first floor were checked, and she was tired and hungry.

The temperature dropped once the sun went down. It was a clear cold night with the moon nearly full overhead, very white and casting shadows on the ground. The sound of her footsteps in the gravel of the parking lot was muffled, reminding her of how the world sounded when it snowed. At the car, she turned and looked across the street at the dark buildings over there, then up at the black sky. The moon was so bright that no stars were visible around it, except for Venus, which shone brightly as the evening star.

No headlights reflected from the rear view mirror as she drove home. Few cars were on the road, period. It was a bit late, and the weather was still threatening. The street lights on the corners of her block did not relieve the darkness of her driveway. Streaks of light glowed between the slats of the venetian blinds at the windows of the living room. At least her timer was working.

As always, Lewis demanded to be fed first thing. He finished his canned food as she started to undress and he jumped up on the bed, demanding the rest of his due. Petting, talking, squirming, not to mention shedding. His fur was soft to the touch, and they both enjoyed these moments when she stroked his back, scratched his ears and under his chin, just the two of them. No cooking, TV, reading, nothing to take her attention away from him. His loud purr, sounding nearly as loud as a Harley Davidson motorcycle in the next block, soothed in the quiet.

Standing, she shook off the drowsiness that threatened to overwhelm her. Finally getting into her fleece lounger, she went back into the kitchen to find her own meal. Canned soup would do for tonight, as she wasn't very hungry. She opened a can of beef barley and dumped the contents into a pan to set on the stove burner.

Having promised Ben that she would call back, she picked up the phone and dialed. They chatted until the soup was hot. She promised she would "keep her head down," and they said good night. She opened the morning's newspaper that she hadn't made the time earlier to read.

The lead article was something about the state budget about to be passed and how it would take more money away from education in the state. A sidebar to that was a description of a bill introduced by Senator Blair for a memorial to his grandfather. Some in the Senate decried it as a waste of taxpayers' money, while others praised both the man and the memorial. If passed, it would be one of the Senator's last acts in the state legislature.

She was too tired to focus on the details. Her thoughts strayed to what she was doing this very evening, the life she was leading, alone and basically very boring. Only her work interested her on a day-to-day basis. Maybe Ben was right. She should move to California, find a job there, take advantage of the weather and the beaches and mountains. Surely there was an archive where she could find a job. Perhaps even a boss who appreciated her. Who also appreciated the collections over which he or she had authority.

Doctor Arnold would probably give up authority over the archives in order to gain a more prestigious position. His wife,

Eleanor Titus Arnold, was socially ambitious. They chose a poor place to make their mark. But her need to interfere, if known to any potential employer, would always be a barrier to his chances of bettering his situation elsewhere. As were his own shortcomings. Intelligent, knowledgeable on many things, his limited skills or experience with archives, and no people skills, made him a less than desirable candidate. The two of them made decisions about organizing the archives and processing the collections that Sydney learned to ignore or work around most of the time.

The only person who knew the full extent of her dissatisfaction with her boss was Ben. He listened when she expressed her frustration with the status quo and offered suggestions only when she asked for them. Of late, though, the two Arnolds appeared infrequently, meaning much less interference from them, for which she was very grateful. Still, she couldn't help wondering what they were doing and when they would re-emerge.

She ate as she finished the paper, then searched the Internet, until realizing the soup was cold. Covering the bowl, she put the remains in the fridge. She poured a glass of water from the filter pitcher and took it into the office.

As she continued the search for information on the Blair Bar Ranch, the computer chimed, indicating a new email. It was on her work account.

> *Still searching for information on the Blairs, I see. Don't make me come over there.*

Her first reaction was to laugh. "Don't make me come over there"? She forwarded the message to Sheriff Otis's email address, with a note about just receiving it. The wording was funny, but the fact that someone knew what she was doing on her computer and knew her email address was disturbing. After all, someone came into her house once, already.

How did they know? It was common knowledge that people could hack into others' computers. If that was the case here, which computer was hacked? The message was sent to the work email address, but that didn't mean anything. She started to shut down the computer, having no taste for continuing to work. However, she remembered something and opened the files on her computer. There she found the "Shared" option and clicked on it. She'd never used it, yet there were two other computers listed. Had she inadvertently enabled the option, or had someone done it for her? Or was it possible for someone to access her computer that way if she didn't close it down?

Sharing was a mystery to her, but she made a note to check it out the next day. For now, it was time to go to bed, where she lay worrying about who was monitoring her computer activity.

She slept poorly, dreaming about someone spying on her through the computers, their blurred faces staring at her from the screen. Once she got to work next morning, she called the IT office for the county and asked for Tamara, who said she would be over a little later in the morning.

The phone rang as soon as Sydney disconnected the first call.

"Sydney, it's Otis."

"Good morning."

"I got your email. Were you on your home computer or the one in the archives?"

"The laptop at home. But the message came to my work email. I've asked Tamara to come check out both. I don't know if she can tell if someone's hacked into it or not."

"Yeah, let her look at it. If she can't tell anything, we need to get someone from the state police to check it."

"Why them?"

"They have people with the expertise. Plus, it's a crime to hack into an individual's computer, moreso when it's a government computer system. It's also a crime to threaten someone."

"I see."

"Have Tamara call me when she's done."

"Will do."

Charlene came in just after they hung up. They worked steadily on cleaning up the mess, making good headway. When Tamara came in, Sydney handed her the MacBook and gave her the desk to work on, where she could also access the desktop computer. She moved the papers and box she was currently sorting over to the table and continued working, but with an eye on Tamara. The computer tech was very good. She had installed the new Mac desktop a year earlier and helped Sydney set up her laptop so that she could access files on the server from home. This particular assignment took a little less than an hour.

"Here it is," Tamara said.

"What?"

"Someone has accessed your Internet activity."

"How did they do that? No one's been in here and gotten to my computer."

Tamara explained the process in very technical terms which Sydney understood only a little. What it boiled down to was that someone was sharing the activity on the desktop in a way that allowed them to "see" everything she did on the Internet. And because desktop computer and laptop were linked, they could also see activity when she was home.

"They actually got into the county system in order to get to your computer. We'll get it blocked, but whoever did it is good. They'll be back."

"There's no way to permanently block them?"

Tamara shook her head. "Even if we block their IP address, they can always set up another one."

"Sheriff Otis wants you to call him and let him know what you've found."

"Sure. No problem. I'll call from here, if you don't mind. He may have questions."

Sydney agreed and left the office. She checked on the work going on in the reading room. Charlene looked up and shook her head.

"Problems?"

"No. Just maddening that someone could be so mean. At least the last two boxes went really fast."

Sydney agreed that it was a mean thing to do, then checked on Tamara. It sounded like the conversation with Otis was winding down.

"He's going to get the state police involved. They should be able to track down the person who hacked in."

"Meanwhile?"

"You might want to give them a day or two to work on it. They need for your computer to stay as it is so they can watch for them."

"If I'm online, does it make it easier to trace them?"

The tech didn't think so, but they'd let her know if they needed anything different. She gathered up her things and left. Since the hackers got into the entire system, a lot of work probably waited for her back at the IT center.

Sydney went back to the reading room.

"Charlene, I think I'm going to do some outside research tomorrow. There's a chance that Doctor Berger may show up sometime this week."

"Okay. I'll keep an eye on things."

She decided that visiting the Kay County courthouse in Newkirk would help keep her off the computer. Plus, she could do research there without being afraid someone else was listening in.

The drive north was uneventful, thanks to good weather. The sun even came out off and on. Sydney walked into the clerk's office and leaned against the counter.

"Hi, Sandy."

The county clerk looked up from her desk and smiled.

"I have the records over on that desk for you," Sandy said.

It wasn't the first time Sydney visited there to do research, either looking for records not yet put online or looking for more detail than was usually posted. As usual, Sandy outdid herself in making the search easy.

First, Sydney looked through all of the records on the Blair Bar Ranch. Property deeds, land sales and purchases, tax information, all in the paper records. That far back it was all written in large ledger books in a fine hand. In spite of the dust, reading the individual listings was a pleasure.

Birth records were on file for all of the Blair children and grandchildren. However, there was no record of Grayson, Sr.'s marriage. At least not under the letter B.

Sydney asked for the records under the letter X. In some offices, records that people wanted to hide were filed there by clerks who could not or would not destroy them. First, she looked in the marriage licenses issued. There were more than expected, but she found what she was looking for quickly.

"X Blair, Grayson, wed to Gladys Smith, 20 August 1940."

The birth record of Grayson, Jr., was right behind the marriage record rather than in the birth records: "X Blair, Grayson, Jr., born 23 January 1941." It listed the parents' names, that they were married, and that the baby boy was "white," brown eyed, and other details. The date of birth was five months after the date on the wedding license. It was not unusual for a bride to be pregnant, not even in the early 1900s. But in this case, the possibility that the father was not the name listed on the birth certificate loomed large. She was beginning to suspect that was the case.

Sydney made notes since she could not get copies of the originals unless she was a member of the family or an authorized representative, such as a professional genealogist hired by them. She always carried a journal for recording information, unlike most people these days who used a laptop or electronic tablet. Writing things down by hand also made it easier to remember later on.

CHAPTER 10

A sign pointed to the right to the Marland Mansion. There was a sad family history if ever there was one. E.W. Marland established the headquarters for his oil company in Ponca City in the 1920s. He and his wife built the mansion, originally with 22 rooms, although they had no children. Eventually they adopted a niece and nephew. When Mrs. Marland died, he married Lydie, his adopted daughter, causing a great scandal.

The home was a showplace for art and architecture, but it was the formal gardens it was best known for. Around 1930, the Marlands moved into a smaller dwelling in town, while he served as a U.S. Congressman from Oklahoma and as governor of the state. Eventually, he lost control of the oil company and all of his money, in part because he would not move the company out of Ponca City to a larger, more accessible location.

The city owned it currently, after its time as a monastery, nunnery, and being abandoned. Sydney always wondered where E.W. Marland's papers were archived, but never pursued an answer. At the moment, she wondered if the Marlands and the Blairs knew each other, perhaps even socialized.

Sydney came to Ponca City because this was where Grayson Blair, Sr., lived after leaving the ranch. Also, Grayson, Jr., was born in the so-called Hospital on the Hill. First thing to check was the city archives. Not the official government records, but historical records.

To find those, she headed to the public library. A separate reading room maintained by the county historical society took up the back fourth of the building, where original manuscripts from various sources were kept. Until now, she had never accessed them. The librarian guided her toward the back of the building. As they went, Sydney explained that she was working on background information on some of the city's prominent citizens.

At first, Mrs. Lawson, the librarian, who had obviously been around a while, was clearly miffed by the fact that the Blair papers went to Filmore County rather than to her library. Sydney let her express her dismay at losing so much local history without comment. However, she mellowed as Sydney asked questions about the Blairs and their place in the city's society.

Mrs. Lawson answered her questions with a slight air of superiority, hoping probably to prove that the papers went to the wrong place. As boxes of files were placed on the library table, and after several questions were asked and answered, Sydney mentioned how sad it was that poor Gladys Blair died in childbirth, or at least within several days of giving birth to Grayson, Jr.

"Oh, no," Mrs. Lawson said, her air of superiority increasing. "That's the commonly believed version. However, those of us who knew the family know that Gladys fell down the stairs in her and Grayson's home a couple of months later. Broke her neck, poor thing."

"Really? Strange that by all accounts . . ."

"It was rather hushed up, you see. There would no doubt have been some talk about suicide and such. Postpartum depression existed then, although we didn't call it by that term."

"Was there an inquest?"

"Oh, yes. It was private, of course, although reporters tried to attend. And a few curious people."

She spoke as if she was there at the time, but judging that the librarian was perhaps in her late fifties, that wasn't possible. She must have heard first-person accounts from someone, though, since she seemed very sure of local gossip as fact.

Mrs. Lawson elaborated on what she knew, and after she left the reading room to resume her position at the front desk, Sydney made notes on everything the librarian said. Then for the next hour, she made more notes and ran copies of pertinent information. There was a lot of material, but only rare bits of any interest, and she was able to get through it in a relatively short period of time.

She replaced all the material in the boxes and stopped at the front desk on her way out to let the librarian know that she was done. Mrs. Lawson had warned her not to put everything away as that was not her job. She either didn't know archivists also earned library degrees, or she didn't care. Before leaving, Sydney asked if the local newspaper had back copies for research.

"Most of their back copies are on microfilm at the Oklahoma History Center in Oklahoma City."

That meant there was no need to visit the newspaper offices. It was already late afternoon, and Sydney decided to start back south. This time of year, it got dark early, and she wanted to get to the Interstate before the sun was down. She would try to get to the History Center tomorrow. There wasn't much more she could hope to learn in Ponca City. She ended the visit, using her GPS, by driving past the house where Grayson, Sr., and Gladys lived when their son was born and where she died.

It sat in a well-established neighborhood of good-sized homes. Theirs was a two-story Prairie School style, painted red with a large stone front veranda. The house sat relatively close to the street with large bushes of different types planted against the wall of the front porch and on either side of the front sidewalk. Although large, the house was relatively modest in appearance. She would have bet that the inside was a different story. At over four thousand square feet, according to the blurb she read in the archives, there were many rooms. The current owner, a prominent lawyer in town, could more than likely afford the best in furnishings.

Sydney sat in her car across the street, studying the facade of the home in which Lily Blair, whom she was coming to believe was also Gladys Blair, spent her final months. She was reaching that conclusion based on facts and feelings.

The old CR-V began sputtering after she got onto Interstate 35. The sun was setting, the sky red in the west and grey to the east. Sydney pulled onto the shoulder and debated whether to turn off the engine. The SUV saved her the trouble, sputtering to silence on its own. She sat in the darkness, silently cursing her luck and watching cars whiz past in both directions.

She pushed the button to turn on the emergency blinkers so other drivers knew she was there. The sky was growing darker every minute. The last thing she wanted was to flag down some stranger and have them turn out to be the very person who was bent on stopping her research.

She dug the cell phone out of her purse. It was charged to eighty percent; at least that was a good thing. She sometimes let it run down to almost nothing before re-charging, and right now she couldn't even use the car charger.

But when she tried to call Triple A, the call wouldn't go through. Checking the signal, there were no bars. Now what?

Maybe she could text Julia.

Stuck on I35 just out of Ponca City. No phone signal. Can you help?

"Text not sent."

Damn!

She tried sending the text again, but got the same error message. Did having no phone signal also mean no access to text messages? She supposed it must.

There was always the 3G network. Maybe she could access that.

She looked under "Settings" and found that 3G was activated. Maybe she could send a plea for help on Facebook. Julia or even Ben might see it. She tried accessing the Internet, but nothing happened. Another try at sending the text message also failed.

"Damn!"

All this technology and nothing worked. What good was it to have it?

Stepping out of the car, she held the phone above her head, further in front of her as she turned in a circle, trying to find a signal. Nothing.

She tried to think rationally as she got back in the car and locked the doors, but the situation was becoming scary. Suspicions that someone might have sabotaged her car crept into her mind. As she held up the phone, moving it in every direction, a car pulled in behind hers, the headlights illuminating the inside of her car and reflecting off her rearview mirror. She lowered the mirror as she prayed it was a state trooper, but there were no flashing lights or spotlight.

She watched in the rearview mirror as a dark figure got out of the car and approached hers. It was dark enough now that she could not even tell if it was a man or woman. He (as it turned out from his voice) rapped on the window next to her head, asking if she was all right.

"Yes, fine," she responded loudly. Even lowering the window a little seemed a very bad idea, which she didn't have to worry about since there was no power.

"Can we help?"

Another tap on the window on the passenger's side. Someone else got out of the car as the first figure occupied her attention.

"No, thank you. I've called Triple A."

"It'll take them quite a while to get out this far."

"Yes, but I can wait."

He straightened up and said something to the person on the other side of the car. Full darkness blanketed the world, the only light coming from passing cars. Traffic was relatively heavy.

"Okay," the man beside her door said. "Be careful."

"I am."

She wasn't certain they had returned to their vehicle until the headlights came on. They pulled back onto the road and sped south, blinking their headlights as they passed.

Several more cars passed her as she considered what her next move should be. What had she read that a woman should do under such circumstances?

Stay with the car, she remembered. Don't try to walk to safety. Don't accept rides from strangers. Wait for a policeman or state trooper. For how long?

There would be one by at any time. But it was getting very cold in the car. She turned the key, but the starter ground a bit without the engine turning over.

How cold was it supposed to get tonight?

She remembered there was a blanket in the back. She kept it back there in case she bought something breakable at a garage sale. For a while she watched cars passing until there were fewer and fewer. The way the old CR-V was designed, the console between the front seats was an add-on that could be flipped down, making it possible for her to crawl to the back seat. Once back there, she could lean over the seat and feel for the blanket. However, she just wasn't as agile as she used to be and crawling didn't appeal to her, even knowing that it would be safer.

With no cars in sight, she could pop the back as she opened the door. She could grab the blanket and be back in the car in just a few seconds. Plus, there was no one around, so it should be safe enough.

She pressed the button for the hatch, then the door lock, jerked the car door open, and slid to the ground. With one hand on the side of the car she went around to the back, raised the hatch, and opened the bottom section for full access. Her hand closed on the blanket just as someone grabbed her around the waist from behind.

It was incredibly cold, and her left side was numb. Even so, sharp bits dug into her arm and side. The air was cold and smelled moldy. Darkness was all she could see, yet it felt as if even darker things stood around her. She lay very still, not knowing where she was or how she got there. She pressed her right hand to the surface on which she lay, feeling damp, cold ground instead of the floor of a car. Her hand was nearly as cold as the ground. Leaves rustled in a slight breeze. The very sound of it made her feel colder.

For a moment she wondered why she thought of being in a car.

"Hello," she called. "Hello."

The words died before they went very far. Apparently, she was alone. But where? And how did she get here?

She raised her head a little. A throbbing pain made her close her eyes. Someone hit her. Or she fell. What was she doing before? Before what? Before she ended up here, of course. There was no good reason for her to be lying on the ground at night in the cold.

Earlier. During the day. She went somewhere. She remembered driving through countryside. And a red house. Where was the red house?

Slowly, bits and pieces of the day came back to mind, driving to Newkirk then Ponca City. The red house was in Ponca City. Someone she knew lived there. No, she didn't know them. Why was the house important?

A scene flashed across her mind, but it disappeared as quickly as it came, leaving behind a memory of darkness and cold different from what surrounded her now.

A blanket. She was trying to get a blanket. In the back of the car. She was on the Interstate.

She groaned at her foolishness as she remembered the details of what happened. How she got out of the car and went around to the back to get the blanket there. The car wouldn't start and she had gotten cold. Someone grabbed her from behind. There was a struggle, but he was very strong. Oh, there were two. She managed to kick one of them on the leg and had the satisfaction of hearing him cry out. The memories were jumbled, recalled in bits and pieces. Kicking the man was the last she remembered.

As the events of the day, of the attack specifically, came flooding back, she wondered if the two who attacked her were the same two who stopped to offer help. Did both of them get back into their car? Maybe one stayed behind in case there was an opportunity to grab her. Or maybe they went out of sight down the road and circled back.

Slowly she turned onto her back and looked up. Nothing but blackness at first, then as her eyes adjusted, pinpoints of light. Stars. They blinked on and off in different parts of the sky. Clouds rolling past, probably. Tree branches swayed in the wind.

Sydney flexed her knees, rolled her ankles, one at a time to see if there were any injuries. Her shoulders were sore, possibly from the struggle with her attacker. She arched her back before trying to sit up. Pushing herself up with her hands, she managed that much, but the pounding in her head returned. She felt her scalp but found no sore spot or lump. Maybe she was given something like ether or chloroform. They might cause a headache. She wasn't sure what was *de rigueur* these days for disabling a victim.

One thing she knew for certain: It was too dark to try to move around. Her watch was gone, so even if she could see it, she couldn't tell the time. Daylight was not too far off, she hoped. In the meantime, she must find a way to keep warm.

At least she still wore her coat. If it was intended that her death look like an accident, not having the coat would make that a little more difficult to believe. In the pockets there were two tissues, a tube of lip balm, and the keys to her car. The last item surprised her, but they were probably left for the same reason as the coat: to make it look as if she wandered away from her car after it broke down. There was nothing else in the coat pockets, nor in the pockets of her corduroy slacks.

She got to her knees and felt the ground all around for her purse.

That was another thing that might have been left with her, but she didn't find it. It was doubtful that there was anything of use in it anyway. She didn't carry matches or a lighter. Her cell phone lay on the passenger's seat of the car.

She stood and stomped her feet, which began to tingle as circulation returned. She stuck her hands under her arms, but to do that effectively, she left the coat open. It was a short pea coat that fit loosely. She took it off, buttoned it up and slipped it over her head. Crossing her arms over her chest, she managed to put her hands under her arms. Her feet were not warming, but if she kept moving, she might at least keep circulation going.

After a while, she ducked her chin inside the coat, the warmth of her breath filling the small space. Every so often she turned, hoping to see a brightening in the sky, as the sun began to rise, to get an idea of direction. She had the feeling that there was no view of the horizon from where she stood and if she didn't keep looking, she could miss the early dawn altogether.

She was exhausted. That and the cold made her limbs heavy, growing heavier with each passing minute. She wanted so much to close her eyes, to sit down and relax. Sleep would solve everything. It was becoming more difficult each moment to tell if she was still moving. She was on her feet, that much was certain, as she fought to keep her knees from bending to lower her to the ground.

A bird began singing. She snapped awake, realizing that she had fallen asleep on her feet. How long she stood there, was anyone's guess. But birdsong meant something. It was important. It meant the sun was rising.

She turned in a circle without detecting a glow in the sky. She continued turning slowly. She stopped. There it was. Yellow glow. It looked so warm. She'd managed to survive the night. And now she knew which way was east.

CHAPTER 11

The sun rose and the world brightened. Even where Sydney stood in the midst of a copse of trees and underbrush. In every direction, nothing but vegetation, black in the shadows. The light did help to define her surroundings more clearly. Too bad nothing in sight told her exactly, or even approximately, where she was. She did know that east was to her left, and to the left of the turnpike. Nothing told her whether she was to the east or west of Interstate 35.

She pulled the pea coat over her head, unbuttoned it, and put it on properly. With her hands in her pockets, she pondered in which direction to walk. She assumed—or hoped—that the Interstate lay not too far away and was her best chance of rescue. In the amount of time from her attack to her being placed on the ground, only a couple of hours might have passed. Thus, she should not be terribly far from the highway. Even two men would be handicapped by carrying someone. Plus, since her car stalled on the west side of the highway, it could be assumed they would take the easier route, rather than crossing the highway, either while carrying her or even transporting her in their vehicle.

She tried desperately to recall maps of this part of the state. She remembered that the Cross Timbers lay in the area to the north of Oklahoma City and west of Tulsa, and she probably was somewhere in there. It was a long stretch of ancient forest spreading north-south from southern Kansas, through the middle of Oklahoma, down into Texas about to Fort Worth. It wasn't very wide, as she recalled, but it straddled the Interstate highway, so that didn't help much. She continued to believe that her attackers took the path of least resistance and left her near the Interstate.

If she was right, she could probably walk back to the highway. She just wasn't positive in which direction to go.

She wiggled her icy fingers in the pockets of the pea coat, trying to keep the circulation going, and discovered what felt like a bit of tissue. She grasped it as best she could and pulled it free. Pinched between thumb and forefinger was one of her gloves. She transferred it to her left hand and reaching back into the pocket, found the other one. She guessed that her hands were so cold the night before that the gloves felt like part of the lining of her pockets. Putting the gloves on was awkward, but she managed it. The material was wool, lined with silk for extra warmth. Hopefully, her hands would be warmer soon.

Feeling cheered even by this small comfort, Sydney brought her thoughts back to deciding in which direction to walk. Her memories of all the maps she ever looked at were muddled. Studying them added to the information regarding many of the creators of the collections in the archive, but the information she'd sought was always of a specific area.

One thing she thought she did remember. She believed that she drove far enough south on I-35 to have crossed the Salt Fork of the Arkansas River, which made a sweeping curve upward from west to east at that point. If that were true, and her attackers chose not to go far, she might be better off going north to find the river. Then she could follow it east or west and eventually come to a town. Any town would do. Or maybe the Interstate.

She began walking, hoping to find some clear ground or, even better, higher ground from which she could see more than trees and underbrush. Thorns and prickles dragged at her trousers and coat. Vines tangled around her feet, and dead twigs crunched at every step.

The going was laborious, especially as her feet remained cold and unfeeling. She tried to step very carefully, but stumbled several times, falling once, bruising and scratching her hands, in spite of the gloves. She came upon a tree branch slightly taller than her, hanging loose in the jumble of dead vines and brush. Pulling it free, she used it as a walking stick to help with her balance. At one point, she jammed it against a rock. It snapped in two, leaving her with two three-foot long pieces of wood, neither of which was of much use. However, she found they were useful in pushing branches out of the way of her feet or her face. The pea coat protected her rather well, but it would take hours to pick all of the thorns and other sharp bits out of the thick nap.

The sudden thought of a warm room, hot soup, and Lewis nearly made her cry. It was the image of Lewis, waiting for his dinner, that was the worst. He must feel so betrayed, even though his bowl was full of dry food when she left yesterday morning.

Just yesterday?

She felt as if she'd been walking for days. And still her feet were like blocks of ice.

She wiped away tears with the backs of her gloved hands and trudged on. Head down, watching for places to step, she walked into the center of a clearing before she realized it.

She first looked up at the sky. Broken clouds scudded across the blue of the background. It wasn't just their beauty she admired. It was the fact that as she watched, she could see in which direction they were moving. And that direction should be to the east. She turned north again.

Sydney stumbled into a particularly dense thicket. Thrashing around, she tried to turn back and find a way around it. In the midst of the noise of fighting the brush, a new sound came to her. An animal sound. Something snuffling, then dry leaves and brush crackling under heavy feet.

The noise came from behind and slightly to her right. Pinpoints of sunlight came through the branches overhead, and as she watched, a form shook itself. More snuffling as it moved toward her at an angle. Did it sense her?

It snorted as if in answer and stood still. Should she run? Try to move away quietly—impossible under the circumstances. Or stand very still and hope it went away.

Whatever it was, it was wild or feral and probably dangerous. Maybe a bear or a wild hog, which she understood lived in the state. Maybe even a feral dog, but its dark form seemed too bulky for that.

It turned away from her at a sound in the brush farther to the right.

Go. Get whatever it is, she urged silently.

It raised its head and tested the air, snuffling loudly.

With its attention diverted, Sydney took a careful step forward. There was no longer time to try to get around the dense thicket ahead of her. She was determined to plow through it at a rush, hoping not to fall. She pushed off her back foot and began running with one arm in front of her face. Still, branches stung as they slapped her cheek and forehead as her arm bounced. Even her nose.

In spite of the noise she was making, she could hear the animal behind, crashing through the brush even faster, pushing her to desperate speed. She decided that the thing was a wild boar. She'd read stories of what one could do to a person if roused, but never heard of any in Oklahoma. This one must have been wakened by her progress through the underbrush, and he sounded in a foul mood.

Suddenly, she broke into the open, running on sand. It edged the river she hoped to find. She turned to find the hog running full tilt toward her, oblivious to the undergrowth. She swung the stick as it got close, striking it on its nose. She turned again and ran into the water up to her knees. Maybe, just maybe, the hog wouldn't come into the freezing water.

She didn't stop to check.

Splashing water everywhere, she waded to the other side where the sandy bank was wider. Hearing nothing behind her, she turned. The wild hog stood there. She could see now that it was a boar, his tusks several inches long and curling upward. It watched her with its little pig eyes, raising its snout to test the air, but made no move to get any closer. Apparently, she wasn't worth his plunging into the freezing water, and she was glad of it.

Shivering now in wet clothes, she agreed about the water. What the cold last night had not done, the wet clothes might do in the early afternoon. Thank goodness the wool coat, at least, was relatively dry and still warm. Even so, she would not survive a second night, wet like this, and the sun would be down in three or four hours.

She set off again, following the river, worrying about quicksand, which she'd only heard about. The wind picked up and the shivering got worse. Yet, the wind dried her clothes, leaving them stiff and cold. She forced herself to put one foot in front of the other, without feeling the ground, a death grip on the short stick. Holding on to it became very important. If she lost it, she would surely never find the highway. She would die of exposure. Collapsing there in the middle of nowhere, her body would never be found. No one would know what happened to her.

If they found her car abandoned, would they search for her? Surely, they would. But who were they? Who would care enough to keep searching? And where was her car?

Ben's face appeared in her mind's eye. His blond hair, greying at the temples, his blue eyes. And that smile. Ah, that smile.

She walked, stumbled, fell, occasionally wandering too near the river and getting her feet wet again. She tried to hold up her right arm to ward off the sun's reflection off the water. She didn't hear the rushing water. She stumbled along the edge defined by sand and rocks and cold water. When she entered total shadow, she stopped. The river continued but the day darkened completely.

Was it sunset already? Did the sun drop below the horizon so suddenly?

She looked ahead; there was light. Raising her head further, she could see that it wasn't the sky overhead, but solid concrete. Behind her, there was more light.

She turned back until the sky was overhead again. Behind her stood a solid structure, arched underneath, straight across the top. Her mind worried the facts of what she saw until it came up with the answer: It was an overpass. The flat top was a road.

Up there was where she wanted to be. People in cars would be passing. That was what she needed.

Turning away from the river, she sought a path up the hill to the highway. A car passed, the whoosh of the air and the roar of a motor. More focused now, she knew that shouting to them from below, would do no good. Finding a way to climb up meant life or death.

She tried a couple of places, but the dirt and rocks just slid under her and she made little progress. So close to finding her way home and she couldn't get up this little hill. Both mind and body rebelled at the task, neither strong enough to make it. She balled her hands into fists to keep from crying.

"Hey! Are you all right?"

The voice came from above, and it didn't sound like God. She looked up and after a moment saw a young man looking down from the overpass. She tried to answer, to say no, she wasn't all right, but her voice failed her. Instead, she sat down and slid down the few feet she managed to climb.

"Stay still. I'll be right down."

Of course, you will. Then we'll both be stuck down here.

Sitting on the incline, she sighed and put her forehead against her knees. Dirt and rocks suddenly slid down past her. In another moment, the man appeared beside her.

"Are you okay?" he asked.

She shook her head.

"I'll help you get up to the highway."

She tried to laugh, sure that they were both trapped where they were. No sound came out, and she wondered how it would be if she never made a sound again.

"Come on," he said and helped her to her feet. He was dressed for the cold in a heavy jacket, gloves, and hat. He led her to the slope and started climbing, holding her hand in his and pulling her upward. With his support, and using the stick she still grasped in her right hand, she got a good start, slipping every so often, but managing to keep going. It was amazing how sure-footed he was.

Finally, they stood on the wide shoulder by the side of the road. Sitting on the ground was a huge backpack from which he took a water bottle. He helped her drink from it, then handed her a granola bar, which she bit into eagerly. While she ate, he tried to flag down a car, several of which passed them by. After several tries, an Oklahoma State Trooper heading south saw them and pulled over onto the shoulder.

"What's the trouble?" the officer asked when he got out of the car.

"I found this lady down there. She looked like she needed help."

The trooper asked more questions, got the young man's name, and after several tries, Sydney managed to tell him hers. He called for an ambulance to meet them and got her into his car. The young man with the backpack waited with her, sitting on his heels just outside the car door. Sydney waved to him as she started into the ambulance. As it drove away, she looked down at the wrapper for the granola bar she gripped and realized she hadn't thanked him.

CHAPTER 12

Once more Julia came to the hospital in Edmond and picked up her friend. Sydney managed to convince the state troopers, ambulance drivers, and whoever else was involved to take her to Edmond rather than one of the towns nearer to where she was found. It was bad enough that she went back into hospital without its being so far from home. It would cost her, they said, but it was worth it.

The EMT let her use his phone for the call. Julia arrived almost as quickly as the ambulance did. Full of concern at first, her friend then resorted to teasing her about this being the second visit in a very short amount of time and she would have to be more careful in future. Sydney agreed, at the same time feeling more than a little embarrassed by it all.

In the meantime, she learned a lot about what happened to her. She was injected with some sort of drug whose name she couldn't pronounce that knocked her out for several hours. She was suffering from hypothermia, many scratches and bruises that would take time to heal, and physical exhaustion that might take a little longer to get over.

With some persuading, she got the hospital to release her and let Julia take her home, not wanting to spend another night away from her own warm bed. The doctors and nurses warned that dire things might occur and made Julia promise to take the necessary steps for Sydney to get over her ordeal.

It was very late when they got to Gansel and into her own house. She wanted most to take a shower, but Julia practically forced her to call Ben and let him know what happened first. He immediately booked a flight, calling back to tell her he couldn't get there until

Sunday. She needed looking after, he said, and he was just the person to do it.

Thursday afternoon, the state police called to say they found her car where she left it. Her purse and cell phone were there and intact, but there was no notebook or journal. Whoever attacked her, took all of her notes on the Blair family. The CR-V was impounded and taken to a lot in Stillwater. She called them and arranged for it to be brought down to her house, for a fee, of course.

Julia slept in the guest room each night, just in case she needed anything. Late Friday afternoon, she stripped the bed, washed the linens, and re-made it, ready for Ben, in case he wanted to sleep in there. Although Sydney slept like a rock most of the time, she did have spells of restlessness, crying out and thrashing about, waking herself. Her heart pounding and her breathing rapid, cold and darkness filling her dreams.

Julia went home Saturday morning to be there when Paul got home. Sydney slept most of Saturday and Sunday. Ben wasn't due to arrive until early evening, and he was renting a car at the airport.

The whole thing was too surreal. Her emotions, her dreams, even her stray thoughts struggled to accept what happened. She'd been threatened before. She was forced to fight for her life. That it was happening again, in an entirely different way, just didn't seem real, in spite of the aches and pains and the cold that permeated her whole being.

When Ben arrived, Sydney called Julia to ask her to come over for a while since she might remember more about what the doctors said. A part of her wanted a buffer between herself and Ben until they became comfortable in each other's presence. She didn't want to be immediately confronted by Ben. It was strange, Sydney knew, but in the end, it made for a lighter atmosphere.

Julia had already heard much of what Sydney remembered, but she listened just as intently as Ben did, adding bits that Sydney had forgotten. When the story came to the part about the river and drinking some of her rescuer's water, he asked why Sydney didn't drink water from the river.

"I'm not sure I didn't," she said. "My memory is vague. But when I got to the stream, I was running for my life." After that, she was plodding along in neutral, her hands so cold that plunging them into freezing water would have been torture.

"But you were so thirsty when he offered you his water bottle."

"Yes, very. It was as if there was no thought of water until that moment."

"Strange," Julia said.

Ben agreed and Sydney shrugged. She had no memory of being thirsty during the whole adventure, not until the young man offered his water bottle. Nor was there any memory of his name, something she needed to find out from the state troopers. She owed him a thank you. His name and address must be in the trooper's report.

Julia fixed them a dinner of an omelet filled with leftovers from the fridge. Sydney managed to eat some, but with little appetite. She was nearly asleep by nine, and Julia helped her get into bed. Once her head hit the pillow, sleep eluded her and she lay there, remembering the feeling of being lost and weak. It was overwhelming after a moment and she started to get out of bed. Then, she heard Ben and Julia talking in low tones and thought better of it.

They were worried about her, she knew. What was happening was almost beyond belief. Three attempts on her life and she did very little to bring on the violence. How could anyone know what she was doing? It wasn't as if she told a lot of people about what was found in the collection, nor what information she was searching for. In fact, she was careful not to tell people.

Just before she dropped off to sleep, she promised herself that she would never again get involved in any more mysteries. It was too dangerous.

When she woke Monday morning, the house was quiet. She lay listening, wondering who might still be there. Ben was supposed to be, and she figured Julia probably left the night before.

She looked over at the clock radio on her nightstand. Eight o'clock. Ben was probably still sleeping in the guest room, since it was only six o'clock where he'd come from.

She lay in her warm, cozy bed, feeling safe and secure. It wasn't just because Ben was in the house, although his nearness was comforting. There was more and she puzzled over what could have that effect on her mental state. Maybe it was whatever drugs the doctors gave her in the hospital. But it was more than that, too. Was it that surviving the wilderness gave her some sense of invincibility? Maybe, but she didn't think so.

There were dreams, she remembered that, but with no sense of what they were about. She continued lying there quietly, not trying to remember. Just letting her mind free wheel, sorting out thoughts and feelings and memories. She relaxed and just as she was about to drift off to sleep, the memories came flooding back.

Breakfast was simple, Ben saying that he wasn't much of a cook. However, he made a decent pot of oatmeal and buttered toast. He also made a great cup of coffee, and she loved her coffee. They talked about his trip and how she was feeling. After they ate, she called Charlene to be sure she was in the archives and everything was quiet.

Doctor Bergen was in, beginning his research on Route 66. He wanted to speak with her, but when he found out she was ill, he said it could wait. She suspected he wanted to know what she had done, if anything, about the crime against Johnny Whitefeather.

Doctor Arnold had called. He heard about her misadventures somehow and checked to see if she was in her office. He never hesitated to call her at home, but there was no call this time. There was no answer when she tried to call him back. It occurred to Sydney that, with all of her time out, although most of it was not her fault, he might be contemplating firing her. The possibility didn't frighten her, although it might later. She needed to know soon, though, if she was to pursue buying a house.

On one level, he certainly had cause to be angry. Her choices made possible everything that happened to her. It wasn't the first time, either, that her research and curiosity brought grief into her professional life, not to mention her personal life. She wondered if a word from Sheriff Otis about how helpful she was in finding information pertinent to the investigation would smooth things over a bit. However, there wouldn't be an investigation if she had kept quiet.

"How are things in the archives?" Ben asked as he refilled their coffee.

She was sitting on the sofa in the living room where she'd carried on the conversation with Charlene. He sat down beside her and lifted his own cup to his lips.

"Seems that everything is going great. Doctor Arnold is probably angry, of course, but I'd love to know how he found out about what happened. Although, I'm not very clear on what he actually has heard."

"Maybe there was a news report on TV. It wouldn't be surprising if some reporter heard about your rescue and made a story about it. It is sort of bizarre."

"Yes, I suppose it is. Wouldn't they contact me, though? To get details?" She shook her head. "I'm beginning to believe that we should stay off the Interstates altogether."

He laughed. "We do seem to have difficulty getting from one place to another without incident." He set his cup on the side table and took her hand in his. "I've been terribly worried, you know. It's not easy being so far away, knowing that someone you care about is in danger."

"I know."

"You don't really, except intellectually. I know that you never intended for things to get so out of hand. I can't understand exactly how that happens, to be honest. But so far, it's happened twice."

"It is strange. I've worked at the archives going on four years now. Nothing ever happened until last year. But . . ."

She hesitated to say what was on her mind. He couldn't understand, even though he was totally involved in the earlier incidents.

"What?"

She settled back against the sofa and pillows and gently squeezed his hand. He looked puzzled and maybe a bit worried about what she was about to say.

"I have to admit that . . . well . . . it's been pretty exciting. Not the danger. Maybe a little. It's just that when I'm researching something important . . . it's exciting. It's important. It's not just looking for mundane facts about someone's life, or some company's history, or how long a particular ranch stayed in operation. I'm not just filling in details, providing background that some researcher might find useful some day."

"I understand that bringing people to justice . . ."

"It's not exactly that, either. That's important, true. But it's history.

It's people's lives. More deeply felt than just ferreting out facts and data. It's completing the story, finding the end and how it got there."

He sat looking at her, searching her face, looking deeply into her eyes. Yet, she felt that he was also looking at his own reflection in her, wondering.

"So, you won't stop pursuing . . ." He paused.

". . . the truth? No. I don't think so."

"I'll have to think about that," he said, shaking his head. "I'd much rather you moved to California and lived with me. I'd at least be able to keep an eye on you, if nothing else."

"You could move here. You have mentioned that before."

"I could. We both have our work. And California's gotten so expensive. But the climate . . ." He left the rest of that thought unspoken, knowing she loved it there, too.

"Well, if Doctor Arnold fires me," she said with a laugh.

Ben smiled and put his arm around her shoulders. Sydney wondered if he wished for that very thing.

Sitting at the desk, looking out on Logan Avenue felt very odd. It was Tuesday and she'd been out of the office since the previous Tuesday. A whole week. It felt longer.

Ben was in Norman, taking care of more family business while he was in Oklahoma. Charlene had worked Monday, but wasn't coming in today. Doctor Berger had worked all the week before, and the part-time archivist left a note that he wasn't sure when he'd be back.

She'd been in the office about fifteen minutes when Doctor Arnold called. He didn't sound angry, but he reminded her how tenuous her employment might be if there were continued absences.

She tried to explain that the attack came while she was out of town doing research for the archives, but he didn't care. She didn't tell him that the whole thing originated with a police investigation, but it seemed that he knew about that.

"Sheriff Otis called me yesterday. He left a message on my cell phone. Something about your finding valuable information regarding a . . . what did he call it? A 'cold case.' Whatever that is. Oh, I know what a cold case is. I just don't have any idea what this case is you're supposedly working on or why you're involved. Eleanor thinks you're going through a second childhood or something. Seeking adventure, looking for fun . . ."

"Doctor Arnold, I almost died last week. I wouldn't call that fun."

"We can't have anything like this past week associated with the archives. Oh, that reminds me. The security installation should be completed this afternoon. Watch for the installer. That should help protect the papers from these rogues you seem to be attracting."

He hung up without a goodbye, how are you, or anything that might show he was concerned about her. His only concern was how all of this might make him look. It was understandable, she supposed. He was not a sympathetic or empathetic person. All of his emotional attention was focused on himself and his wife.

There was a lot to dislike or ridicule about both of them. Both grossly overweight, sloppy in appearance. He with a beard that always seemed to have crumbs in it. She nearing sixty with fiery red hair in a helm cut of some sort. There were better bosses. Somewhere. On the plus side, their interference in the work itself was becoming rarer, and she loved the work. Research, history, primary sources, all under her care. What could be better?

All of that served to fortify her lack of desire to move to California. Even if there were open jobs available there, now or in the future, no one could guarantee she would be hired.

If Ben moved to Oklahoma, that would also change everything. Some good things, some bad things. Both prospects scared her.

While she considered her situation, she was setting up boxes and folders to re-organize. The last of the mess was in sight and she was determined to finish it that day. Charlene worked wonders while Sydney was out. All but three of the boxes were replaced and the new box list looked good.

The installer for the new alarm system arrived just after eleven. Near noon, Ben called to see if she wanted to come out for lunch, but she had to stay in the office while the installer was there. Ben arrived at twelve twenty-five with sandwiches, soup, and Perrier he picked up on his way back from Edmond.

"That was quick."

"I was lucky," he said. "The café wasn't terribly crowded."

The day started eye-watering cold and had not warmed. By

having it double-bagged, the food had not cooled off, in spite of the frigid temperatures.

They ate in her office at the desk, the table to the side being exclusively for sorting and organizing. The same held for the reading room. No food or drink was allowed in there, and a cube organizer stood to one side where patrons stored their backpacks, purses, coats, and other things they brought with them. All that was allowed on the tables with the archival material were laptops, notepads, and pencils. Even cell phones were banned from the room, except sometimes when a frequent visitor was in there alone. But they weren't allowed to use any type of camera. Not yet, anyway; the rules were changing in the field due to pressures from researchers and the prevalence of electronic devices. Still, the papers were her most important responsibility, and they must be protected.

Sydney worked to keep the conversation on subjects other than the weekend. She told Ben about several articles she read recently on changes that were being made in rules in archives overall. Some were allowing cameras now, as long as they didn't interfere with other researchers. Hand-held scanners were still banned since there was the potential for damaging papers. Most of this information came from newsletters, blogs, and websites associated with professional memberships. Every year she hoped to make it to national and regional meetings of professionals, but it didn't happen often. Her contract provided for funds and time off to attend once a year, but something always came up. They were mostly held in larger cities where hotel rooms were expensive and flying there was both an agony and costly. Still, she managed once in a while.

"Are there ever any conferences in California?"

"I think there's one this summer in San Diego," she said. She dug into the files in her lower desk drawer. "Here it is." She handed him the flyer she'd printed off the Internet.

She'd finished her lunch and sat back in her chair while he read. She studied him while his attention was diverted. He wore glasses to read, wire rimmed, that didn't hide his eyes. The lids were lowered as he looked down at the flyer, but she could see how blue they were in her mind's eye. His eyebrows were dark, even though his hair was blond, except for the grey at his temples. Like so many men, he looked more rugged as he aged. Few wrinkles marked his face, just enough to let one know he wasn't young, but not old. She suspected it would be many years before he looked "old."

At nearly six feet, compared to her five-foot-six height, he often seemed much taller, in part because he bore himself upright, yet without seeming stiff. Fully dressed, he appeared slim and fit. Under the clothes, he was tanned and muscular. He worked out regularly in a gym back home and ate healthy. Where he lived, fresh produce was nearly always available.

She felt dumpy standing beside him sometimes. She'd put on weight after she quit smoking fifteen years before, and those pounds were still with her, in spite of efforts to get rid of them. Sedentary work and a love of reading weren't conducive to a physically active life, although she tried to exercise at a gym or at least walk regularly. Oklahoma summers weren't friendly towards outdoor exercise of any kind, and in winter, the cold, especially when the wind blew, could be discouraging. Then, too, the nearest gym was in Edmond, and it was a bit of a drive to make three or four times a week.

What she found most attractive about Ben was his intelligence. They often discussed philosophy, politics, art, history, science, and he knew as much or more than she did on many subjects. On the subjects where her knowledge was greater, he wasn't shy about learning from her.

He finished reading the flyer and looked up to catch her studying him. He smiled.

"What?"

"Just watching you. You're so intent sometimes."

He handed over the flyer and shrugged. "Sometimes. Why don't you come out to this conference this summer? Or should I ask first if Arnold would let you have the time off?"

"Time for attending professional conferences is in my contract," she said. "There's a small provision for travel funds."

"I could . . ." he began. Seeing her frown, he changed tack. "*We* could share the expenses at the hotel and meals. I know you'd be attending sessions and such, but it could be fun. I haven't been in San Diego for a while."

"Do you like baseball?"

"Yeah. Not a regular fan, but I enjoy a game now and then."

"We could see the Padres while we're there. I've never seen a professional baseball game."

"Done. You make whatever plans you need to and let me know."

"Sure." She looked at the clock on the computer. "I'd better get back to work. I want to finish this today."

"Okay."

He told her his plans for the afternoon, and promised to be at her house after five. He kissed her and left, taking the trash with him so there wouldn't be food dregs in the building, and she checked with the alarm installer to see how he was progressing. Because of the age of the building and some of the wiring, he was having to work around a few problem areas. It just might take him until five or later to finish.

Instead of getting back to the boxes and folders, she sat for an hour trying to reconstruct the notes she'd made in Ponca City and Newkirk. Having written things down by hand helped her remember much of it. There was only half as much as in the original notes, but she wasn't thinking about going back north. Not yet. What she managed to re-construct from memory would have to be enough for the moment. She supposed that whoever was responsible for the whole misadventure had destroyed her material. It would be safer for them. Besides, her time would be better spent at this stage at the Oklahoma History Center looking through the newspaper collection.

Reading back over what she'd written on the legal pad, her memory was stimulated into remembering a few other facts which she added. Finished for the time being, she made a copy of the notes and put the pages into a folder. In the vault, she kept a manuscript box in which she put files of her own for safe-keeping. These included the deeds of gift for several of the collections and legal documents regarding others.

She sat at her desk for a short while, enjoying the warm afternoon sunshine slanting through the right side of the window. Several cars drove by, heading west across the railroad tracks. On that side of town, most of the businesses dealing in farming and ranching sat close to the tracks. In the old days, most of the products of the county were taken there to be loaded on train cars and shipped across country. That function was moved some years ago, but its current whereabouts were unknown to her. Much of what she knew about Gansel and Filmore County she got from the papers she processed, and the story they told was an earlier one, so far. The rest she got from researching on line, through newspaper morgues, and history books, but so much related to specific people and time frames.

Thinking of which, she was reminded that she needed to get back to finishing cleaning up the Blair collection.

She moved her desk chair to the table and slid a folder in front of her. So far, nothing looked even remotely related to the part of the family history she was checking out. Most of the information was contained in Carl Blair's journals. It was still surprising that he had written so openly about Johnny Whitefeather and Lily. Yet, there was nothing in any of them about what happened after Lily supposedly disappeared.

Before she realized it, the material in the box was finished. She pushed the last folder into it and sat back, feeling relief. Her mind was still working on the mystery as she put the box on the shelf.

On her way back to the office, she stopped at the vault to retrieve the box of journals. Sorting them into date order, she made a list of them, realizing when she was done that there was a gap. At least one journal was missing. If it ever existed. There was nothing to say that he stopped writing for a period of time, but it seemed unlikely. The known journals covered twenty-five years or more. The missing one would have begun in 1939, around July or August. Why hadn't she noticed the gap before? Did the intruder find that particular journal and take it with him?

No, she was certain that every journal mentioned in the original box list that came with the collection was in the box in the vault. Looking through the copy of the inventory that she used, every mention of a journal was checked off. Now, she took the list into the stacks, along with a book truck. With the list in hand, she pulled out every box that was not checked off as having a journal, or had not been pulled out by the intruder, set it on the truck, and looked through it.

In box number forty-eight, listed as containing documents dated 1947 through 1950, she found another journal. Its notations included the dates listed on the box list, not the 1939 dates she was looking for. In box fifty-two, she found two journals. At first she thought neither of them was what she sought. The first showed years 1950 through 1952 on the first page, and when she leafed through there was nothing else. But the second journal held a surprise.

The years noted on the first page were 1938 through 1939. Some of the dates overlapped those in other journals, but when she leafed through it, notations for late 1940 and 1941 took up the last pages.

She gathered up all of the newly found journals and took them to her desk. Would one of them contain the information she was missing? If so, why would Carl have mixed up the entries? Most of what she'd read was in perfect date order.

With some trepidation, she began reading. She became so totally engrossed in its content that she didn't hear the alarm installer coming down the hall and jumped when he rapped on the door frame. Her first inclination was to cover up the journal lying on the desk, but that would call attention to it. Instead, she slipped a strip of paper between the pages and closed it.

"I've finished getting it all in, but I need to work on a couple of the connections," he said. "I'll be back in the morning to finish up."

"Thanks for letting me know," she said. When he arrived earlier in the day, she had let him know that she should be informed of any problems or changes. Clearly, he had heard what she said. "What time do you expect to be here?" She stood and moved to stand between the door and her desk. He seemed not to notice.

"Should be around nine. There's not much left to do, but I need some parts from the shop, and it's after five now. They'll be closed up."

Surprised, she looked at her watch. It was indeed after five. Just then the phone rang.

She reached over the desk to pick up the handset, noting from the readout that the number was her home phone.

"Ben?"

"Hi."

"I'll call you back in a minute, Okay?"

"Sure."

She hung up the phone and turned back to the serviceman. "Can we turn on the system tonight?"

"Yes, most of the openings are covered, but it's not active in a couple of areas."

"Which ones aren't?"

"Mostly on the second floor."

He told her which windows were not yet hooked up, only one of which was in the stacks on the first floor. It was a window that had been painted shut many years earlier and still stuck when anyone tried to raise it. She thanked him again and moved to the door to let him out. His truck was parked at the curb, and she waited only a moment to see him stow his tool box and belt in one of the compartments. Closing the door, she locked it securely.

As she gathered her things, she called home. Ben answered quickly.

"I'll be home in a few minutes. I found another journal, and I'm bringing it home to read tonight."

They hung up after a few words about dinner, and she finished putting everything to rights in her office. The journal was inside her book bag with the other material she often carried back and forth, including a new composition book for notes since the one she'd been using was stolen.

Making the usual rounds, she checked the reading room and the processing room downstairs. Setting the alarm, she left by the side door opening out onto the small parking lot. She'd gotten a rental car paid for by the insurance company for a few days, until her CR-V was returned.

Once home, she was greeted by both Ben and Lewis. The cat demanded her attention, even though he'd been getting lots from Ben, who also loved cats, thank goodness. But Lewis was accustomed to being fed immediately after she got home. Once he was munching happily at his bowl, she fixed some fried potatoes and scrambled eggs, adding leftover kielbasa from the refrigerator. While they ate, Ben described his day in Norman, where he'd finished up some family business.

"The lawyer seems to think that my stepmother may be very ill. He's just heard through the grapevine about her bad health, but hasn't spoken to her directly."

The second Mrs. Bartlett, Ben's stepmother, led to Sydney's meeting

Ben when she donated his grandfather's papers to the archive. At the time, Mrs. Bartlett stated that she was the last living relative, seeming to have forgotten about Ben and his brother.

"Do you ever have any contact with her?" he asked.

"No," she said. "Not since the gift. Actually, I've hardly met her. Doctor Arnold handles all of the gifts and official paperwork."

He shrugged. His father had been dead for a number of years and his stepmother was a non-entity in his life. It wasn't that he didn't care about her. He simply did not know her.

While he cleaned up the kitchen, Sydney took her shower, afterward wrapping up in her soft, warm robe. As he was wiping off the stove, she sat on the sofa and opened the journal to the entries made the first week of August and noted mundane events on the ranch. Then Carl had written:

Chester found the body out around Potter's Creek. Could not bring it in without a second horse. He'd been dead a few days, he said. Me and Grayson will go have a look tomorrow.

She could guess that it was Johnny Whitefeather, but without it being stated, there was no proof. Carl didn't give her the satisfaction of writing the name, but described wrapping the body in a piece of oil cloth and tying it over a pack horse. All three horses were very skittish on the ride back to the house. However, it was the next day's entry that added to the circumstantial evidence.

Lily found out. Can't imagine how. Someone had to tell her, of course, but who—don't know. Maybe her mother. She nearly broke down her bedroom door trying to see for herself. Hysterical women.

Alice spent most of the night on her knees praying. She is distrawt enough I will have to do something about her or she will let the cat out of the bag. Not that it matters much. Whitefeather was only a half-breed.

Alice, his wife, was apparently unhappy about Johnny's murder or . . . Sydney continued reading, seeing Ben come into the living room, out of the corner of her eye. He picked up *The Oklahoman* and soon became engrossed in the day's news.

Got the burying done out on the prairie. Shouldn't have bothered bringing the body in since it created a scene. Carmela says Lily collapsed sometime during the night and does not seem to know where she is or what's going on. Alice still praying—all night she prayed. Damned women.

Getting the preacher out here on Friday. The marrying has to be done and quick. Not sure how to keep him from knowing, but I will think of something.

Sydney lay the journal in her lap and considered what she was learning. Before, it seemed that the great secret was that Grayson, Jr., was the son of a half-breed named Johnny Whitefeather. That was still part of the story. However, the rest of it was the man to whom Lily was married, and to all appearances, against her will. Although from what Carl wrote, she had no will left by this time. How devastating it must have been to know that her father and brother killed the man she loved.

She read on, almost fearing that what she suspected would be confirmed in the next pages.

CHAPTER 13

"You don't know that's what happened. You may never know for sure."

"What else would be so serious to Carl Blair? Or, more importantly, to Grayson, Junior?"

It was after midnight, and Sydney had just told Ben what she learned from the new journal. She'd closed it up at eleven, being too tired to understand what she was reading anymore and eyes too blurry to see the words.

"I'm done for the night," she'd said.

"What did you find out?"

Ben asked questions as she told him, not all of which she could answer yet. Facts turned to speculation, and then to a discussion. They hadn't exactly argued, not in the angry disagreement sense, but they discussed her assumptions from the facts at great length.

Ben was adamant that until she uncovered all the facts, she could not "know" what happened. The ideas that she came up with were clearly unsettling to him. It wasn't until they were in the middle of the discussion that she'd realized that he was a Catholic, a fact that colored his perception of the past events.

He hadn't seemed particularly surprised or upset to learn that she was not religious on any level. If anyone asked her to classify her beliefs she might call herself a deist if anything. Raised Methodist, her parents never pressed her to accept their religion or beliefs. They let her experience it and several others for herself. By the time she married Leo, religion held no interest for her, except as an historical study.

Sydney felt it was imperative to steer clear of any discussion of the possible events based on religion. The Blairs were also Catholic.

Sydney suspected that Alice may have been Hispanic, perhaps Mexican, in spite of her name, which may have been Anglicized. The few photos of the children showed dark hair and hints of that heritage in facial structure. That fact could explain why no one questioned Grayson, Jr.'s lineage.

It was becoming more and more evident that Lily was forced to marry her own brother under an assumed name. She could list several reasons for thinking this, in spite of that scenario requiring circuitous thinking on the part of Carl Blair. She explained her own thinking to Ben.

"First, he could not let the family be disgraced. Not only because of Lily's being pregnant without the benefit of marriage, but also because the father of her child was of mixed parentage. Johnny Whitefeather was half black and half Indian. I suspect Ponca. Sheriff Otis is still checking on him. Had he been a more explosive personality, Carl might have killed Lily, too, but apparently he controlled his anger when he wanted to. Plus, he would have killed his own grandchild at the same time. Instead, he killed Johnny, whom he blamed for seducing, perhaps even raping, his daughter."

Ben started to say something, but she held up her hand.

"Let me finish." Ben nodded and sat back.

"Second, he couldn't abort the baby. As a Catholic, that was a mortal sin, one that he figured his whole family would balk at. Murder was one thing. Abortion, quite another. Also, although Johnny's death was a probability, given the beating he and Grayson gave him, he was alive when they put him on his horse and sent him away."

Ben nodded again.

"Third, a ceremony was performed at the ranch in which Grayson Senior was wed to an unknown woman. Carl worried about keeping the priest from knowing something, except that his future daughter-in-law was pregnant and they wanted the wedding to be a quiet one. I don't think that was the only reason for secrecy.

"Fourth, Grayson Senior's first wife died in an accident in their home, shortly after Grayson Junior's birth. The official cause was given as death from childbirth, but some accounts say that she fell down the stairs. Now, if Junior was as horrified by what Lily had done as their father was, I doubt that being married to her sat very well. Plus, she was his sister . . ."

"Something that would be deeply frowned upon in the church."

"Yes, I know. But until this time, no mention has ever been made about his courting a woman, or even knowing any women."

"He was gone from home for a while, you said."

"Yes, trying to start his own oil business. But he didn't bring a woman home with him. Carl mentions nothing about him and a woman."

"Does he mention his elder son and any women?"

Sydney thought for a moment. She'd paid little attention to Lawrence, the elder son. So far, he was mostly absent from the journals, and there seemed no reason to think that the difficulties involved him.

"Not much about Lawrence and nothing about a woman associated with him, either."

Ben nodded and thought a moment. "You're trying to have some of the facts both ways. You believe that Carl wouldn't agree to abort Lily's baby because it's a mortal sin, yet you think he would have married her to her brother, which is also a sin. And that may have been more difficult to hide."

"But he did hide it. And the sin was theirs, not his. After Grayson was married, he and his wife never appeared together. In fact, she never appeared at all. Nor did Lily. She disappears from all records, at least those I've been able to find, and she was legally disinherited. Search as I might, I was totally unable to identify where Grayson's wife came from. Nothing."

"Still . . ."

"I know. I have no proof for any of it."

"No." He looked at his watch. "It's nearly one-thirty."

She nodded and they made ready for bed. It took Sydney a while to get to sleep as possible scenarios kept rolling around in her mind. There were conclusions other than the one she came to, but she wasn't ready to let it go.

By Friday, she was used to the routine, both at work and at home. Work routines in the archives were ingrained. However, Ben opening the door for her when she got home each evening was not routine, and she looked forward to seeing him. He brought work with him, and the family matters he was still trying to resolve would take a while longer, including trying to get in touch with his stepmother. He still didn't know how her health was, but he intended to continue trying to find out.

He wasn't due to head back to California until Wednesday of the next week, so they could enjoy each other's company the whole of the weekend plus a couple of days. The time was short and Sydney probably would not feel the frustration at not having her own space to herself. He'd stayed with her before for as many days, and this time she was more relaxed about it.

It was quite possible, of course, that it was their regular discussions about what she was learning from the journals and other research that helped her accept having someone else in her home and in her life. Plus, Ben was better at checking out certain types of information than she was and found a few things on his own.

One thing he'd discovered was the identity of the preacher who married Grayson, Sr., and his wife. Being Catholic, one would have expected the priest at their church in Ponca City to have performed the ceremony, but that wasn't so. They brought in a preacher from a very small town just over the state line in Kansas. Presbyterian, not Catholic. That in itself made him start to believe Sydney's suspicions, and by Friday night, they were again discussing the possibilities. By Saturday morning, they determined that they should drive up to Ponca City and see if they could find her grave.

They drove north in his rental car rather than hers. Mostly, she didn't want to drive that road just yet, although driving her rental would have been easier, emotionally, than her own car, which was still in custody. They were told there was not much wrong with it, but the OSBI still needed to complete their examination. Reading between the lines, she was guessing that they were interested in how the car was sabotaged in a way that allowed her to drive it out of town before it conked out. They promised on Friday that it would be finished by Monday.

It was a cold February day, but the sky was bright blue. Wind blew from the north and they could feel the strong gusts shake the car as it tried to push them off the road. In the quiet moments, when they found nothing to talk about, she kept thinking about California, in and around Hollywood where Ben lived. It was dry and sandy there with palm trees. The land she looked out on this morning was prairie, bare and brown now, but it was green in spring. There were trees of numerous kinds, even though the despised red cedars dominated in places.

Going north toward Kansas on Interstate 35, they passed through the Crossed Timbers. It didn't look so forbidding as her memory of it as the area in which her attackers left her, possibly to die. Once she'd looked it up on a map, it was easy to see approximately where she woke up and why the going was so rough.

At the time she came upon the first water, she thought that it was the Salt Fork of the Arkansas River. However, she began her eastward trek farther west, coming upon Deer Creek first. It emptied into the Salt Fork where the river turned back south. That stretch of the river was a wide bend going under the bridge where she was found.

She shivered, remembering how cold and afraid she'd been. The drugs she'd been injected with made matters worse than they might have been, and lying on the cold ground most of the night gave her a chill that still made her shiver.

Ben reached over and took her hand in his. "Is this the overpass?"

With her thoughts turned inward, she was startled to realize that they were coming up on the very spot.

"Yes. This is it."

It was behind them in an instant.

"I still have to find out the name of the young man who helped me."

"Next time you talk with the state police."

She nodded, trying to remember the face of her rescuer. Even the memory of the face of the state trooper was vague. Everything about that day was vague, as if seen through a haze. Except in her dreams. Then, she saw everything too clearly. The trees and the darkness when she awoke. The chill of the ground under her cheek. She felt it all, saw it clearly. In her dreams she never got to safety. She always woke with a cry before reaching the bridge. Sometimes before even reaching the river.

One day, she knew, they would stop. Now, although she was

frightened in her dreams, when she woke and reached over and touched Ben lying beside her, she felt a new joy in being alive. Gradually, she wakened to sunshine and felt glad. His calm presence helped.

They turned off the Interstate onto Highway 60 toward Ponca City. She pulled the map out of her purse that she'd printed off the Internet. It showed the streets of the town with circles she drew around the locations of some of the cemeteries within its boundaries. From the obituary for Gladys, she guessed that the burial was probably at Greenfield Cemetery, half of which was used by Catholics. After a couple of wrong turns, they found it.

Ben stopped the car just before driving between the two brick posts on either side of the road. The cemetery name arched over the entrance in a filigree of wrought iron. Sydney looked over the street map and then turned to the map of graves within the cemetery. Areas were marked with the dates of burials. The oldest graves, 1890 through 1940, were marked in the northeast corner, spreading outward from there. Since the city wasn't founded until 1893, Sydney did wonder about the accuracy of the dating.

Being somewhat directionally challenged, she checked with Ben, who agreed that the northeast corner was to the right and toward the back. Very slowly, he drove in that general direction, a direct route made impossible by numerous curves and meanderings of the gravel road. They passed a sea of grey headstones, most of them either plain or with ordinary urns or pediments mounted on the top. Ahead, they could see a few taller, more elaborate monuments, and Sydney guessed that was where some of the wealthy families of the past were buried. Which most likely included the Blairs.

They stopped the car and got out, pulling their coats tighter around them. The wind blew lightly, but it penetrated their coats, quickly chilling them. They confirmed they were in the general area for the years they wanted, then started on opposite sides of the road, working up and down the rows of markers. A few were engraved so long ago that the carvings were dimmed by wind and sand abrading the stone, or by discolorations from rain and lichens. Ben called to her that he'd found Carl's, and when she joined him, she took out her cell phone and took a picture of his gravestone. A small host of Blairs were buried in a line on either side, with Gladys's near the edge of the group. Grayson, Sr., was laid to rest on the opposite side of the group with his second wife, Clare Dixon Blair.

Sydney photographed each, ensuring that the engravings were as clear as possible, some better than others. Finding that Gladys's was unclear, she stooped down to read the inscription. At her request, Ben returned to the car to get her book bag. He set it down next to her and she drew out a large piece of paper, folded several times, and a roll of masking tape.

"What's that?"

"The paper is used to make a rubbing of the inscription and whatever else is on the marker. The tape holds it down so the wind doesn't keep blowing it away."

He helped her hold the paper against the stone and firmly pressed tape along the edges. Still, the wind got under it, and the tape didn't stick well to the rough surface. He pressed the paper down with his hands, trying to keep the wind from getting under it.

Using a piece of black charcoal designed for making drawings, Sydney rubbed across the paper, creating a negative of sorts of the engraving. She worked quickly as her hands were becoming too cold to hold the charcoal firmly and the wind was picking up. She was shivering badly by the time she finished.

"Let's check this in the car?" Ben suggested. His lips were nearly blue and his words were slurred slightly because his mouth was cold. She agreed, and loosening the sheet of paper, they folded it roughly and ran back to the road, the wind at their backs. Inside the car, he started the engine. "We should have left it running," he said. She agreed wholeheartedly.

It felt good to be out of the wind, but it took several minutes for the car to get warm. When it did, they both held their hands up to the vents while still in their gloves. Having to take off the gloves in order to make the rubbing left her fingers numb, and it took several minutes to get much feeling back.

Spreading out the rubbing in the confined space of the car was awkward. They managed it in the end, with only one slight tear on the edge. She read the inscription out loud:

"'Gladys Smith Blair, Died January 29, 1940, Mother and Wife, Rest in Peace.' There's no birth date."

"Nothing much new there," Ben said.

"No. I'm not sure what I thought we'd find."

She started to re-fold the paper, but stopped suddenly, and looked more closely at the right bottom corner. It looked like a further inscription, but was very faint.

"Can you read this?" She turned it so Ben could see the smudge. He looked keenly, then put on his reading glasses.

"Not really, but it does look like something is there."

"I need to re-do that section."

"It's too cold."

She folded up the large rubbing and grabbed the book bag.

"Stay here and keep the car running," she said as she started to open the door.

"You'll need help in keeping the paper in place. We won't be gone long. I'll leave it running."

She grinned at him as she opened the door and stepped out.

"Who could have done it?"

"It's rough, so it could have been done by almost anyone who with a sharp tool that would penetrate the surface of marble."

"It probably sounds silly, but I think Alice did it."

"She was in a home of some kind."

"She didn't die there. She was living at home for a while. She may even have seemed well enough to drive herself. Or someone took her out to the cemetery and left her alone for a while. I can see her using a metal nail file or something to scratch that name into the stone."

They discussed the small inscription on the grave marker most of the way home, speculating on who did it. Why had they done it? Was it really what they thought it was?

Using a smaller piece of the paper toward the lower edge of the headstone, Sydney had rubbed the charcoal over the paper at first gently then harder and harder. Eventually, she made a mess of it and had to start again. The second time she got a clearer copy. She also took a close up picture of that section of the stone. Then they'd run to the car and jumped in to get warm again.

"It looks like it says, 'Lily,' doesn't it?

Ben agreed, but argued that it wasn't clear enough to be certain. She got the camera and studied the picture on the camera viewer.

"Can't tell much here," she complained. "I'll have to look at it on the computer to see if it's any clearer there."

All the way back to Gansel, they argued both sides. It *was* the daughter's name. It couldn't be. And all the reasons why it was or wasn't. They were still arguing when they got back to her house.

"The only way it makes sense is if you're right about Grayson Senior marrying his sister. But I still don't think there's enough proof of that."

"I know it's bizarre."

"More than bizarre."

They set all of the bags, maps, and rubbings on the chair in the living room and took off their outer gear. The house felt warm and cozy after having been out in the cold. The car never seemed to get warm enough.

"I'll make some hot chocolate," Sydney said as she handed her coat to Ben to hang up in the coat closet near the front door. She filled the kettle, setting it on the stove, then sat at the kitchen table, elbows resting on the top and her chin supported in her hand. Her eyes were unfocused as the facts as they knew them spun around in her mind. Ben was right: her assumptions were too bizarre.

How could a family force son and daughter to get married? The one saving grace might be that the child she bore wasn't fathered by her brother. Wasn't there a better way to handle Lily's pregnancy though? It wasn't unusual to send pregnant daughters back east to homes for unwed mothers. Did Carl Blair have an enemy who could use the fact of the pregnancy against him in some larger way than usual?

Too many questions still unanswered. But she wasn't finished.

CHAPTER 14

Sydney placed the last of the re-filed boxes of the Blair collection on the shelf with a sigh of relief. She finished it on the previous Friday, but on Monday morning, she made some last-minute adjustments. The cleanup was completed. Charlene came in early to pick up her check for the week before and went away happy. Most county employees were required to use direct deposit, but part-time employees were allowed to opt for real checks. Although she preferred to work very little, the extra money probably looked good.

Stretching her arms overhead, Sydney sat down at her desk. After the drive up to Ponca City, she was still tired, especially after standing out in the cold so long. Sunday night was quiet and she slept well. If she dreamt, she didn't remember, making it the first night there were no bad dreams since her latest misadventure.

She felt guilty about all of the time she'd been away from work. Her own paycheck might be affected next time. But there were more important things to do for now.

The old clock in the hallway chimed ten. Ben would be leaving Gansel, on his way to Tulsa to try again to speak to his stepmother. He managed to find an address, the last place she was supposed to have lived. He'd tried to call her several times over the weekend, but never got through.

For herself, Sydney intended to look through the journals again, at least scanning every page, if not reading every word. It might also behoove her to look through other papers. Perhaps the hospital records of Gladys's confinement were in one of the boxes, but it could take hours and chances were pretty slim. Certain areas of record keeping were scanty in the collection, while others were filled with minutiae. However, she had just spent days looking through several boxes in some detail, and with the rearrangement she and Charlene finished, along with the new box list, her chances of finding papers from a specific period were improved.

She started with the earliest journals, determined to work her way through every page in date order. She was a fast reader and she was now familiar with Carl Blair's handwriting. With her familiarity with events as he described them, she sped through.

At the end of a journal dated 1935 through 1937, she came across notations of a slightly later date. It appeared that Carl went back to use up the blank pages, beginning on 28 January 1939. It wasn't a normal thing for him to do, but she could imagine several scenarios for doing so, from being frugal to not wanting to make an extra trip into town to pick up another blank journal. He could have written the brief notes out of sequence in much the same way that county clerks filed some records under "X", so those bits were more difficult to find. Carl couldn't seem to keep from writing everything down, but it wasn't because he wanted others to read of his day-to-day activities. They were for his own personal use. She didn't want to believe that he enjoyed revisiting his cruelty, but that might be a possibility.

Try as she might, she could not make sense of much of what he did. Still, if he wrote the journals just for himself, there was little chance of someone else seeing anything he wrote until after he died.

She shrugged the questions away. Whether he ran out of journals or was trying to hide the passages didn't make a difference in what he wrote. In this case, the misplaced passages were not helpful. Nor was her understanding of his thinking process increased.

By the end of the day, she finished going through half of the journals. She couldn't help feeling guilty for spending so much time on Carl Blair, but it was part of her job to know the collections and the people represented by them.

Just after four o'clock, the doorbell rang. When she opened the door, Doctor Arnold stood just outside.

"I forgot my keys," he said as he pushed past her.

"Of course."

He went directly into her office and sat down in the visitor's chair. Every time he deigned to come into the archives, she half expected him to take her chair behind the desk. She took her own chair, clasping her hands on the desktop.

"How are you, Doctor Arnold?"

"Fine. Fine. I needed to check on your status after your recent absences," he said. "I've been unavailable for a few weeks, but I was informed of what's been happening."

She kept him informed through voice mail, of course. Yet she felt that he knew details she hadn't given him.

"Everything has evened out," she said. "I don't think . . ."

"Thankfully, this has not been a busy time for the archives. But we do need to be more careful in future." She nodded, ignoring his interrupting her. "I thought I'd check to see what you're working on these days. And I wanted to see how much damage occurred during that break-in."

"Charlene and I have taken care of the boxes that were emptied, and they're all back on the shelves. No permanent damage was done."

"How is the new alarm system installation working out?"

"Fine. They finished the install. Of course, there have been no attempts to break in since it was finished. As far as we know."

"That should take care of things, I suppose."

"It should."

He sat, steepling his fingers, and looking at everything in the office, but her. Sydney kept her eyes on him, trying to gauge his attitude, wondering why he was really there.

"Let's have a look around, then." He stood up, indicating that she should lead the way.

For the next twenty minutes, she took him on a tour of the stacks, pointing out the boxes of the Blair collection, then collections that needed to be re-processed, those not yet touched, and the larger number that were completed. Arnold acted as though he was seeing some of the boxes and shelves for the first time. A few of the older ones were very familiar to him. He even patted some of those boxes as if they were old friends.

The processing room on the lower level was relatively clear since there were no new, large collections. Two smaller ones—one with eleven boxes and one with seventeen—were preliminarily inventoried and put on those shelves with others still to be processed.

The large room was clean and organized, ready for whatever might be on its way to them.

"Very good," he said in a low voice.

When they went back up toward her office, he seemed as pleased as he ever was at conditions in the building and with the collections. Without saying much else, he walked by her office door and made for the front door. She unlocked it and let him out.

The visit left many questions unanswered. That night as she described the visit at dinner, Ben suggested that Arnold's bosses may have told him he needed to be more aware of matters concerning the archives.

"That might explain it," she said. "I do hope it doesn't mean he's going to be around more. He and that wife of his know nothing about archival best practices, even though she thinks she knows everything. I can do without their help."

The visit added one more mystery to her life and worrying about it kept her from sleeping that night. Rather than toss and turn, she slipped out of bed, trying not to waken Ben, slipped into her robe, and padded barefoot into her office, leaving the door slightly ajar. She turned on the laptop, and while it was booting up, she went into the kitchen to make herself a cup of tea. Water boiled quickly in the electric kettle, and with the tag of a ginger peach tea bag dangling over the edge of her favorite mug, she sat down at the desk.

Her first inclination was to try more research on Carl Blair, the Blair Bar Ranch, and Grayson, Sr. However, she had spent so much time on them already that it was unlikely much new information could be found on the Web. What other angle could she try? There was almost nothing on Lily, so that wasn't a good angle.

Grayson, Jr., was something of an enigma, even though he was a politician of many years' standing. He'd been in office for—she checked her notes—over twenty-three years: twelve as a representative, eleven as a senator. With term limits that began in 2004, he was no longer eligible for re-election to the state senate. He once indicated a desire to run for governor. A scandal could ruin any chances for election and most decidedly would ruin his reputation, something that was very important even to outgoing politicians. However, as long as he'd been in office, he might be untouchable. That depended on how convincing any evidence might be.

Did he know about the possibilities concerning his mother? Would his family have told him who his mother was? He probably believed the stories that were concocted for the world's benefit. Why would anyone tell him otherwise? There was a streak of cruelty running through the family.

If he didn't know or have any suspicions, there would be no reason for him to resort to violence to keep the facts from being revealed. Who else would want the facts hidden?

She looked down the lists of people he worked with: family members, people associated with the family, a few workers on the ranch, which was not as large as it once was. Then there were those who worked in his legislative office and who worked on his campaigns. She was still filling these out, but their histories were peripheral to the main subject.

The one important person on whom she found little information was Grayson, Sr.'s, brother, Lawrence. Again, she consulted her notes.

Lawrence was born in 1914 and now lived in a senior community in Ponca City. For the next hour, Sydney tried to fill in the blanks of his long life. It became clear that, as she suspected, he was not the star of the family, even though he was the eldest son. After spending a few years working alongside his father on the ranch, he went to the University of Texas, studying law. His going that far for school was only a bit strange, but with the University of Oklahoma so close, why had he chosen to go to Texas?

Maybe OU hadn't accepted him. Or maybe they didn't have a law school so early on.

Having read so much about the elder Blair's attitude toward his children, it wasn't hard for Sydney to believe that any of his children might go far to get away from the strictness and abuse of their father. She made a note to look for notations in the journals about Lawrence's decision to become a lawyer. Until now, most of her attention was fixed on the Graysons, father and son.

Even using all of her skills at finding data on the Internet, it took more than half an hour to find information on Lawrence's family. He was also married twice. His first wife was Matty Winston who died in childbirth. The child was stillborn. His second wife, Mildred Petty, gave birth to five children, two of whom lived to adulthood. There was a son, named Carl II after his grandfather, and a daughter, named Lily.

So, there were two Lily Blairs: a daughter and a granddaughter. Sydney sat back in her chair and studied the screen. Why was it so difficult to find information online for Lily Blair if there were two women with the same name? Did something happen to Lawrence's daughter before she managed to make any sort of name for herself?

Seeing the door to the office swing inward out of the corner of her eye, she stopped breathing and swung around in the chair. Ben shuffled in, looking very ruffled in his pajamas and very sleepy.

"Hey," he said.

"Hey, too. Did I wake you?"

"No. Got up to pee, saw you weren't in bed and the light was on in the office. Made a brilliant deduction."

She smiled. "I have some tea. Want a drink?"

She picked up the cup and realized the tea was cold. She apologized and offered to make him a fresh cup.

"No. I'm going back to bed. Are you staying up much longer?"

It was two o'clock in the morning. Time for both of them to be in bed. She began turning the computer and everything off. "I'll come with you. Otherwise, I might never be able to get up in the morning."

He put his arm around her and they made it back into the bedroom. Once under the covers, though, they were no longer sleepy. She rolled over toward him and kissed him. His response was tender and warm. Her hands stroked his back, moved down, as they continued kissing. He pulled her close against him, his own hands finding her sensitive places. Another hour passed before they fell asleep, exhausted and content.

"I need to go down to Oklahoma City." Sydney was almost dressed for work. Ben still lounged in bed.

"What for?"

"I need to check the newspaper morgue." She told him about finding there was a second Lily Blair. "There must be an article on Lawrence's wedding, engagement, or something."

"Are you sure they were married in Ponca City?"

"There's reason to believe that. But, no, there's no direct evidence.

Even if they got married somewhere else, their engagement would most likely have been in that paper."

"Do you dare go? Getting in to see the microfilm has to be done during the week, and you aren't on the best terms with your boss right now."

"I know. The only other way to get what I want is to pay for someone at the newspaper to do a search and send me copies."

"What about me? I've got two more days."

"I hate to ask. It's pretty boring looking through page after page of old newspapers. It can take hours."

"I know. But you have approximate dates, so that narrows it down some."

They discussed his going until Sydney had to leave for work. At the last minute, she agreed that he could serve as her surrogate. In the back of her mind was the memory of his being attacked the year before, when she was trying to figure out who killed her intern in the archives. She didn't like putting him in danger, especially when he was so concerned for her safety and kept warning her not to get involved.

Even so, he was right that she shouldn't take more time off from work under the circumstances. Plus, finding articles in old newspapers was more a matter of perseverance than knowledge.

"Come by the archives in an hour or so and I'll have a list of dates and other information written down for you."

He got out of bed and put his robe on. At the door, he kissed her goodbye just before she slipped out. The car windows were covered with frost, and she started scraping them clear. As she worked on it, Ben stuck his head back out the door and hollered, "Need some help?"

"No, I'm just about done."

He laughed. "My timing's always been good."

She waved to him and smiled. The rime was thin and with the defroster heated up, she was done in a few minutes. Ben stood in the doorway as she drove away, and he waved goodbye.

She started on the list for Ben right away in order to have it finished before Doctor Berger arrived. He was due in at nine-thirty, and she wanted to have the boxes he wanted ready for him when he arrived. She finished the list by a quarter to nine, giving her enough time to get the boxes out of the stacks. This was the first time in a couple of weeks they would be in the archive together, and the good doctor probably would want to talk to her about whether she reported the flogging of Johnny Whitefeather and to whom she reported the incident. He should be satisfied that she'd called the sheriff and talked with him about it.

Ben arrived at five after ten. It took five minutes to go over the list with him. As she watched him drive towards the Interstate, she couldn't help feeling apprehensive. Surely this time wouldn't be like the last.

Doctor Berger arrived promptly at nine-thirty. They sat together in the reading room and discussed what he'd found and what had happened since. She left out many details, relating the conversation with Otis and his interest in finding out what happened. Simply put, there was no real need to tell the good doctor and make him worry.

In the end, he was pleased that she reported it. His article on the Blair Bar Ranch was nearly finished, and he promised to get her a copy as soon as it was published. That was one condition of doing research: a copy of any publications that resulted would be provided to the archives. Not every researcher followed that rule, of course, but he was prompt in providing copies. Right now, he was eager to begin research on Route 66, his new subject. She still couldn't figure what unique angle he might find, but that was his concern, not hers. In minutes, he was happily going through boxes of material.

Her own concern was to finish reviewing the entire texts in Carl Blair's journals. So far, after 1939, there were few words written about Lily. As Sydney worked her way through, trying to find anything about the daughter, the granddaughter loomed large in the back of her mind. Carl must have been furious at Lawrence for naming his daughter after her disgraced aunt. Lawrence must have been very fond of his sister for him to stand up to his father like that.

With every passage read, the more apparent it became that Carl favored his younger son. Lawrence seemed to be a great disappointment to his father. He was less athletic, less interested in the ranch. Even though Grayson left home to start his own business, Carl approved of the venture, and he remained the favorite.

In September 1936, she found an entry that caught her attention. Lily, his daughter, went to a college dance where she imbibed alcohol. She didn't get drunk, but Carl was furious, giving her a tongue lashing that night after she got home, threatening to get his whip and teach her how to be a lady. Lawrence stepped between them, challenging his father for what might have been the first time.

Carl was taken aback at first, surprised at Lawrence's standing up to him. Then he became furious.

He stands up to me and what is it about? His whore of a sister. Never once has he stood up for himself or his brother.

His use of the word "whore" startled Sydney. It was indicative of how little he respected her and probably other women, but to call her by that name when all she did was have a drink was surprising.

The scene got worse. In the end, he beat up his older son, leaving him on the parlor floor.

He's no son of mine. Defending his sister like that. Ending up on the parlor floor with his mother on her knees beside him. And Lily gone up to her room.

Sydney stood and walked into the hall. The scene was upsetting. She knew there were men like Carl Blair, men who bullied and abused their families, not only because they were mean sons of bitches, but also because society allowed, even encouraged them. Her own childhood wasn't a bed of roses, but her father never raised a hand to her or her mother. He was kind, even though he felt women had their place. It was always difficult for him to accept his own wife's sense of independence, and he did his best to squelch it. He gave up on changing his daughter very early.

What was interesting in what she read, once she got past her emotional reaction, was that Lawrence took a beating for Lily. Deciding to jump ahead in the journals, Sydney flipped through pages, checking the dates, until she found the years in which she thought Lawrence got married the first time.

Two journals contained most of the records of those years. She scanned the pages quickly, looking for key words: wedding, marriage, Lawrence. It wasn't until she came to the pages dated December 28, 1941, that there was any mention of Lawrence's wedding.

> *One hell of a year soon to be over. Lawrence married. Good girl, knows her place. Grayson married then widowed. Grandson born. What a monster he is—never amount to much. Could be worse. He takes after his mother more than his father. With her gone he will never know.*

It could be assumed that the grandson's taking after his mother meant he was more light-skinned. She turned to her notebook to find—yes—Carl died three years after Grayson, Jr., was first elected to office. Was that success enough to raise his grandfather's opinion of him?

There was no mention of Johnny Whitefeather's flogging or death, nor any details about either of Lawrence's wives. An occasional word about his own wife, Alice, who was hospitalized for long periods in the last years of her life. Sydney couldn't help but believe that her collapse was due to the circumstances of Lily's marriage and the birth of her grandson, then her daughter's death. The poor woman must have been horrified at the way her daughter was treated.

The doorbell rang, startling Sydney from her musings. The visitor was Sheriff Otis, whom she invited into her office. Before he could tell why he was there, Doctor Berger came to the door.

"Sorry to interrupt, but I need to leave early today."

"Right now?"

"Yes. I just remembered that I'm supposed to see my dentist."

She smiled. In some ways, Berger was a typical absent-minded professor. As she rose from the desk, he asked if he could leave the folders on the table in the reading room. He'd straightened them so that they were in piles, but . . . She told him that she would take care of it.

As she let him out the door, she couldn't help wondering if he'd heard that the new visitor was the sheriff and the good doctor didn't want to be questioned on what he'd found in the papers. She didn't blame him.

"There's been a new development regarding your kidnapping," Otis began without preamble. "A body has been found near where you were rescued."

Her heartbeat quickened and she swallowed hard. It felt as if she was choking, and she took a drink of cold coffee. Thank goodness Ben wasn't on that road.

"When?" she managed to ask.

"Early this morning."

"Where?"

"Near where you were found. He'd been there a day or two."

"Oh, you said that. Who is he?"

"We're hoping you can give us a clue about that."

"You think it's one of the men who attacked me?"

"You'll have to tell us."

"Now?"

"Yes. The OSBI and state police asked me to bring you up."

"Right. Give me a couple of minutes to see if I can make arrangements."

The chair creaked as he pushed himself to his feet. He stepped out to his SUV parked at the curb at the front of the building. The first thing Sydney did was call Ben on his cell phone. He didn't answer and she guessed he was probably in the History Center with his phone turned off. She left him a message, then called Charlene to see if she could come in. She couldn't come in until one, which was okay with Sydney. Last, she called Doctor Arnold to let him know that, once again, she would be out. As usual, she got his voicemail. She deliberately didn't tell him why to see if he found out on his own.

She hung up and grabbed her purse and turned out all of the lights. Otis opened the door on the passenger side of the SUV while she locked the door behind her.

As they started east toward the Interstate, Otis told her what little the state police found concerning the investigations, reminding her that there were two with which he was involved. He hadn't managed to find out much about Johnny Whitefeather's death or his relationship with the Blairs. Tribal records for that period, particularly those of the Ponca Tribe, were somewhat scattered. Still, they determined that he was a member of that tribe and that he'd worked on the Blair Ranch for over a year before he was found with Lily Blair.

As for the attacks on Sydney, he and other investigators found them a bit curious. The poison put into her food was definitely pokeweed, every bit of the plant being poisonous to humans, but rarely fatal, meaning that the plant could be dormant. That dashed her hopes that it was a simple case of food poisoning. Now it was clear that it was put in the dish deliberately since there was no other way for it to have gotten there.

As for the kidnapping and leaving her in the wilderness of the Crossed Timbers area, it was clear that she was not left far from the Interstate. Circumstances and probable ignorance on the part of the kidnappers made the incident more dangerous for her. They probably had no idea how much of the drug they gave her would be dangerous, especially for a person suffering hypothermia. Plus, she was already weak from the poisoning.

"The theory, again, is that there was no intention of killing you, only putting you out of commission for a while. The thinking is that whoever it was gave you too much of the drug to knock you out so that you lay on the cold ground longer than they expected."

"Were they wanting to get me out of the way or scare me? If we accept that they weren't trying to kill me. Just incapacitate me. I can't imagine why anyone would do that. Twice. I mean, what would alarm someone so much about my researching the Blairs? Clearly, they are a family of historical significance within the state. They're wealthy. They've held some amount of power, politically and financially, beginning with Carl. But his papers are in the archives, available to anyone who wants to read them."

"Maybe it's some old grudge. I figure it's something very personal. Not just something the family is trying to hide."

"Like the Johnny Whitefeather murder."

"We don't know yet that it was murder. But, yes, once you began looking into his death and such, it must have come to someone's attention."

"Like Grayson, Junior."

"Maybe. But we've found no connection with the attacks on you."

"I'd really love to know if they know about Carl's journals."

"Maybe you can ask 'em."

"I don't know how. If they are the ones behind the attacks on me, they won't likely be welcoming me to their homes."

Otis shrugged. They'd been on the Interstate for a few miles. The SUV, heavy as it was, rocked with wind gusts out of the northwest. Prevailing wind patterns were usually out of the south around to the west, but winter storms and cold weather often came out of the north.

Her cell phone sounded with Ben's ring.

"Hey, got your message. What's up?"

"I'm with Sheriff Otis," she said. "I'll tell you all about it tonight."

"Okay. I'm still at the History Center, taking a break. Wish me luck."

"Good luck."

They said goodbye, and she turned the phone off so that she wouldn't be tempted to answer any further calls. Not that she got many on her cell phone. She tended to use it more for other things, like getting directions or addresses, and quite often for taking pictures on the spur of the moment.

They drove on, Otis working against the wind to keep the vehicle on the road. After they crossed the overpass, he used one of the official turnarounds to get on the southbound side. When he pulled over, Sydney was apprehensive. He parked on the wide shoulder of the overpass where she was found.

"Where is he?"

"Down near the river."

"I'm not getting out."

Sydney wanted to be brave, to do what was necessary to help both the police and herself, but this didn't feel like the time or place.

"It's all right. I'll be with you the whole time, and no one is going to let anything happen."

"It's this place, not what might happen."

"We need your help, Sydney."

He opened the door and stepped to the ground. Coming around to her side, he opened her door and undid the seat belt. She and Ben drove over this overpass on Sunday, and she remained calm. Now, stopping on this very spot, her hands were suddenly ice cold as Otis took them into his own. Her mouth was dry and felt as if her lips must have turned blue. Her heart beat hard enough to break through her chest. Otis helped her to slide off the seat, holding her arm as she stood stiff-kneed, trying so hard not to collapse.

Being thoroughly frightened was neither totally new nor strange. The attack by Violet Parsons and her grandson in the archives the year before came so suddenly, unexpectedly. There was no time to be afraid, not until after it was all over. Her reaction to the site of the attack was familiar ground—her own archives. In contrast to that, she hardly remembered what this area looked like. Only how she'd felt while waiting for the ambulance to drive away, the immense relief as the vehicle turned onto the highway and sped south.

This was necessary, she knew that, and she made herself walk toward the bank without falling. Sliding in the gravel as they climbed down, Otis and a state trooper helped her make it to the river below, then into the shadow of the underpass, out of the wind. The darkness surrounded her, every movement echoing from above punctuating the murmur of the river as it flowed through.

Several officers prowled around, looking down for any evidence that might have been left behind. Otis and the trooper led her toward a group of three men, one officer in uniform, who stood a short ways back, and two men in some sort of environmental suits. She guessed they were the medical forensics team, whether medical examiners or coroners she didn't know.

"They need you to identify the man if you can," Otis said quietly. "He was pulled out of the water, so he will look strange. Do your best."

The body of the dead man was not covered as she'd half expected. It lay darkly wet on the wet sand, where they must have pulled it to get it out of the water. The face, however, was so white it almost glowed in the light of the flashlights. Standing beside this dead thing, looking down at the white face, with its eyes open and almost colorless, its grey lips swollen as if they would burst, she fought the urge to look away.

As she bent over slightly, she cried out in recognition, surprise, and grief. The body was that of the young man who first found her and gave her the granola bar.

CHAPTER 15

"I'm sorry, Sydney."

Otis drove south, toward Gansel. All she wanted was to be home, to wrap herself in her blankets and hide in bed.

"Couldn't I have identified him after they moved him?"

"That won't happen 'til tomorrow. They needed you to see him before he . . ."

"Before he looked any worse?"

"Yeah."

That might be logical, but she resented it. She sat in angry silence, feeling the wind buffeting the SUV. It was again out of the north, sending clouds scudding overhead. Occasionally, blue sky peeked out between and through them as they moved, thinned, swirled. As much as she disliked hot weather, she longed for the cold to end. Wearing heavy coats, scarves, and gloves grew old.

She looked down at her hands. They were red after being out in the cold under the bridge because she'd forgotten her gloves. Her hands were already dry from the winter cold, soaking up hand lotion like a sponge. As she searched for the small bottle of lotion in her purse, she recognized what she was doing. It wasn't just trying to protect her hands or wishing for spring. She was avoiding the subject staring her in the face. A young man was dead, and in some way, it was because of her.

"Do they know his name?" she asked Otis.

"Not really. He gave the trooper a name and address when you were rescued, but it didn't check out. There's no identification . . ."

"So they knew it was probably him when they wanted me to come out and identify him."

"Yeah. That's why they asked for you to come."

Anger gripped her again and she sat up straight, determined not to let emotions get in the way. *So much for your curiosity*, she thought. *This is taking the good with the bad. Move on.*

"We know his death has something to do with me. I'm the only link. We could assume that it also has something to do with the Blairs."

"You know what you do when you assume."

She smiled. The old saw went, "When you assume, you make an ass of u and me."

"It's a perfectly good word," she said. "And about all we have to go on right now are assumptions."

"We?"

"I'm the one who started this whole thing."

"You and that professor of yours."

"He's not involved. Only you and I know about him."

"Neither are you. Involved, I mean."

"Of course I'm involved. Maybe not in the same way you are, but I'm the one who's gone out and found the information."

"What information?"

Uh oh, she thought. *I didn't tell him about what I found in Ponca City or Newkirk.*

"Well, you know that I've continued reading through the journals. I've found some facts there."

"Where else?"

"I've only . . . well . . . I went up to Newkirk and did some checking in the records in the county courthouse. You know, births, deaths, marriages. That sort of thing."

"Newspaper articles?"

"No, they're in the History Museum in Oklahoma City." She didn't mention that Ben was looking there.

"What have you found out?"

First, she told him what facts she knew or could remember off the top of her head.

"All the dates correlate?" he asked when she finished.

"Pretty much. There are a couple of glitches. The one thing I wasn't making allowances for was that Lawrence named his daughter Lily."

"Why is that important?"

"For one thing, I should have found more information on someone named Lily Blair since there were two of that name. Plus, a couple of assumptions. First, Carl would probably have been angry at Lawrence for naming his granddaughter after his disgraced daughter. The fact that Lawrence did that, probably knowing how his father felt meant he either loved his sister very much, he hated his father that much, or both. There was that time when he faced up to his father because of Lily."

He asked what that was about, and she described the fight on the night of the party, when Lily had been drinking.

"Nothing in all of that we could take to court," he said. "Unless you have more than assumptions."

"Not yet."

"You aren't involving yourself anymore. It's gotten too dangerous."

"Are you going to take the time to read through the journals? I'm the logical person since I have daily access to them. Plus, I already have so much background information and know what could be important when I see it."

"Okay. I'll give you that. But no more looking through records in courthouses or newspapers. You keep making yourself visible in this investigation and I figure someone will decide you're too dangerous. They haven't tried to kill you. Yet. But they have killed."

"I'm very aware of that, Otis. And it does frighten me."

"Good. You stay frightened. At least enough to keep you at home and in your damned archives."

She smiled. It wouldn't make either Otis or Ben happy, but she figured that she had permission to investigate now. She'd never knowingly carry it so far as to endanger the sheriff's job or endanger Ben's life again. Of course, she hadn't considered herself in much danger either. What happened so far was someone trying to warn her off. From now on, she would try to be less obvious.

"Your house or the archives?" Otis asked as they turned off the Interstate.

"Archives. My car is still there."

He nodded and steered the car toward downtown. It was past five o'clock, and she should check inside to see if Charlene made it in and that all was well.

Otis stopped the SUV at the curb and she got out.

"Mind, you be careful," he said before she shut the door.

She waved, and he waited while she unlocked the building's door. She waved again as she stepped inside and he drove away.

The building was dark except for the new night lights that shone from corners of the reading room and in the stacks. A separate one illuminated the stairs to the second floor. She checked her watch. Five-twenty. Unlocking her office and turning on the lights, she moved around to the computer and switched it on. The message light blinked on the phone. Ben's voice said that he was on his way to the house and should be there around five-thirty.

She realized that she had not turned her cell phone back on after talking to him earlier. When she did, there was a message from him there, too, identical to the one on the office phone. On the computer, there were no emails to be taken care of; the only other message was on a slip of paper in the middle of her desk. It startled her for a moment that someone got into her locked office. But she remembered almost immediately, that she left the office door open for Charlene in case a researcher called, or possibly Doctor Arnold who was out of pocket more than usual. Charlene locked the door before she left as she was supposed to.

The note read: "Senator Blair called and wants to come see you. Please call to set up appointment."

This was an unexpected development and one Sydney viewed with considerable trepidation. Was the good senator planning on using his powers of persuasion to stop her from pursuing information on his family? Would he threaten to close down the archives? How much did he know about what she'd discovered?

The front bell rang, putting an end to her speculations. Who in the world would be here at this time of day? She looked out of the window facing out to the street, leaning as far to the left as she could, trying to catch a glimpse of whoever it was, but they were standing too close to the entrance for her to see them. A blue Lincoln was parked at the curb.

The light was on in her office, so they knew she, or someone, was there. Shrugging, she went to the door. Pulling the key down from its place on a peg next to it, she unlocked it slowly, prepared to slam it shut if necessary.

Standing on the stoop was Senator Blair.

"Missus St. John?"

"Yes."

"I'm Grayson Blair. May I have a word?"

Caught so off guard, she started to say, "We're closed," but thought better of it, saying instead, "Of course. Come in."

Opening the door wider, she stepped aside to let him pass. Closing the door, she motioned toward the door of her office. "Please."

Unlike many Oklahoma officials, Blair's reputation for dressing very stylishly made some people think of him as too formal. It was clear that everything from his Italian shoes to his silk tie was very expensive. As he passed, she got a whiff of his cologne. Although not an expert on colognes, it seemed expensive as well, although how one could tell she wasn't sure. She only knew that it was pleasant.

He sat in the visitor's chair across from her desk without waiting to be asked. She sat in her own, pulling up close to the desk and clasping her hands on the blotter.

"What can I do for you, Senator?"

"It has come to my attention that you've been . . . uh . . . researching my family's background."

"I gather information on the families of all . . ."

"We both know that this isn't your usual research. At least the reasons aren't the usual ones." He crossed his legs and for the first time, Sydney got the impression that he wasn't comfortable being there. "As you may have heard, I will not be running for another term in office. I'm in my final term. It's important to me that this final term be successful, especially as it is my last chance to promote certain items of legislation. There are always people who will use any bits of information that could indicate a scandal against me or anyone in politics. These days . . . well . . . anything goes."

She detected only a slight Oklahoma twang as he spoke in a soft voice. There was a sense of gentleness and gentility in his manner and the way he spoke. He adjusted his overcoat and glanced out the window. This was proving difficult for him, and Sydney wasn't inclined to make it any easier. She was too curious about what was going on.

"You also may be thinking of running for governor. Or at least, that's the rumor."

He shrugged, neither denying nor confirming the rumor.

"Your efforts have given some people the idea that I . . . that is, my family is trying to hide something. We've been in Oklahoma since before it became a state, as you know. We've owned property and run businesses and held political offices. These things can make enemies. There are probably incidents and people that I'm not even aware of in our past. You know all of this, of course. You probably know more about the family than we do by this time."

She sat back in her chair, trying to relax. "What exactly do you want, Senator?"

He gave her a puzzled look, as if he thought she knew exactly what he wanted. Maybe he thought she knew more than she did. In that moment, she guessed that there might be a lot he didn't know about his family, perhaps even his own unique story.

He nodded, as though he'd reached a decision.

"It has come to my attention, obliquely to be sure, that there are some people outside of my own circle who are upset with your efforts. I have gotten the impression that they will do almost anything to curb those efforts."

"Even resorting to violence?" she said.

"You're referring to the attack on the Interstate near Ponca City?"

That surprised her, but she tried not to show it.

"That and later developments," she added.

"Such as?"

She shrugged. "A man has died, Senator."

He looked startled as if this was news to him.

"Who?"

"The young man who rescued me at the underpass on the Interstate. He was a hiker, or at least appeared to be."

"His name?"

"I don't know. He gave a false name to the state troopers at the time. I don't think they've identified him yet."

Blair rose and made for the door, then turned back to face her.

"I came to warn you that some people may want to stop you. They might do anything to keep you from searching for further information. It would seem that I am too late."

"Who, Senator? Who would harm me to keep me from finding out things? What are they afraid I might find?"

"As to the what, I don't really know. At least there seems to be more than I've been told. The who? I'll have to keep that to myself for the time being. Now, I must get back to the city."

She rose and followed him to the front door, which she'd re-locked automatically when he came in. He jiggled the doorknob and she touched his arm as she took down the key.

"Here," she said, fitting the key into the lock.

The door opened and he stepped out onto the sidewalk. Turning toward her once again, he said, "I'm sorry. I'll be in touch as soon as I get more information. Be very careful, Missus St. John."

He got into the back seat of the blue Lincoln parked at the curb and it drove away. She watched him out of sight, wondering what he was sorry for.

"That's all he said?"

Ben was stirring gravy in her cast iron skillet on the stove. The odor of roasting pork filled the kitchen. Dinner was nearly ready, and she sat at the kitchen table. While he tended the meal, she told him about Senator Blair's visit.

"Pretty much," she said in answer to his question. "I got the impression that he really didn't know why someone was trying to discourage me from continuing with the Blair family research. I mean, he figures that maybe it's someone wanting to ruin him. I also got the impression that he has his suspicions."

"Do you think someone else is trying to protect him and his reputation?"

He turned off the flame under the skillet, still stirring to prevent lumps.

"Why else would what I'm doing be so important? It seems like they know about skeletons in his closet."

"You mean the matter of his birth and all."

"More than likely."

"Would it be possible that someone is actually trying to use that information, which they already know, to ruin his reputation?"

"If that's what they want, why would my research be a threat?"

"Timing. Timing is everything."

"I don't understand how that would figure in. Either the story comes out or it doesn't."

"But who lets the story out and when might make all the difference in the world. If you do it, through police officials or whatever, the whole thing could be buried in the inside pages of *The Oklahoman*. Someone else lets the cat out of the bag, and it gets great attention."

He took the pork roast out of the oven and set it on the counter, where he carefully transferred it to a platter. He let it sit for several minutes while they continued talking. The odors of fried cabbage and the roast filled the kitchen. Sydney took a moment to thank the gods that Ben was a better cook than he'd admitted. He poured each of them a glass of merlot.

"I'm just saying that your actions might be disturbing someone's plan to harm Blair's reputation."

"Wouldn't that be a bit too coincidental? Someone is looking to harm the senator and I just happen to find something in the papers that could lead me to discover something else, which could harm his . . . You see what I mean?"

"I do. But remember. You aren't the one who made the discovery. Doctor Berger found it first."

"You mean he was looking for it?"

Ben shrugged and got up to carve the roast. Sydney thought back to Berger's research, the reasons he'd given for looking into the Blair family and their ranch. The good doctor was a legitimate scholar. Over the years, several articles resulted from his research in the archives, not to mention parts of two books. He was about to retire, but said that he would continue to research Oklahoma history and write about it. That was what he was about. And the Blair Bar Ranch fit into his stream of subjects. Most of what he wrote concerned pre-1950s state history. Except that now he was going to start on Route 66, which was later, 1950s through 1960s.

She tried to think back to when he first started talking about the Blairs and their papers in the archives. Was he steered in the direction of their history? If this whole thing with the Senator was a setup of some kind, either Doctor Berger was in on the setup, or he'd been pointed in that direction by someone who knew his interests. She was inclined to believe he came to it on his own, given his field of study and after having worked with the good professor for some time now, and valuing his scholarship. Except, how could anyone know that he would not only find the bit about Johnny Whitefeather and Lily, but that he would also take some sort of action regarding that? They couldn't.

As these thoughts and considerations came and went, Sydney and Ben ate dinner with Lewis going from one to the other, begging for what he considered his due. Sydney made it a policy not to feed him at the table, but she did put chunks of meat in his dish once the table was cleared. They disappeared in record time.

That night, she lay awake, trying to understand what Senator Blair hoped to accomplish by visiting her in the archives. The more she thought about it, the more convinced she became that he wanted her to stop, for her own safety or his, maybe both. There simply wasn't enough information. Clearly, if she kept trying to find information, she could be in danger. She knew that, not because of the senator's actions, but not least because of the murder of the young man on the Interstate.

Who was he? How did he figure into the whole situation?

Another question nagged at her: Was her savior also one of the men who kidnapped her, leaving her in the middle of nowhere? She could have died out there, reminding herself that the kidnappers had not known the possible effects of the drugs they gave her.

She was lucky to have survived, although that was due in part to the fact that they never intended to kill her. They'd wanted to scare her away from looking into the Blair family history. If she died in the process, well, too bad.

The Blairs must have known someone would research them sometime. Carl's papers sat untouched in the archives for more than a decade. Anyone close enough to the family must know that.

All families have secrets, of course, but when the family is a prominent one, they can be more damaging than others. Politicians were vulnerable almost by definition. They must live in fear on a daily basis. Or did most of them believe they'd covered their tracks too well? It was human nature to believe that while others might fail, you wouldn't.

Eventually, Sydney fell asleep. Her last thought was that she felt sorry for Senator Blair. Her whole being believed he was not the one to threaten someone like her.

CHAPTER 16

Ben kissed Sydney at the curb, picked up his bag, and headed into the terminal. He was returning to California as originally scheduled. He would have stayed longer, except one of his clients needed his attention. The IRS had called for an audit of the client's tax returns and it was Ben's responsibility to be there as the accountant who had filled out the tax returns for the past three years.

He turned and waved at the door, then disappeared inside. She stood at the back of the CR-V for a moment, finding that she was already missing him. He tried to get out of leaving, but in the end he admitted that his client needed him there. The danger emanating from the Blairs was starting to pale, with no sign of anything more deadly than a brown recluse spider in the stacks in the archives.

Still, she felt uneasy at the thought of being alone in her house, where she usually enjoyed her time alone. What was happening was exactly what she feared: she was becoming used to his presence in her life, felt safer when he was there, missed him when he was gone.

Sydney shivered and stepped away from the back of the car. Security might be watching her right now, getting ready to approach and tell her to move along.

She climbed into the warm vehicle and pulled away, heading toward I-44 and I-35. It was over an hour's drive to Gansel from the airport, giving her lots of time to think. The Blairs were pushed from her mind by thoughts of her relationship with Ben. They were spending more and more time together—he'd promised to return as soon as his client's audit was completed—which could lead to some sort of permanent relationship.

That in itself didn't bother her overmuch. It was some of the changes that went with it that worried her. Only she had responsibility for herself for a very long time. Depending on others scared her. Their priorities weren't hers, and her priorities weren't theirs. If she couldn't get something done, she could only blame herself. If he didn't get something done . . . As much as she'd loved Leo, those times he wasn't there when she needed him, and there were many, caused the most arguments between them.

She really didn't want to face all of that again. But if she and Ben did make a life together, she would have to make changes in her own way of thinking. She cared for him very much. Even Lewis was fond of him.

The preoccupation with Ben and their relationship made her lose track of the miles, and she pulled into the archives parking lot in what seemed a very short time. It was earlier than she usually arrived in the morning, but with all of the time she'd missed lately, it wouldn't hurt to get started before eight o'clock.

The quiet in the old building was broken only by the ticking of the school clock on the wall outside of the reading room. That seemed to emphasize the cold silence. When she was alone in the building like this, either early morning or late at night, she expected to see the ghosts that must live there.

The bank was originally built in the late 1890s, and even at over a hundred years old, it was in good shape. Repairs were constantly required, of course, and they were kept up throughout most of its existence. There was a word in Spanish that she thought described the relationship between her and the building: *simpatico*. They respected one another and were comfortable together. Most people would think she was crazy. What would they think if they knew she also talked to trees?

Smiling, she unlocked the door to her office. Her plan for the day was to finish reading the journals—there wasn't much left—then continue looking through boxes for papers dating from the 1920s and the following decade. It was nearly eleven o'clock when she found a note that made her heart beat faster.

It was a slip of paper folded up and slipped inside a journal dated in the 1940-1941 timeframe. Some of the explanation came from the journal pages.

Lawrence was foolish enough to try to enlist in the army this week. He thought I wouldn't find out. At his age, he is exempt from the draft, at least for now. I told him not to try it, but did he listen? They rejected him, of course. I could have told him that would happen. I always knew there was something wrong with that boy. Now he knows it, too.

Grayson would never have tried such a stunt.

When she unfolded the loose paper, she understood what Carl meant. Lawrence was turned down by the Army due to the results of his psychological testing. He was found to be unstable, and the terms schizophrenia and depression were used. The important thing was that Lawrence suffered from mental illness. Whether it was genetic, induced by mistreatment by his father, or a combination of causes was not clear from the details in the draft board's report.

There was also no indication, as yet, that Lawrence received any specific treatment for this illness. The death of his mother and the situation with his beloved sister could have pushed him over the edge. His father's bullying would not have been any help to him. She was beginning to believe that Lawrence was as much a victim as Lily was.

What she really wanted was a journal or diary written by Lawrence. That would be very revealing. Not having that, she turned instead to the newspaper articles Ben copied. She'd done some research on the elder brother, but it was time to pursue that more.

An article from 1943 reported that Lawrence was charged with beating his wife, but as was usual in those days, the charges were dropped. Given his probable standing in the community, she was surprised that he was even arrested.

Another of the great things about newspapers in the past, though, was that they often printed stories about social events. Who hosted the event, who attended, where the festivities were held, even what people wore and what they ate and drank.

As a prominent lawyer and businessman in Ponca City, the Lawrence Blairs appeared in many newspaper articles in that part of the state, stories about them and their entertaining. From these, Sydney learned that Lawrence's second wife was Mildred. Reading through several such stories, she realized that most of the other Blairs rarely attended the events. Grayson, Sr., was mentioned once in two years and Carl not at all.

A small story that must have been buried deep in the paper looked promising. Lawrence was again arrested, this time for disturbing the peace. He had tried to force his way inside his brother's house. Banging on the door, he repeatedly called out his dead sister's name, demanding to see her. The police reported that he was inebriated, which made him "forget that his sister was dead." A curious way to phrase it, since no record of her death existed anywhere in the state, as far as could be determined on the Internet or in searches through county records.

Sydney checked out the date. It was nearly two weeks before Grayson, Sr.'s first wife, Gladys, fell to her death. And on the same night as one of Lawrence's parties. The police took him home, where the party was still in full swing. Nothing else was printed for the next few months; however Sydney did not presume that nothing else happened. Everyone involved would have made every effort to keep the events hidden and forgotten as if it never happened. No trial, no charges, nothing.

The fact that Gladys died within two weeks left Sydney with an unsettled feeling. The accumulated details suggested that Grayson, Jr., may have pushed his wife/sister down the stairs. He was in love with another woman (maybe) and the marriage to his own sister became intolerable (maybe). He was a man who when younger, lived life to the fullest, but during his first marriage, his life resembled that of a hermit. Little was written about him as a businessman and nothing about them as a couple during their marriage and for a short period after Grayson, Jr., was born. That all changed when he re-married.

Sydney went back through her papers, searching for Gladys's obituary. As she did, she noticed that the clock on her computer said it was 5:46. She'd eaten leftover pork roast in her office as she worked on the computer. Time passed too quickly. She'd have to get home soon. Lewis would already be very unhappy and Ben had called earlier to let her know that he'd arrived at home. He probably would call again later. Besides, she was getting hungry.

Quickly, she glanced through the remaining articles when she found the obituary. Just what she'd been hoping would be there. It was best to take it home to read, along with the rest of the papers relating to the Blair family. She gathered everything up, evened out the sheets of paper in folders, put the journals back in the vault, then locked up. It was dark and gloomy when she stepped outside, a brisk wind penetrating her coat almost as if she wasn't wearing it. She let the CR-V warm up a bit before backing out of the parking slot and heading home.

A few drops of rain hit the windshield about halfway there, and she wished that she had checked the weather forecast sometime during the day. She'd missed the forecast on the radio by a few minutes. If there was a freezing rain, she wouldn't be going into the archive in the morning until the roads were safe. Overnight, though, she would have to set the faucets to dripping to make sure the pipes didn't freeze.

She considered putting the car in the garage for the night, but decided not to. There was no garage door opener and standing out in the rain, now falling harder, held no charms for her. The last thing she wanted was to catch another chill. It meant, of course, that she might have to scrape car windows again in the morning. One task was as onerous as the other, and she opted for immediate gratification in the warmth of her home.

Blessing the timer that turned on the living room lamp, she dumped her purse and book bag onto the sofa and took off her wool coat. She put it on a hanger and hooked it over the shower curtain rod in the bathroom. Through all of this, Lewis wound around her feet, trying his best to either trip her or guide her footsteps toward the kitchen. When she finally started opening the can of food for him, he was bouncing up and down in anticipation. His deep purr could be heard over the chiming of the mantle clock as she set his dish in its accustomed place on the floor beside the stove.

For herself, she opened a can of tomato soup, warming the contents in the microwave oven. As it heated, she lit a fire in the fireplace, then pulled the folders out of her book bag and brought them to the table. She'd finished eating when the phone rang. It was Ben calling to chat. It was strange to both of them to be so far apart again, yet also natural. She settled onto the sofa, wrapping the afghan around herself, the warmth from the fireplace letting her relax. He was tired, so they only talked for fifteen minutes before saying good night.

She roused herself and returned to the kitchen. She fixed a cup of tea. At least she no longer felt hungry, and she was warm inside and out.

After cleaning up the kitchen, she went back to the sofa with her tea, laptop, and the small piles of papers. Although she found several bits here and there, the information was terribly sparse. Lawrence didn't show up on the Internet much, and finding information in the papers was like gleaning a wheat field.

When she got up to make another cup of tea, the clock on the stove showed ten-thirty. She was tired, both from having to concentrate so hard to find something and sitting for so long. Once more, she straightened the papers and put the computer away. After tending to the fireplace, she headed to the bedroom. Propped in bed, she tried to read the latest novel selection, but kept dropping off, so she gave it up.

Lewis lay stretched out along her left side, seemingly sound asleep. However, his ears moved as if tracking every sound like radar. She stroked his long, thick fur and he purred without raising his head or opening his eyes. She turned out the bedside lamp and slid under the covers. Lying in the dark, she listened to Lewis's purring as a counterpoint to the sound of sleet against the windows and the roof. It was going to be a bad morning.

It was very dark and very late when she was awakened by Lewis's suddenly raising his head and growling. Cats growl deep in their throats, a sound both primitive and frightening, and she knew better than to touch him. He would not know it was her hand.

She lay very still, listening, trying to hear beyond his continued growling. Sleet rattled against the windows. Then she heard, very faintly, what sounded like the creaking of the boards of her front porch. They moved off the porch, she thought, but they were competing with the sounds of the storm, making it difficult to be positive about the direction.

She got up and groped her way into her robe. After taking the gun from the drawer in the bedside table, she moved into the living room. Through the venetian blinds, she was in time to see a car pulling away down the street, its headlights out, but the automatic driving lights on. Brake lights glowed as it turned left onto the last street.

Turning on the porch light, she looked through the windows but couldn't see anything other than the bare porch, the first two feet glistening with water. She would have to open the door after all. She gripped the pistol as she unlocked the door.

The porch roof kept the sleet from hitting most of the porch and the storm door, but cold air rushed in as if the house took a deep breath. The porch was clear except for a package leaning against the wall on the floor next to the door. She opened the storm door slightly, looked around quickly, and reached down to pick it up.

Leaving the porch light on, she closed and locked the doors, then took the package into the kitchen, laying it on the table while she turned on a light. Shivering, she filled the kettle for tea. She was awake now, her curiosity roused, and it would be a while before she could sleep again.

Lewis wandered in, stretched and yawned. He sat down on his haunches with his tail curled around himself, waiting for an explanation. She leaned down and scratched his head, then sat at the table, intent on finding the explanation herself.

The package was a large brown envelope bursting with paper. On the outside, her name was printed in block letters with a black Sharpie pen. It was closed with the metal tab, and she pulled the flap loose. She gripped the edge of the envelope and tugged the papers free with her other hand. She ruffled through them. Copies of newspaper articles, official forms, letters, some with clear printing on them, others dim and difficult to read.

The kettle began whistling and Lewis ran out of the kitchen. He hated that sound, probably because it hurt his sensitive ears.

She put a spoonful of loose tea into the ceramic pot and poured out a mug after it brewed for several minutes. Standing at the counter, she considered who might want her to have more information. Was there much information in the envelope that was new to her? It certainly was a large pile of papers.

She stirred honey into the steaming brew and sat down. A second look in the envelope produced a bright purple sticky note stuck to the inside. She pulled it out. No note of explanation of what the papers were or what she was expected to do with them.

"LAWRENCE" was all that was written on it.

She set that aside and began looking through the stack, page by page. At first, she intended to scan each page briefly to see what the whole thing was about. Instead, she found herself becoming more and more engrossed in the details, sometimes using the magnifying glass from her desk to read the dim print.

Halfway through the stack, she sat back and rubbed her eyes. She'd drunk two cups of tea, and filling her cup and going to the bathroom were the only movements for the past—she looked at the clock on the stove—two hours.

Someone, for their own reasons, came out in the cold, wet weather to leave copies of forms she should not be seeing. Psychological appraisals, admittance forms, medical records that most often are purged before a person's papers would be donated to an archive. These weren't even records of Carl Blair, the creator of the Blair collection, but of his son, who was still alive.

Normally, she avoided papers of this sort at all costs. This time, however, the circumstances were different. A crime was discovered and she'd been asked to do the research into it. Her interest in everyone involved was legitimate, both then and now. Her motives were clear: She'd been nearly killed because of what was in the Blair papers and the further information she'd gleaned in Ponca City and Newkirk. What about the motives of whoever left the envelope on her porch in the middle of the night in an ice storm?

Now the biggest problem was to tell Sheriff Otis what she read and what she did. Reading them might be a criminal offense. If so, that would reflect badly on the archives if it became known.

Most of all, she wanted to warn Grayson, Jr., about his uncle. Everything in these new papers showed how much Lawrence hated both his brother and his nephew for what they did to Lily. A rational person wouldn't blame the senator since he had no say in his own birth or who his parents were.

The inescapable question, however, was, why did he wait so long to cause trouble?

Other questions needed answering. Most importantly, was everything that happened over the past few weeks due to Lawrence's scheming? The papers lying in front of her indicated that someone else was trying to maneuver her in his direction. But now, someone else was seemingly trying to discredit Lawrence, himself.

At one moment it appeared that someone wanted to prevent

the story of Grayson, Jr.'s, parentage being revealed; the next, it appeared that someone was hoping to make sure all of the details were revealed, but not by her.

The possibility that she might be housebound in the morning was frustrating. She needed to call the senator's office and try to get an appointment to see him. She also needed to call Sheriff Otis first thing to let him know everything discovered so far.

She glanced at the clock. It was three-thirty. She should try to get some sleep before anything else.

Tired as she was, she tossed and turned for nearly an hour. So many questions that she couldn't answer, not just why Lawrence waited until now to wreak some sort of revenge. One question without an answer was, why didn't Lawrence's psychiatrist do something himself to fend off any future violence? Could a doctor, sworn to protect his client's privacy, have done anything without that client's consent? Without that consent, whom could he tell? The doctor, if he was still alive, probably felt justified in having done nothing, since Lawrence never fulfilled the promise of vengeance he made, both to the doctor and to himself.

Even Lawrence's first wife sensed his state of mind. She left him once after a beating, stating her fear as the cause. Was she also aware of his obsession with his sister? Gladys's death hit him very hard and his behavior became frighteningly erratic. At the graveside, he wept so hard that he fell to his knees. He'd been carried to the waiting limousine and it appeared that he was taken directly to the hospital where he was committed by his family. After a month, he simply walked out.

The scene at Grayson, Jr.'s house was described more fully in the doctor's notes. In her mind's eye, Sydney saw Lawrence standing outside like Marlon Brando in *A Streetcar Named Desire*, yelling, "Stella!" She fell asleep finally, with that name, that voice in her thoughts and in her dreams.

The morning was grey, every surface covered with a glistening layer of ice, including the sidewalks, trees, everything that was exposed to the elements. Black ice covered most streets and highways. Freezing rain still fell. On the radio and television, every police spokesperson and city official called for everyone in central Oklahoma to stay home. Filmore County offices were all closed, which included the archives, so no need to call Doctor Arnold and let him know she was staying home. Driving, even walking outside was too dangerous.

Sydney called Sheriff Otis, but he was out on calls. Even people in a small town like Gansel believed they could go out in this weather without consequences. Sharon, the deputy who manned the radio in the office, told her there were several accidents in town, with one fatality. All other deputies, all state police officers, were out helping, saving, directing people.

She left a message for Otis to call her, but accepted that it might be a day or two before he could call back.

Next, she called Senator Blair's office to try and make an appointment with him, but not surprisingly, no one answered. Their offices were officially closed in this weather. She left a message on his voice mail, wondering afterward if he would actually check it today or even tomorrow. Was the state legislature in session this time of year? She tried but couldn't find his home phone, so she left it for the moment.

The lights flickered for the first time as she was clearing the breakfast dishes. Rain and sleet throughout the morning promised more ice, adding weight to the power lines. The outside temperature hovered around twenty degrees. The house might not be cozy if the power went out and stayed out, but with the fireplace and plenty of wood, and the gas cook stove, she wouldn't be cold. It would be necessary to keep one or two of the faucets dripping, though, to make sure the pipes didn't freeze. She'd done that last night and the plumbing fared well.

Pouring her second cup of coffee, Sydney pondered on how to spend the day. Several ongoing projects would keep her busy, like organizing her personal photographs. Most were stored loose in boxes, unlike those in the archives. She could re-organize her books on the shelves, something she did periodically. There was always research on the Internet for one collection or another, as long as the power stayed up. G3 on her computer and cell phone would help keep her connected, although the signal was often erratic. There was no way to re-charge her electronics if the power went out, though.

With all the possibilities of keeping busy, it was the package still lying on the table that beckoned. She had read only half of the papers. She couldn't ignore the lure of learning more about the Blair family.

She dressed in her warmest sweater and jeans, slipper socks with non-slide soles, and tackled the papers. With a yellow legal pad in front of her, and a full pot of coffee in the machine, she first organized everything by date. They were given to her in no specific order, making her wonder how they were gathered together in the first place. That and all other questions disappeared as she became more engrossed in the contents.

The dates ranged from 1939 to 1943, nearly four years. As copies, they would be useless in a court of law. A biographer would have to verify much of the information with originals. In the end, even she would have to be careful about relying too much on the information before her. But this, plus what was in the archives, would create a clearer picture of events.

At nine o'clock, the house phone rang. Caller ID said it was Ben.

"How are things at your house?" he asked. "I saw on the news that the weather has gotten bad."

"Lots of ice. It's still raining and sleeting." She opened the front door and looked out. There was so much ice everywhere that if the sun came out, the glare would probably blind everyone. "I'm not going anywhere today."

"Good. Hope you're staying warm."

"So far." She might have gone on to say that the power was still on, but the one superstition she believed in was to not say a word when things were going well. "I won't ask how the weather is there."

He laughed. "Better not. Otherwise, you might be on the next plane out here."

She found herself wishing that she could.

"My client and I meet with the IRS agent later this morning. I don't think there will be a problem, but the IRS didn't give us enough time to review all of his earlier returns. It could get interesting."

"Not too interesting, I hope."

A silence fell between them, which was unusual. Most of the time their chatter flowed effortlessly, but the existence of the information lying on the kitchen table overshadowed the small talk. She wanted to talk to him about it, but with his own concerns at the moment, she hesitated.

"Ben, something has developed," she said, deciding it was important that he know. "Last night, as a matter of fact. I know you've got a lot on your mind, but would you . . . are you able to listen objectively to . . ."

"Nothing dangerous, I hope."

"No. At least in itself, it's not dangerous. It's a bunch of records on Lawrence Blair."

"He's the . . ."

"He's Senator Blair's uncle. The older son of Carl."

"Where did the papers come from?"

"Someone just put them on my front porch."

"Have you called Sheriff Otis about them?"

"Yes, but he's out of the office. The weather, accidents."

"Of course. Any idea who left them for you?"

"No. There's no note or return address. Nothing."

"Tell me about what's in them."

She began describing the contents, telling him first what the time frame was. When she'd finished, there was silence. The first thing he said was, "Should you have those psychiatric records?"

"No, not as an archivist. Maybe not under any circumstances."

"But you think it's okay because of Johnny Whitefeather and Lily and all of the things you know?"

"I wouldn't have read them otherwise. But I think it's all that I was looking for. Something to give me an idea of who . . ."

"Which crime are you looking into? The one in the thirties? Or the attacks on you?"

"All? Both? I asked myself the same question. Right now it all seems so intermingled."

"I know, but you don't want to be accused of invasion of privacy. What about your job? Your reputation as an archivist?"

"I know," she said. "That's why I wanted to talk with you about this. I should turn it all over to Otis when I can finally see him. I tried to get in touch with Senator Blair, too. He needs to know that he may be in danger."

"Let the sheriff tell him. Give all of those papers to him as soon as you can. Too much knowledge can be a dangerous thing. Especially when someone with power is involved. Blair won't appreciate your knowing so much about his family."

That was true. All of what he said. Yet at the same time, she knew that she would read the rest of the papers. She'd already gone too far. Now, she wanted very much to know it all.

Even so, she promised Ben that she would give them up at the first opportunity. That time wouldn't come for another day or two, given the weather.

CHAPTER 17

The opportunity to give up the papers came sooner than she expected, announced by a knock on the door. Sydney looked at the clock on the stove from where she sat at the table. One o'clock. Outside, rain and sleet still fell, although not as hard. The afternoon was already dark enough that she'd turned on the overhead light in the kitchen.

As she rose from the table, the knock came again, then the doorbell rang. "All right. I'm coming," she called out.

Her knees were slightly stiff from sitting so long, and she took short steps at first. By the time she crossed the middle of the living room, the doorbell rang a third time.

She went to the window to look out onto the porch. A man of average size stood there, rocking back on the heels of winter boots. His overcoat looked expensive and warm, but his head was bare. She didn't know him and was more than a little nervous about opening the door. He looked up and saw her in the window. He smiled and wrapped his arms around himself, indicating that it was cold.

She held up one finger, letting him know that it would be a moment. Hurrying back into the kitchen, she swept up the papers, including the envelope, and put them in the oven.

There was nothing to use as a weapon that wasn't pretty obvious. The gun wouldn't fit in one of her small sweater pockets. Plenty of knives lay in the drawers, but answering the door with one in hand wouldn't work. The best thing was a tall walking stick, which she kept beside the door.

Going toward the door once again, she looked toward the walking stick to be sure it was still there. The deadbolt was ice cold as she unlocked it; the doorknob was too. Frigid, damp air blew in and she shivered. She braced her foot against the bottom of the door to hold it open only slightly.

"Hello," the man said, coming close to the opening. "I'm from Senator Blair's office."

"Do you have a card or something?"

"Yes. But may I come in? It's very cold out here."

She considered his request. Even if she shut and re-bolted the door, it wouldn't take much to break it down. Plus, she was beginning to shiver.

"Certainly," she said, backing up and opening the door wider.

He stepped inside. His black all-weather coat glistened with moisture, rivulets running down to the hem and dropping on her rug. He shook himself, water drops flying over the room and her, and she scowled. That was pretty thoughtless and made her inclined to tell him to leave.

He reached into a jacket pocket and pulled out a business card.

Jason Pickett
Legislative Aide
Senator Grayson Blair, Jr.
Oklahoma State Senate

A phone number she recognized was printed in the lower right corner under the mailing and email addresses.

"What can I do for you, Mr. Pickett?" She closed the door and put her back against it. If necessary, she could grab the walking stick from there.

"The Senator got your message about some papers and he asked me to come up and pick them up. It's a bit too dangerous out there for him today." He nodded toward the door.

"I'm sorry you came all this way, but Sheriff Otis picked them up a little while ago."

She wondered if the senator really did send him or if he heard the message and came on his own. If the senator didn't know about the call, it was possible Pickett sensed a threat to his boss's reputation or career. He might be devoted to Grayson, but she cynically guessed it was his own ambition that pushed him. She could only hope that Pickett would believe she had done as she said.

A sudden roll of thunder rattled the windows. Startled, she looked toward the window. She was further surprised to see what appeared to be a man's form pass by it. Or was it a shadow from the wind blowing debris around?

"Missus St. John, it doesn't seem likely that the sheriff would have come out in this weather to pick up some papers."

"Why not?" she asked, her ire rising. "You did."

"True. True. He took everything?"

"Of course."

"Do you mind if I look around? Just in case."

"I most certainly do." She turned and grabbed the walking stick, holding it in one hand. "And now I'd appreciate it if you would leave."

He held up a hand, surprised then amused. He was more than twenty years younger, and her martial arts training was more than a year ago.

"There's no need to be afraid," he said as if talking to a child. "I have no intention of hurting you."

"And I have no intention of letting you have free rein in my home. I'll ask you again to leave."

He still held up his hand, palm facing her, and took a step forward. "I'm afraid you have no choice."

Sydney turned the walking stick to hold it in both hands and pointed the small end at him as she'd seen it done in class and in movies. She hoped she did it with enough ease to make him think he might be ill-advised to come any closer.

"Does Senator Blair know that you've come to threaten me?"

"He sent me to get the papers. He believes they are his to begin with and that they contain important information."

"I can give you Sheriff Otis's number, although he is still out on calls and may not answer. They're very busy what with this storm and all."

She kept talking as steadily as she could, trying to sound confident, and hoping to block him if he should rush her. Hoping more that she could convince him to leave. She kept her heel wedged against the bottom of the door, to keep the other man outside.

"Yeah, I'll do that," Mr. Pickett said.

He took a step toward the door and lunged for her. He got a

whack on the shin for his efforts, which stopped him. He shouted in pain, bending over and grabbing his left shin. In defending herself, she stepped away from the front door. It burst open, hitting her in the back and knocking her forward. The living room was instantly ice cold. Strong arms grabbed her from behind, pinning her arms to her sides. The cold of the body behind her chilled her to the bone. She still held the walking stick, but was unable to swing it in any direction.

Sydney let out a huge sigh, relaxed, and slid down, out of the intruder's grasp, dropping the stick. She scrambled on all fours, trying to get away. The two men grabbed at her. She kicked, scratched, and screamed, all the while one of the men shouted, "Be still!"

She fought until the phone rang. It was all just too silly all of a sudden. She collapsed in laughter and the two men let go of her. They probably thought she'd lost her senses.

The phone rang until the voicemail picked up the call. "Help me up," Sydney said and raised her hand to one of the men. He obliged, totally nonplussed.

"All right, you two Neanderthals. What the hell do you want?"

"All of your research on Senator Blair," Mr. Pickett said.

She shook her head. "I've researched Carl Blair and his family, not just the Senator. Most of my notes were stolen from me a few days ago." It wasn't the exact truth, but it seemed a simpler way of dealing with his demand. "Anyone can find out what little I still have. There are dozens of boxes in the archives. Records in the county offices. Articles in the newspaper files at the History Center. Hundreds of pieces online. It's all out there for anyone to find."

"That may be true," Mr. Pickett said, "but you've summarized, connected . . ."

"The Senator himself might not want to know what I've learned," she said, interrupting him. "I went too far in my research. Or at least I might have. Sheriff Otis has that information. So, it's not going anywhere. I have no intention of giving out or using what I've found out in any way. This . . . " she waved her hand to include both of them . . . "is more likely to cause the senator trouble. Even in Oklahoma, invading a widow's home and threatening her is not good for anyone's career."

A car pulled up in front of her house, colored lights blinking, lighting the whole neighborhood. She shivered and watched the doorway, standing agape and letting in the frigid air. Sheriff Otis's large bulk appeared on the porch, first in silhouette, then lighted by the glow from inside.

"What the hell's going on here?" he asked as he glanced at the open door. His hand was on the butt of his gun that was no longer strapped into the holster. "Sydney?"

"First, let me close the door," she said. She started toward the open door, but her knees buckled, and she nearly went down. Otis stepped forward and steadied her.

"Have they hurt you?"

"No. At least not much. Close the door, will you?"

He eased her down on the sofa then did as she asked. Hopefully, the house would get warmer soon. The fan on the furnace was doing its utmost.

Otis motioned for the two men to sit down, which they did, one on the easy chair and the other on an antique bench to one side. Sydney got a good look at the second man for the first time. She didn't know him at all. Both men looked out of their element. Pickett looked angry, even belligerent, in spite of his obeying Otis's orders. The other kept his gaze down, looking a bit like a frightened boy.

"All right," Otis said.

She told him what happened, and the two men stayed silent. Mr. Pickett watched her the whole time, and the large, unnamed man never looked up. She had the impression that he was a gentle man under ordinary circumstances. The room was finally starting to warm up.

Sheriff Otis shook his head. "I told you not to get too involved."

"Yes, and you also asked me to find out what I could about the Blairs."

"True." He filled the easy chair, his big hands wrapped around a cup of coffee.

Deputies, who arrived very quickly, took Pickett and his colleague away, charged with breaking and entering for starters. She made a fresh pot of coffee while they and the sheriff handcuffed the men and led them to the waiting police van.

As they drank, she told him what the two men did and said. Then she told him everything that happened before her visitors arrived. Fetching the papers out of the oven, she set them on the table. They were stacked every which way, and he left them like that as he began to scan through them.

"Someone just left these on your porch?"

"Yes. Last night."

"You've no idea who?"

"Otis, I have no idea about anything any more. I have the feeling that there are two sides working at cross purposes. Or actually focused on one thing—me and my research—one trying to stop me, the other feeding me information, both for their own reasons. No one meant me any real harm, even those two who broke in here tonight."

"Still there was always the possibility."

"True."

She sat silently, rubbing her upper arm where the second man had held her. Memories flashed through her mind of waking in the dark in the woods, wondering where she was, cold and frightened. She shivered violently and shook her head and took a sip of the warm coffee.

"What happens now?" she asked.

"The state police will talk with Senator Blair and Lawrence and others in the family. I have to wonder if the Senator sent Pickett out here to try and get those papers. Do you believe he knew what was in them?"

"I wouldn't think so. The only way they knew I had them was from the message I left for the senator. Unless he knows who left them, of course. We know now that it wasn't him."

Otis set the mug on the end table and got up.

"I'd better be on my way. I need to get those two booked and you're probably exhausted. You'll need to come in and sign your statement as soon as the weather allows." Standing in the middle of her living room, he looked around. "You might think about finding yourself a more secure place. This one seems awfully easy to break into."

She laughed. "Tell me about it. I'll probably have to build one if I'm staying in Gansel."

He looked down at her.

"You thinkin' of movin'?"

Sudden realization hit her. She was thinking of the possibility. But she said, "I don't know. After everything that's happened . . ."

Otis nodded and left the house. Alone finally, and standing in the middle of the kitchen, Sydney pondered what to do next. The newest bundle of papers was gone, the house was warming up, and the weather outside was still dismal. The sun was down, but looking to the west, the sky along the horizon was lightening. The rest of the sky was dark grey. Looked as if the falling weather was moving east.

Lewis appeared, meowing his displeasure at not only having his home invaded, but also at being ignored through it all. She picked him up, and nuzzling his neck, she sat down on the sofa with him. He was content for a while, purring his pleasure at the attention, but eventually jumped down and sat looking at her with displeasure. It was past time for his food and he was not amused.

CHAPTER 18

The archives were chilly when she opened up the next morning. Salt and sand worked on melting the ice and snow on the streets and sidewalks, and she had waited for that to take effect.

The first thing she did was try to call Ben. The phones at home went out during the night, which was distressing, but the power stayed on. Even her cell phone gave a busy signal each time she'd tried that. The office phone gave her a dial tone, though, but the call didn't go through.

It was disturbing. There were so many ways in which to keep in touch, but a storm could bring it all down. The landlines were out all over town due to a major junction having been hit by lightning, of all things. Cell phones were blocked in the area, probably due to increased traffic. Even her Internet was down at home, so no email.

Once in the archive, she found the furnace running continuously, although her office was quite chilly. The coolness attested to some sort of problem. When she went to the closet where the furnace was hidden away, she found a note on the door from Clarence, the county maintenance man who took care of county buildings. Apparently, power went out in the downtown area during the night, and he had checked the furnace and breaker box, both when the power went down and when it came back on.

The day started dark and grey, but by eight o'clock, the sky cleared and the sun shone. Rather than warming the world below, bright light reflected off of ice and people's exhalations in the cold air. The few people who were out looked as if they were moving in a personal bubble of steam. The wind was calm, at least, which was a blessing, although wind would help to dry out the landscape and chase away those clouds of steam.

When she found the phones working, she dialed Leonard Leeds' phone number, this time with success. He was the handyman she called on when she needed something fixed around the house. Surprisingly, he was home.

"I can't come until tomorrow at the earliest," he said. It seemed that others got to him first, although she couldn't figure out how if the phone lines had just come back up.

"As soon as you can, Leonard. I know there's a lot of work around town, but not having a front door working is a pain in the you-know-what. Right now it's kept closed with a bit of wire and a heavy chair against it."

"Yeah, I'm sure it's a problem. I'll call first."

"Thanks. I appreciate it."

Next, she called Ben's number again, and this time it rang. She dreaded telling him about yesterday's misadventure, knowing he would tell her, "I told you so." But the voicemail picked up and she left a message for him to call her. "Use the office number. The cell phones in the area are still down."

The computer booted up and she sat looking at it, wondering if she even wanted to check email, Facebook, Twitter, or any of the other outlets to the rest of the world that were so useful in keeping up with events in her professional world. When she checked, though, she found an email from Ben.

> *I've dropped my cell phone and can't get it replaced until tomorrow afternoon. Heard about the ice storm—sounds bad. Guess it's the reason I couldn't get through to you last night. Let me know if everything is okay. Please.* ☺

She quickly typed a reply, saying her cell phone was down, so she couldn't get through before. She was fine, she said, and would tell him all about the storm when they finally could talk. She mentioned the voicemail, although he wouldn't be able to get to it.

It felt good knowing that someone out in the world cared about her well-being after so many years of relying on no one. She reminded herself that there were others as her phone rang.

"Sydney, there you are," Julia's voice said. "I was sure you would be fine, but I couldn't get hold of you."

"Thanks. Yes, I'm fine. How are you?"

"I'm okay, but I couldn't go anywhere. Still can't. Believe it or not, my garage door is frozen shut. At least four inches of ice."

"Makes me glad my car was outside."

She hadn't felt that way earlier as she chipped away the ice on the windows and door handles of the car. It took half an hour, leaving her hands and nose like blocks of ice. She left the motor running until the defroster melted the ice on the windshield enough to make it easy to break up. Light from the porch and the streetlight at the end of the street helped her find her way. But, fortunately, the streets were clearer by the time she finished with the car.

Except for her own street, most were sanded and provided a modicum of traction. Still, she'd slid through one intersection unable to stop. Thank goodness there were no cars crossing in the other direction. Go slow, keep it in second gear, and be careful with the brakes, she'd told herself.

Driving the few blocks to the archives, she'd passed downed trees and large limbs both in the road and on the ground. The visible damage was extensive, but there would be other repairs and cleanups, including frozen pipes and damaged roofs.

She commiserated with Julia and guessed that Paul hadn't gotten home because of the road conditions.

"No, he's in California right now."

"Wish I was."

"I'll bet you do."

They discussed conditions, outages, and how they planned on spending the rest of the day, perhaps the week, cleaning up and making sure houses, and in Sydney's case the archives, in Julia's case, the flower shop, were in good shape. An ice storm like this one could cause serious damage. Downed trees and fallen limbs, as well as downed power lines, were just the start.

They hung up after another ten minutes of catching up, planning to have lunch one day during the week if the weather didn't get bad again. Sydney made a deliberate decision not to tell her friend about the events of the night before. No need to worry her further, and it would all come later. Their friendship was a close one, but there were long periods of time when they didn't see one another. When they did get together, it was as if the time between was a matter of days rather than weeks. And then, Sydney would realize how much she missed their conversations and laughter.

She straightened in the chair and looked around the office. For now, though, a workday lay ahead of her.

First thing, she wanted to review where the current projects stood. She kept a chart, but with everything going on with the Blair collection and the weather and her own misadventures, status of everything was a little unclear.

She was soon deeply engrossed in the chart and planning details for the next few days. Getting everything organized was necessary. Except for those times when Doctor Arnold interfered, she exercised complete control over the day-to-day planning. As much as anyone does when working with researchers. Most of the people who came to the archives, though, were regulars, people who knew the routines, the collections, and what they were looking for as much as anyone could. Doctor Berger was the most regular and she wondered when he might drop back in. She still wanted to ask him what prompted him to research the Blairs and how far he'd gotten.

She jumped when the doorbell rang. No one had scheduled an appointment for the week, and with the weather, a drop-in researcher wasn't likely. She stood and looked out the window over her computer that faced out onto the street. A large grey sedan sat there, not quite a limousine, and familiar to her, even if only vaguely.

The silhouette of a man darkened the frosted glass of the door. She took the key off the hook, and opening the door, found Senator Blair waiting to be let in. She stood aside, muttering a greeting while she looked to the car to see if there was a driver. The windows were dark and there was no way to tell.

"I'm surprised to see anyone out this morning, Senator. Do come into the office. Have a seat. May I get you a cup of coffee?"

As he passed she felt an aura of cold. They took seats in the office, and even the room grew cooler. He was wrapped in a black wool or perhaps cashmere overcoat, leather gloves, no hat. His expression was passive, except for his eyes. They were narrowed to slits. The senator was angry.

He refused the coffee with a wave of his hand. They sat across from each other as before, he straight and still, she with back straight and hands clasped on top of the desk. His hands gripped the arms of the visitor's chair, belying the casual words he spoke first.

"I understand that some of my staff visited you last night in your home." His voice was higher than she remembered, another indication of the stress he was under.

She nodded.

"I'm here to apologize for their behavior. They overstepped their authority."

"Did you send them to see me?"

"Yes. I was informed that certain papers were sent or given to you and I needed to know what they were. I only wanted to see them. Pickett was to ask to see them or determine they were in your possession, then negotiate with you on my behalf."

"The other man?"

"A friend of his. Apparently, Pickett associates with people I know nothing about. I told him to offer payment if necessary, not make threats. I guess my instructions were not specific enough."

"I left a message on your office phone," she said. "I gather you heard it."

"No."

During their first meeting, his speech was fairly typical of an Oklahoma native, with that pleasant mixture of southern and western twang that she rarely noticed anymore. Now, however, his speech was very formal and precise, leaving no doubt that he was there on business.

"I see," she responded.

He sat silently waiting for her to say more. Perhaps he expected accusations, curses, something to show her anger. Instead, she was silent, waiting for him to continue.

"Do you still have the papers?" he asked when he realized that she was not going to say more.

"No, I don't. I gave them to Sheriff Otis, as I told Mr. Pickett."

"That's a shame. I really would have preferred that no one else saw them."

"Do you know what's in them?"

"Just a vague idea. This whole thing has been so nebulous. Vague accusations. Veiled threats. Suggestions of impropriety."

If her understanding of what occurred all those years ago was correct, impropriety hardly described what Carl Blair did to his children, particularly Grayson, Sr., and Lily. Lawrence was almost ignored in comparison, yet his mental instability made his abuse all the more telling.

"Senator Blair, do you have any idea who might be trying to ruin your reputation? Or why they would act now, knowing you would be retiring?"

"No idea really. I do have my suspicions, of course. Those who would like to see me fail . . ." He shrugged. "Well, they surely would have acted before now."

"Was there anything different about this last session of the legislature? Were you planning anything unique or controversial in your final term?"

In her research, she figured out that he was a moderate Republican with political enemies in both parties. He worked for ecological issues within the state, spoke out against pipelines crisscrossing from border to border. He also abstained on many social issues rather than fully supporting his party.

The senator shrugged. "More of the usual, really. I haven't planned to introduce many bills in the next term. There's one to protect the Crossed Timbers region, which is in danger from builders."

Sydney's heart skipped a beat at the mention of Crossed Timbers.

"I also planned to introduce a bill to fund a memorial honoring my grandfather, Carl Blair. But you know who he is."

"Did your family know that you planned to do that?"

"Yes, I told them when we were all together at Christmas. It wasn't universally popular."

She would have bet on that.

"What did Lawrence, your uncle, say about it?"

"He was furious. He became so angry that it affected his health and he was hospitalized. I believe he was in the hospital a month or more."

That would help explain the timing of events. If Lawrence was behind what had happened, the announcement and his being hospitalized might have set everything in motion. However, Lawrence's health would also make it difficult for him to have been directly responsible for any of the assaults on her and the archives. He was over ninety years old, after all.

"He has children and grandchildren, doesn't he?" She knew, of course, that he did, but she wanted the Senator's reaction.

"Yes, he has a son, Carl, named after our grandfather. And a daughter, Lily. She's the younger, named after my aunt."

"Is your uncle able to get around on his own? He's in his nineties now."

"What is this interest in my uncle? He's old and feeble. He can't drive on his own. He couldn't possibly have anything to do with anything that's happened."

"Maybe not directly. But we both know that people can be hired to do almost anything."

"Uncle Lawrence and I may never have been on the best terms, but he would hardly sabotage my career."

A dozen more questions needed to be asked, but the doorbell rang. She excused herself. Her mind was so busy considering what the Senator told her so far that her attention was not on what she was doing. She wasn't even curious about who else might have come out on such a dreary and dangerous day to gain access to the archives.

"May I help you?" Sydney asked the older woman standing just outside. She was wrapped in a fur coat, whether real fur or fake was difficult to tell. She wore a matching fur hat and leather gloves. Her hair was platinum blond, her boots leather, and her makeup looked as if she'd stepped out of a 1930s movie. Everything was very expensive and too big for her small frame, as if she'd recently shrunk. Once very fashionable, the clothes and the bright red lipstick now accented the wrinkles in the face and how out of touch with current fashion she probably was.

"I'm Lily Blair Thompson." The voice was low-pitched and scratchy, as if she'd smoked for many years. "I believe my cousin, Grayson Blair, is here. Senator Grayson Blair."

"Yes, ma'am, he is. Please come in."

Sydney shivered, both from the cold air that came in with the woman and from finally meeting one of the Lilys in the family. It was beginning to seem that she would never be warm again.

She went into the reading room and pulled over the straight-backed chair she used at the work table. Grayson stood when the two women entered the office. He probably heard the newcomer introduce herself. Was that why he looked paler? They all sat down. The Senator looked uneasy. Lily held herself stiffly, red painted lips pressed tightly together. Sydney clasped her hands together on top of the desk again to keep them from shaking.

"How can I help you, Miz Thompson?"

"I came to see my cousin and find out from both of you what's going on regarding our grandfather's papers."

"We're currently re-processing his papers to get them in better order and to weed out duplicates and such," Sydney answered, using the archival "we."

"Gray?"

The Senator shrugged. "I'm just here to try to find out who may be wanting to sabotage me and my career."

"Sabotage? What a word to use."

"It's the best one to describe what's been happening."

He shrunk into himself, becoming smaller while she appeared to have grown in stature, as if she was sucking the life out of him. Had these two grown up together? Or were they more strangers than friends? At the moment, he did not look like a man for whom many people would vote.

"Now why would anyone want to sabotage you of all people? You're retiring at the end of the current term." There was no threat or condemnation. Just a statement of fact. After a pause, Lily continued. "Of course, before you decided to air the family's dirty linen . . ."

"What dirty linen? A powerful family has its secrets, true. But there's no dirty linen in the Blair family."

"Are you totally blind?"

He looked from Lily to Sydney. "What is she talking about?"

Instead of answering him, Sydney turned her attention to Lily. "You know about your namesake, I take it."

The older woman nodded, smiling, as if she were a child enjoying putting one over on the adults. "Most of it, I believe," she said, sounding smug.

"And you believe that the Senator knows everything?"

"Of course. Who better to have been in on the secrets of his own birth?" She shook her head. "We are a naughty family."

"What are you two going on about?" Grayson blurted out.

"There are no secrets regarding my birth."

Lily ignored him, continuing to talk to Sydney. "I hired a genealogist a few years ago to fill in many of the blanks, but even she couldn't confirm everything. Some of the story came from my father, of course. He's too bitter not to let things slip out, although he never told us everything."

"Us?" Sydney asked.

"His children. Me and my brother, Carl. He's dead, you know. Died in 2003 from a stroke."

Sydney held her expression, trying not to register surprise.

Lily's eyes lost their focus and she seemed to lose touch with the present. Sydney stayed silent, waiting for what might happen. Very soon, Lily shook her head and looked from Sydney to Grayson.

"What was I saying?"

"Your brother, Carl, is dead. But your father is still alive." Sydney prompted the older woman. She was eager to find out what Lily knew about the family's secrets.

"I think my father hired some people. After Gray announced that he would introduce that bill to put up a memorial to our grandfather. He really should have been put in a home. Maybe that would have kept him out of mischief. But he insisted on remaining in his own home. My husband and I live there, too, you see."

Sydney glanced at the Senator, who seemed frustrated at being unable to take control of the situation. How in the world did this man manage to be elected to the state senate?

"It's the memorial that started it all. You've no idea what you set in motion, did you, Gray?"

He shook his head. "Is that what this is all about?"

"Of course. Father couldn't have you heaping praise on the man who'd ruined your mother's life. Although, I suppose Grandfather would have said she ruined her own life. I was named after her as a sort of revenge. Grandfather refused to call me by that name, and since I've no middle name, he called me Kip, after one of his hunting dogs."

"I remember," Grayson said. "As a child, you thought that was funny."

"Yes. It was an insult to my father, but I never let it be an insult to me. Grandfather hated that I didn't let it bother me."

"Do you know what happened to your Aunt Lily?" Sydney asked the senator.

"No, not really. Everyone said she ran off when she got pregnant. We never knew who the father was or if what we were told was even true. The genealogist was very upset, considering that a challenge to her skills. But she never found out about her, either."

"And your mother, Senator?"

"She died right after I was born."

"Do you know where she came from?"

"Chicago, I think. Somewhere in the Midwest."

"Why?" Lily asked of Sydney.

"Oh, I couldn't find anything on her either."

"That came to Father's attention. That you were checking on family records. He has spies everywhere, you know."

"I imagine he does."

Lily nodded. She opened her purse and took out a pack of cigarettes.

"I'm afraid there's no smoking in the archives," Sydney said, automatically.

"Ah." She put the cigarette back in the pack and set her purse on the floor. Settling back in the chair, she pulled the fur coat more tightly around her.

Silence fell again. The moment was awkward, as if no one knew why they were there. The Senator sat, legs and arms crossed, looking as if trying to protect himself. He looked at neither of the women, staring instead down at the floor. Lily looked from one to the other, her posture more dynamic in spite of her diminutive size.

Sydney wasn't sure how to get them talking again about what they knew of the family's past history. Clearly, they both came to the archives with some goal in mind. How to get them to make clear what that purpose was? Lily indicated that she knew more about the Senator's birth and his mother, then seemed to forget that she knew. Finally, Sydney asked straight out.

"Senator, Miz Thompson." They both looked at her. "Exactly why are you here? What did you want to see me about?"

The Senator's expression changed to one of concern, while Lily looked as if she'd experienced an ah-ha moment.

"I wanted to warn you," Lily said. "My father . . . I told you I thought he hired some people." Sydney nodded. "Well, he wants them to stop you from releasing any information about Grayson's parentage. It's too late to ruin his career in the Senate, with this being his last term. Father wants to ruin the moment for him. His retirement."

"The moment?"

"The moment when he thinks he has the memorial all set. Perhaps even when the plans are made, the contract let, the design approved. He's afraid that you will let the information out beforehand, and that will ruin his plans."

"I wasn't planning on telling anyone anything," Sydney said. "I don't even have all of the facts. As you said, there is no way to trace of what happened to your Aunt Lily."

"Father isn't certain what you've found. He does know that you've discovered a lot and you could have found out everything."

Sydney nodded and turned her gaze on the Senator. "Senator Blair, what do you know about your Aunt Lily and your parentage? Did your grandfather tell you anything at all? Or your father?"

"Only that my mother died soon after I was born, like I said. As for my Aunt Lily, well, she ran away. She'd shamed herself, although it was never spelled out. We always guessed that she'd gotten pregnant like Lily said, which would have been not just shameful, but also a sort of . . ." He searched for the right word. "A rebellion against his authority. His children and his wife were to obey at all times, abide by his rules. Any deviation was not tolerated."

"And this is the man you want to honor with a memorial?" Sydney asked.

"In spite of how he was personally, he was an important rancher. He served two terms in the state legislature. He's the father of two important businessmen and politicians. And . . ."

He stopped. What he started to say distressed him, and he refused to say more. Sydney wondered if he worried that not promoting some sort of honor for his grandfather might reflect badly on him, as the one person with the authority to arrange for such an honor, and then didn't. People might begin to wonder and start digging into the past.

"What is it you two think happened?" he said after a time.

Sydney looked out the window behind her computer. It was now a cold blustery day, the wind having come up, driving bits of trash down the street, people bundled up fighting the wind no matter what direction they were headed. They walked carefully, trying to avoid slipping, even though the sidewalks were mostly slush now with a few bits of ice. A couple of pickup trucks passed by slowly, the sound of tires running through more slush very loud. The roads would be even rougher tomorrow if the temps fell again tonight and froze the tire tracks.

What should she tell Grayson Blair, Jr., about his past? About his parentage? How much did she really know? Then the thought returned that nibbled at her since these two showed up: she should call Sheriff Otis. Let him decide what should be told and what shouldn't. Yet, this part at least was probably not a matter for the sheriff. It wasn't a legal problem by itself. Only the attacks on her that were indirectly caused by events from decades earlier, carried any legal repercussions.

Except, of course, for the death of Johnny Whitefeather.

Knowing what sort of man Carl Blair was, she didn't approve of the idea of a memorial being raised to honor him. She knew him too well. He was a bully and a misogynist, possibly even a masochist. But the decision wasn't hers.

She turned back toward her visitors. They seemed to be trying to stay as far apart as they could. Again, she wondered if they were ever friends.

"Senator, why don't you take your cousin, Lily, for a cup of coffee. The two of you need to talk about this. Once you know what she knows and what she guesses, then you can decide what you want to do about the memorial, about your uncle."

"Yes, Gray. Why don't we go somewhere and talk?"

Lily reached over and took his hand in hers. The Senator nodded. "All right."

He stood and helped Lily get to her feet. He gave her a kiss on her cheek, then turned to Sydney.

"I thought this all would be so simple," he said.

"It still may be."

"Not yet," Lily said. "My father's hired thugs may be coming here. I overheard him say that he wanted all of the records taken out of here. He wants them under his control."

"Really? I guess I'd better make some arrangements of my own, then."

The Senator straightened, put on his gloves, and escorted Lily outside. After a short discussion, they got into their separate cars, him in the driver's seat of his vehicle, and her helped into the back of the dark grey limousine. There was no time to wonder where they might be going for coffee. Sheriff Otis must be notified that there might be more trouble brewing at the archives.

CHAPTER 19

"I didn't realize things had gone so far," Otis said.

He called back after the Blairs left. Apparently the proposal in the legislature was not widely known.

"The Senator has no idea about some of the things his grandfather did." She glanced out the window. "That's odd."

"What?"

"Their cars are still here."

"Whose?"

The doorbell rang and she stood, glanced toward the two chairs to see if her former visitors left anything.

"I'll call you right back," she said.

"Sydney . . ."

She hung up and made her way to the door. A male figure was outlined on the frosted glass. She took the key down, thinking it was the Senator coming back for some reason, and unlocked the door, leaving the key in the lock. As she turned the knob, it slammed back against her hand and she cried out.

The man pushing the door wider was definitely not someone she knew. She tried to put her foot against the bottom of the door to prevent its opening further, but his size and her surprise gave him the advantage. Holding her injured hand, she wondered if anything was broken. More importantly, she wondered who the man was as he looked at her, then around the entry.

Straight ahead was the hall leading to the reading room on the left and the vault at the end. To the right was the wall of her office with the door at the far corner. To the left was a narrow wooden wall where the key usually hung on a hook next to the door. On the other side of that wall was a counter from the original bank, where bank customers once filled out deposit slips. A wide opening led into the first floor stacks and a short space farther on, the door to the reading room.

The man went to the opening into the stacks and looked around.

"Anyone in there?"

"No," Sydney said.

"How 'bout in there?"

He pointed toward the reading room further in, closest to the vault at the end of the hall.

"No. There's no one here but me."

She stood to the left of the door, her back against the wall. The man gave her a look that seemed to say, "Don't move," and leaned out the doorway. His voice was vaguely familiar, but she couldn't concentrate on that right now.

"Bring 'em in," he called to someone outside.

The Senator and Lily were guided back into the building by two men holding onto their arms. The Senator, looking very small beside the other man, frowned, probably never having been manhandled before, at least not since his grandfather died. Lily looked bewildered.

"In there," the first man said, motioning toward the open door of her office. He seemed to be the one in charge. He looked through that doorway, too, as he walked down the short hall. He motioned for Sydney to follow the other two. His companions now stood in the hall. As it was, the office was crowded with four in the room. She squeezed past him to sit behind her desk.

"Now," he said, "I'm here to get the papers belonging to Carl Blair. Every box, every page, every item."

Sydney made note of how he was dressed, how he carried himself, as well as his appearance as he spoke. He reminded her of Julia's husband, Paul. She knew that not all drivers were big and strong, but Paul and these men were. The leader wore jeans, a button-up shirt, and a sport coat, even in the twenty-degree weather. His boots were black, the kind she'd seen bikers wear. The other two wore heavier jackets, but were dressed the same way otherwise, except that one wore a beard and the other wore a baseball cap.

"Do you have a truck?" she asked.

He turned his head toward her, a warning in his expression.

"I just mean that there are one hundred twenty-nine boxes in that collection, give or take. If you only have a car, even two, you won't be able to take them all in one trip." A desperate exaggeration, but even with the truth, he would need something bigger than a pickup to take everything.

He looked over at his henchmen, then pulled a cell phone from his inside jacket pocket. He stepped into the hall and spoke to someone in a voice too low for her to hear every word. She guessed he was explaining what she'd told him. She could just catch a glimpse of the other two, wondering if any of them carried a gun, or if they depended on their size as a weapon.

The leader came back into the office.

"We want the papers describing Carl Blair and his family," he said. "The personal ones."

She exhaled loudly. "They're everywhere. The collection is organized by year," she started to explain.

He turned his back and talked into the phone again. He was still talking when her desk phone rang. Automatically, she started to reach for it.

"Leave it."

"Of course," she said. Hopefully, it was Otis calling to see why she hadn't called him back. If she didn't answer, he would get suspicious.

"We wait," the man said, turning off his phone and putting it back in his jacket pocket.

Were they waiting for a phone call or for someone to come, Sydney wondered. Either way, it could be a while.

She couldn't help thinking how ill-prepared these men were, not to mention the person who sent them. They knew very little about what they were after or how to go about getting it. That meant they probably weren't the ones who'd ransacked the place before. It was true that their taking the whole collection would cause great inconvenience to the investigation, not to mention the archives. However, the journals in the vault, her notes, and the information in her head were safe. She didn't want to think about the possible alternatives.

What was being considered on the other end? Hiring or sending a truck? Maybe setting the archives on fire. The latter would be disastrous, even if the fire was put out. Flames, heat, or smoke would cause the new fire suppression system to come on and that could be deadly for any people in the building.

"What kind of system do you have in case of fire?" the leader asked, as if reading her thoughts.

"A combination of sprinklers and Halon gas."

"Where's the control panel?"

"In the closet."

"Where? Show me."

She stood and led the way into the cross hall where the janitor's closet opened just behind her office. He moved past her to open the door and flipped the light switch on. He opened the cover to the panel and studied it for a minute. The panel was on the left and the gas cylinders stood against the back wall. He snapped the panel cover closed. Satisfied, he motioned for Sydney to go back toward the office. As she neared the door, she could hear Lily talking.

"I never thought Father would go this far," were the first words she could hear. "He's really serious about ruining you, Gray."

Sydney walked into the office and made her way to the desk. "Are you all right, dear?" Lily asked.

"Yes, Lily. I'm fine."

"I was just telling Gray that I didn't expect Father would go this far to be sure he got his way. I know he can be ruthless, but he's never been so to his own children. It was as if he tried to prove something."

Maybe that he's different from his father, Sydney thought.

"I do know that once he's started something, he intends to see it through. But he won't harm me. Now you, on the other hand," she said to Gray. "Oh, how he hated your father. And his father. I think the only one he ever loved was Aunt Lily."

The three men who watched over them ignored what she was saying as if it was nothing to do with them. Sydney figured they were told only to get the papers, but not why. Only that their employer wanted her stopped. It was amazing to her that the timing of the Senator's ruin was so important.

"What about his mother?" she asked Lily.

"What, dear?"

"How did your father feel about Alice, Carl's wife?"

"He's never talked about her much. She didn't seem to have much effect on her children, and after a while, she wasn't around very often."

Sydney knew that Alice Blair was powerless against her husband in a time when women were not much more than chattel. Carl would have expected her to be silent and do as she was told. When he forced Grayson, Sr., to marry his sister, it was more than his wife could bear. From the little evidence found in the papers and records, it was easy to assume that the mother lost her mind with the shock of it. What if she'd tried to keep him from accomplishing his ends in his own way? Given the times and her history so far uncovered, that was probably why his wife was put away, "for her own safety." He could have done that without much hassle, and there was a lot of evidence in the papers that she'd spent time in mental institutions.

Every time one of his children tried to assert themselves, he squashed them in a way meant to make them afraid to rebel again. He would most certainly have done the same to his wife.

They all sat silently. The leader of the crew looked at his watch periodically. The other two stood in the hall, shifting positions every so often.

Sydney kept expecting to see Otis coming up in his black SUV. Where in the world was he?

How far did Lawrence have to come? If she was to believe he was coming. If he did, it would be her first time to meet him in person. Carl's only surviving child would be in this room with two of the grandchildren. If she could just get him talking . . . Or, if Otis could get there first.

"Would anyone like a cup of coffee? I'd like a cup." She faced the man holding them prisoner. "I'll bet you'd like a cup."

"No."

"The coffee maker is in the break room just down the hall. Across from the closet. It will only take a few minutes to make a pot."

She wanted desperately to normalize the situation, ease the tension. This wasn't like the confrontation in her living room, when it became so ridiculous that she couldn't help laughing.

He looked toward the men in the hall and nodded. "Go with her."

Sydney stepped around her desk, into the hall, and toward the break room. It felt good to stretch her legs. One of the men followed.

While the coffee brewed, she did a couple of stretching exercises. The pot made ten cups, so it took a while.

Why wasn't Otis here? It seemed as if an hour or more had passed since she said she would call back, a little less time since the call she'd guessed was him. He'd probably gotten busy. The roads were still bad, after all, and other emergencies always occurred in this kind of weather. While they waited, different scenarios went through her mind. She wanted to be brave and wished again that she still studied martial arts. That was a foolish thought, of course, but her mind always got creative when confronted with an insoluble problem.

The coffee maker burbled and hissed. She took down a tray from the cabinet and six mugs. The sugar bowl needed filling before placing it on the tray along with the cream in the carton. Two spoons would have to do. Supplying the break room was catch as catch can.

The tray was heavy, but her guard didn't offer to carry it. He did step aside to let her move through the doorway and out into the hall. At the door to her office, the second guard also moved aside. Once in the office, there was nowhere to set the tray.

Not a gentleman among them, she thought.

"Could someone move those things to the other side on my desk?" she asked.

The Senator and Lily looked at each other, then at the guard who accompanied Sydney to the break room. Their leader nodded, and her escort began pushing everything to the far side of the desk. Sydney cringed at the callous handling of papers and tools, but said nothing. It was her idea to get coffee, after all.

As always, the temperature in the archives was kept low, and she was looking forward to hot coffee. The circumstances certainly weren't designed to make anyone feel warm and fuzzy. Lily still wore her fur coat, which she held tightly around her, and the Senator wore his overcoat, all buttoned up. The three men wore their jackets. As for Sydney, she always dressed warmly for work, but today she felt chillier than usual, probably because she wasn't moving around a whole lot. Not to mention her fear, not only for herself, but also for the archives.

As she poured coffee for everyone except the leader, she thought of Doctor Arnold for the first time. Where was he? This was a great time for him to pester her. He would certainly be very upset with her once he heard about today's events.

With everyone settled with their coffee, she sat down facing the window, and took a sip. It wasn't long before a large blue sedan pulled up to the curb across the street. In a few minutes, an old man was lifted from the back seat to a wheelchair that was taken from the trunk, and was being wheeled across the street toward the front door. As they drew nearer, she saw that the man was on oxygen. Their captors stood too far from the window to see the car arrive and they jerked their heads in sync toward the door when the bell rang.

"It's your employer, I believe," Sydney said.

The leader crowded against her and the chair to look out the window. "Open it," he said, motioning toward the front door.

A shaft of bright light pierced the hall nearly to the end when she did as she'd been told. The sound of the wheelchair seemed to push the two guards ahead of it as they backed out of the way toward the reading room. The man behind the wheelchair turned it into the office doorway.

"Cozy," Lawrence Blair said. He motioned for the three hired men to move out. The wheelchair was pushed over the threshold and backed up against the work table. The brakes were set on the wheelchair and the man remained beside Lawrence.

"Hello, Father," Lily said.

Lawrence Blair hardly looked at his daughter. Instead his gaze settled on his nephew.

"Lily. And you, Gray. What are you doing here?"

"Checking on Grandfather's papers."

"I'll bet you are."

"And you, Miz St. John. What are we to think about you?" Although his voice shook, it was strong in volume.

"Nothing, I suppose. I'm just a civil servant doing her job."

He harrumphed, then began coughing. The cold air certainly wasn't having a good effect on his well-being. He must feel it deeply in spite of the cowboy hat on his head and the cashmere muffler wound around his neck. He started to unbutton his dark grey overcoat, but his hands were either too cold or too stiff from arthritis to manage it. Lily started to get up to help him, but he waved her away. Instead, he unwound the muffler, folded it in half and lay it across his lap.

"Take my daughter and nephew outside," he said, addressing his man, but not looking directly at him. "Go home," he ordered, glancing at both. The man nodded and motioned the two to stand, then escorted them from the building. The door closed, leaving just the two of them in the office.

"I'm told that the papers I want are too scattered among the boxes of my father's collection to be easily gathered together and hauled out of here."

His voice grew raspy with each word. He looked straight into Sydney's eyes as he spoke.

"As I told your hired men, the material is organized by date. Some boxes might hold two or three years' worth of papers. Other years might be spread across three boxes. It's a large collection."

"Not as large as you said." He was thinking of the figure she gave his hired man. "My father was a busy man." He finally pulled off the leather gloves and laid them on top of the muffler. "I do not want certain facts spread about just yet. In fact, not for several months. And here you are, ferreting out information that could destroy my plans."

"Does it really matter so much when it comes out?" Sydney asked. "I understand you have plans and you want revenge for your sister . . ."

"You know nothing." There was no anger in the statement, only a blunt statement of truth as he saw it. "I've been planning this for some time. I came into possession of additional information a few months ago, the last pieces, and realized that, with them and what I already knew, there was enough to ruin Gray's and my father's reputation. Certain events have been set into motion."

"And your health?"

"What about my health?"

"Are you that certain that you will live long enough?"

"Of course, I will."

"It's just that you seem rather frail." If she could plant a seed of doubt in his mind, perhaps he would be satisfied to know that an earlier revelation of his information would be satisfactory enough.

"If it all comes out earlier, your nephew probably won't be able to push the issue forward. Wouldn't that be enough?" She intentionally avoided the word "memorial."

"No. It's the humiliation I'm after. For someone to propose a memorial to a man like his grandfather, a man whose very existence is an affront to decency . . ." He took a deep breath and coughed.

"Does Grayson, Junior, know any of this?"

Lawrence thought for a moment, as if speculating what his nephew might actually know.

"If he knows anything at all, how could he possibly propose a monument to his grandfather. The man who . . ." He broke off, looking pained, emotionally or physically was impossible to tell.

"Haven't enough people been hurt by your father? Your brother, Grayson, your sister, Lily, your mother . . ."

"Don't speak of my mother. She was weak. Never could protect her children. Never even tried."

"What would your father have done to her if she tried?"

"If she didn't learn not to . . . He probably would have killed her. Eventually."

"In the end, even Lily found out what it meant to try to rebel against him."

He turned his head to look at her, his expression fierce and angry this time.

"You know nothing of Lily, what she went through. What she wanted. How she . . . how she . . ."

"How she died?"

"What do you know of it?"

Sydney couldn't tell if he was stressing that she knew nothing or if he was asking what she actually knew. She believed that she knew much more than he suspected, yet some things she only suspected. Maybe she could find out the whole truth now.

"I know that your father forced her to marry her own brother when he found out she was pregnant. He picked Grayson because you were so jealous of him. In the end, it was punishment for all three of you, not to mention Grayson, Junior."

"A half-breed," Lawrence spat out. "A nobody, unworthy of Lily."

"No one was worthy of Lily, were they?"

"You know nothing," Lawrence said for the third time. "Lily

was pure, sweet, a joy. She lit up a room. Everyone noticed her."

"Even Johnny Whitefeather."

"Yes, except she said she seduced him. That was just her way of trying to protect him."

"You and your father flogged him."

Lawrence shuddered, remembering that day, that act of violence and revenge.

"He deserved it."

"After you found out Lily was pregnant."

"She wanted to have the baby. I wanted her to get an abortion. Father wanted only to punish her."

"Was that the reason he forced her to marry her brother?"

"He wanted to be certain that she and the baby bore the Blair name. And, yes, to punish her and him. And me."

"After they were married, after her son was born, she fell down the stairs. Was that suicide?"

Lawrence's expression changed. He looked at her under lowered eyelids, cunning now. At first, he was eager to talk about the events that led to this moment, but now he wasn't so sure.

"She wouldn't leave her son. And the only way she could try to protect him was to stay with Grayson. I tried to get her to leave, but she wouldn't. I would have done anything for her."

It suddenly occurred to her that she might have some events totally wrong. Particularly Lily's death. Because of what she found, she became convinced it was not because of childbirth as noted on the death certificate, but suicide, or that Grayson, Sr., killed her because he was in love with someone else.

What if Lawrence loved her too much?

"Lawrence, what happened that night you pounded on Grayson's door? Was Lily home that night?"

"Maybe. I don't remember."

"Was Grayson at home?"

"I didn't get into the house."

Suddenly, Sydney wanted to draw back, to stop asking questions. It would be better for the police to ask the questions, record the answers, so they could use them in prosecuting Lawrence. Or for putting him in a facility that would protect him from himself.

She looked out the window as she always did when confronted

with a question she couldn't readily answer. Downtown Gansel always appeared calm when she looked out. Dark grey clouds scudded across the sky and she realized it was getting late. Her heartbeat quickened when she also saw Sheriff Otis in his official SUV.

He saw her looking out the window. The big man opened the door and slid out of the vehicle, closing the door behind him. He waved to her and she wondered how long he'd been there waiting for her to notice. Maybe he'd just arrived. She'd find that out later.

She nodded to him, hoping he knew that meant she was all right. He walked across the street toward the door that was still unlocked. She turned back to Carl's eldest son, feeling sorry for him and not a little bitter. Something in his tone gave her different possibilities to work on, each more unnerving than the last.

Would he have knocked Lily down those stairs when he tried to convince her to leave? If so, it could have been an accident. It could have been rage. It would never have been pre-meditated. If she refused to leave because of her son, Lawrence might blame him for her death, no matter what the circumstances were that day.

But, clearly living with her death, and how it happened, ate at him all these years. Unstable at the best of times, at least according to what she'd read of his history, such an event would only have made his mental health tenuous.

The front door of the archives opened, the sound all too familiar. Otis spoke to someone in the hall, and she realized the two men were still there. She heard something about everything being all right. The door from the parking lot to the side of the building opened a moment later. Footsteps indicated that at least two more people walked toward the office.

"How . . .?" Lawrence began.

"It's Sheriff Otis," she said. "He's a friend."

Lawrence looked angry at first, then his expression softened and he nodded.

"It's good to have friends."

CHAPTER 20

Sydney wrote everything down, all that she could remember that Lawrence Blair told her that day in her office. But the police couldn't act on any of it. There was no proof and everyone present in the office that afternoon denied it all, up to and including being there.

For whatever reason, Sheriff Otis decided not to pursue any charges having to do with Johnny Whitefeather's death. He seemed to think that after all these years, it would sort itself out, although he did turn over all the information on the current crimes to the State Police for them to do whatever they wanted.

A few days later, Sheriff Otis called the archive.

"Lawrence Blair died early this morning," he said. "I thought you'd like to know."

"Oh. Yes, thanks. How did he die?"

"Meanness probably. Nah. He left the old folks home, got in his car and drove away. The car slid on some black ice right into the path of an oncoming car. The other car only tapped his back fender, and he hit a tree, instead."

"Will there be an autopsy?"

"Probably not. The doctors taking care of him listed many pre-existing conditions. At his age, he shouldn't have been driving anyway."

"What do we do about . . ." She didn't know exactly what to call what they knew. The situation? The crime?

"Nuthin' I guess. There's no one left to prosecute. You never saw the men who abducted you. Oh, Mr. Pickett and his friend will be charged with breaking and entering, causing bodily harm. You'll have to testify if it comes to trial."

"Maybe they'll plead guilty."

"Probably." There was silence for a moment and then Otis said, "Sydney, Lawrence did leave a statement. He didn't address it to anyone in particular. I got a copy of it, and I thought you might like to read it."

Again, that feeling that she knew too much already came over her. Most of the time she was certain there was no such thing as too much information. In this case, and for the first time, she wasn't certain. But, since she started down this path, she might as well see it through to the end.

"Yes, I'd like to read it," she heard herself say.

"I'll be over momentarily, then."

The phone went dead, but it was several seconds before she hung up. For a while, she thought she knew everything that happened, or could guess accurately enough about some bits and pieces. In the end, though, she could imagine too many possible endings to the Blair saga, none of them pleasant.

It was twenty-five minutes later when Otis arrived. She let him in.

"I can't leave it with you, since it's official," he said. "I'll wait while you read." He handed her a folder, like those used in business for bound reports. The first page bore the title "Statement of Lawrence Broom Blair," with the date and Ponca City printed in the lower left quadrant.

"Read the first couple of pages, then start on page twelve," Otis said.

It opened with a brief history of the Blair family, where they lived, and how they made their living. It was the first time she'd seen his mother's last name, Broom, which was also his middle name.

She skipped to page twelve. There he told the story of Lily and Johnny Whitefeather, that she'd become pregnant and how Lawrence and his father flogged the half-breed. He was put on his horse and sent out onto the prairie afterward, but they knew he later died from the beating.

Lily became hysterical when she found out and tried to run away. Grayson, Sr., caught her at the train station and took her home, where she was locked in her room. The scheme to marry her off to him, and keep it all in the family, was hatched sometime in the next few days, something no one but Carl was happy about. As Sydney suspected, Grayson, Sr., was in love with someone else and had asked her to marry him. Lawrence couldn't stand the thought of his lovely Lily being treated that way, but most of all, he couldn't stand the thought that his brother, the favored son, would have her all to himself. Lily tried to kill herself by taking pills. Alice, Carl's wife and Lily's mother, said very little, although she'd been the one who got Lily to the train station when she tried to run away. Carl beat both of them for that.

The story played out almost exactly as Sydney pulled it together. Until she got to the part where Lily died.

> *I went to the house to take Lily away,* Lawrence wrote. *It was all set up. She would travel by train to Chicago, assume another name. Letters of introduction gave her entrée to a company where she would have worked. I planned to send her money. She could have disappeared in such a large city and lived her own life. Only I would have known where she was.*
>
> *"What about Gray," she'd asked. "I can't leave my son." I reminded her of his father, that he was a half-breed, a nothing, but she would have none of it. She would not leave without Gray. She ran upstairs and tried to close her bedroom door against me. I pushed in. She ran back out, but I caught her on the landing. We argued. I shoved her away in disgust. She fell down the stairs.*

"Like some old black and white movie, isn't it?"

Sydney looked up at Otis, still stuffed quietly into her visitor's chair. He nodded and she looked back down at the statement.

> *I called the police and an ambulance. Told everyone I'd come to see my brother and found Lily at the bottom of the stairs. Grayson was so good at showing grief he didn't feel. Father would sometimes look at me as if he knew the truth. We buried Lily. She died because of that son of hers and our father. He died a horrible death from throat cancer, vengeance enough. But Gray, my wonderful nephew, the senator, lived happily ever after. It was his fault his mother died. He will pay one day.*

With a sigh, Sydney closed the folder and sat back. That Lawrence may have killed Lily occurred to her when he was in her office, telling her so much, admitting very little.

"What will you do? Or is there anything you can do?"

Otis shrugged. "It's all over, essentially, as I said on the phone. I suspect that Lawrence wanted everything in place to ruin the Senator and the plans for the memorial at a most embarrassing moment. We'll just have to wait and see."

"I guess. Maybe the Senator will give it up."

It was all very depressing. She should be satisfied that it was over, but not all threads were tied up.

"We still need to know some things."

"Like what?"

"Like who kidnapped me on the Interstate and left me in the woods in Crossed Timbers."

"Oh, that was one of the guys who was here in your office that day and another guy he'd hired. The dead guy was him, the young guy hired to help. He was hitchhiking through, just like he said, they offered him a couple hundred to help them. His name, we've since found out, was James London, from Texas, and heading north for a job."

"Why'd they kill him?"

"We're guessing that he got spooked when you didn't come out of the woods as fast as they figured. He'd hung around to make sure. That's why he was on the overpass."

"All right. Who was feeding me information on the Blairs? That envelope left on my porch and so on?"

"Don't know. Someone may own up to that, just like someone may someday tell us they were the one feeding information to Lawrence."

"You know, this is the second time information has gotten out to someone from my office. The same happened when we were looking into Violet Parsons and Josiah Bartlett."

"If you're thinking there's a leak in my office . . ."

"I don't know, Otis. But something's happening."

They talked about possibilities for a while, then he left for lunch. She called Ben to let him know how it was all ending, then called Julia to see if she would like to meet her at Molly's for chili.

The archives settled back into routine.

As promised, Senator Grayson Blair, Jr., proposed a bill for the raising of a monument to his late grandfather, Carl Blair, rancher, businessman, politician, father, and husband. Shortly after, Lawrence's estate released the information he gathered about the Senator's parentage, about his own father, ruining his nephew's and father's reputations along the way. The release was very public, making it impossible for anyone to cover it up.

The bill was defeated. The senator retired early, fully disgraced, although not all his doing. Lawrence exacted his revenge, nearly erasing the Blair family from history. Except in the Filmore County Historical Archives in Gansel, Oklahoma.

That summer, Ben came in August, staying for the whole month. It was hot as hell, something Sydney enjoyed for the first time in so many years.

ABOUT THE AUTHOR

Cary Osborne's tastes have always been eclectic, due to her varied background. Because of that, she has written in several genres, including science fiction, fantasy, and horror. Recently, she delved into the fictional world of mysteries. She won an honorable mention and was a finalist in the Writers of the Future Contest for short stories. Having lived all over the country, she recently moved from New Mexico to Oklahoma.

Book List:
The Iroshi Trilogy
Iroshi
The Glaive
Persea

The Deathweave Series
Deathweave
Darkloom
Winter Queen

The Sydney St. John Mysteries
Oklahoma Winds

Curious about other Crossroad Press books?
Stop by our site:
http://store.crossroadpress.com
We offer quality writing
in digital, audio, and print formats.

Enter the code FIRSTBOOK
to get 20% off your first order from our store!
Stop by today!